EARL
OF
DESTINY

A LORDS OF FATE NOVEL, VOLUME 2

K.J. JACKSON

First Edition: October 2015
ISBN: 978-1-940149-12-7
http://www.kjjackson.com

K.J. Jackson Books

Historical Romance:

Stone Devil Duke
Unmasking the Marquess
My Captain, My Earl
Worth of a Duke

Paranormal Romance:

Flame Moon
Triple Infinity
Flux Flame

Be sure to sign up for news of my next releases at
www.KJJackson.com

Dedication

– As Always,
For my favorite Ks

PROLOGUE

NORFOLK, ENGLAND
NOVEMBER, 1820

No.

The one word reverberated through her body.

Past the pain.

Past the blood pooling around her foot.

She strained to lift her head, forcing herself to crack her eyelids.

No.

Impossible, what had just happened.

Her love. What he had said to her. What he had done to her.

"Stupid girl—you are nothing—nothing more than a plaything."

She gasped for breath, focusing through the tears clouding her vision.

Her father.

His body was still there. Limp. Not the slightest shift of his limbs, of his head, from when she had closed her eyes to the horror. The blood spread—spread and soaked into the stone just below his neck.

She couldn't even go to him, couldn't even see if he was truly dead, or if he could be helped. The ropes around her wrists, around her ankles were far too tight, far too secure.

She knew that after hours of trying to escape.

A scream ripped through the dank bowels of the abbey. It should be her own voice, but it wasn't.

Slowly, her mind molasses, she turned her head to the sound.

Her sister stood at the door. Screaming. Again and again and again.

Hell.

Please let him be gone. Please let him have disappeared. He couldn't take her sister too. Not her sister.

She tried to open her mouth, to tell her sister it would all be well. To tell her to shut her eyes. To tell her to leave. To quiet her screams.

But she couldn't make her own mouth move. Couldn't make her head move. She had no way to make that happen. Not after this. Not after losing everything. Not after her own stupidity.

Her father dead.

And the one man she had loved—body and soul—gone.

Gone.

And he took his knife with him.

CHAPTER 1

LONDON, ENGLAND
JUNE, 1822

His back against the mahogany wainscoting, Sebastian Rallager, fourteenth Earl of Luhaunt, wedged himself along the wall behind Lord Crungel.

Crungel's girth would serve him well—Sebastian would be mostly hidden from view of the evening's last desperate bids of matchmaking mamas.

Sipping claret, he focused past the crush of couples comically attempting to dance with nary a space to step. His gaze landed on Miss Silverton's brown dress camouflaging her into the dark wainscoting.

Standing on the opposite end of the ballroom, her back against the wall, she blatantly ignored the gentleman talking into her left ear. Miss Silverton's eyes were trained, as always, on her laughing sister in the middle of the dance floor.

The man leaned closer to Miss Silverton's head, apparently thinking he could get her attention if he talked louder.

Sebastian smirked. The poor bastard.

For a fortnight he had studied this scene. Everything about Miss Silverton screamed that she did not want to be approached. Did not want to be talked to. Did not want to entertain the slightest bit of attention from the opposite sex.

From the drab brown dress with a neckline choking her well above her clavicle, to her light brown hair tightly pulled back in the most severe bun he had ever seen.

She had appeared at every ball, every dinner, and every party exactly the same—her dress never changed, her hair never altered, her light blue eyes never veered from her sister.

It was a shame that none of that could stop the hopeful fools. And Sebastian had come to pity them and their hope, because no amount of steely coolness could hide Miss Silverton's inherent beauty, no matter all she did to deny its existence.

The man next to her stopped talking, perplexed, and looked out to the dance floor. With a shrug and not another word to her, he moved away, shaking his head.

Sebastian took another sip, watching Miss Silverton's shoulders relax ever so slightly. It was subtle, but he had learned to pick up on the tiniest movements her body made—a must, because absolutely everything about her was incredibly controlled.

"You stayed longer in town than I had imagined you would, Seb." Rowen Lockton, the Duke of Letson, settled himself next to Sebastian at the wall, wine in his hand. "More than a fortnight— this is the longest stretch of time I have ever known you to willingly stay in one place."

His friend scanned the crowd. "And not only have you stayed here in London, but you have been attending function after function. Your mother is well? Nothing is amiss?"

"My mother?" Sebastian's eyes flickered to the duke and then back to Miss Silverton. "No, she is the same as always."

The duke's eyes trailed out into the sea of people, trying to pinpoint what Sebastian watched. "Then you must finally be pondering a wife?"

Sebastian squelched his own reaction and looked at his friend. "Why do you say that?"

"Why else attend these blasted things?"

"To be reminded of what I like to avoid." Sebastian turned to the duke, his shoulder bumping into the fleshy back of Lord Crungel. "I assume that to mean you have had enough of the season, Rowe?"

"I would happily be up at Notlund right now." The duke tilted his head in the direction of his duchess across the room. "But my wife had other plans for our two charges. This is all the younger one wanted—a season—and Wynne adores them and wanted to make it happen for them."

"It can be a bugger, having a wife you want to make happy?"

"Yes." The duke shrugged. "But the good outweighs any of the drudgery. So pick wisely when you do finally come to it, my friend. At least tonight is the end of it."

"This is your last function in London? Are you back to Notlund soon? I had planned to be up there in a week or so as I have some business with those Berber fillies and their new residence."

"Lord Granger will be coming for them? He has been more than anxious."

"Yes. And I believe he intends to bring his third cousin. I have not met him, but the man is interested in several of our studs. He wants to assess them, so it will be good for you to meet him as well."

"I warn you, it will not be the usual peace at Notlund." The duke's forefinger swept around the room. "This madness is to follow us, on a smaller scale, of course—or so I have been promised. Wynne and the Silverton sisters have concocted a full summer of visitors—all of the top suitors from the season will be clunking through the estate."

Sebastian sighed, shaking his head with a feigned frown. "That is unfortunate." He sipped his claret as his attention went back to the crush. "But Notlund is large, so I am sure I can stay out of the fray."

Sebastian's eyes landed on Miss Silverton once more, now chatting with the duchess. She looked parched, as she always did at this point in the night. Miss Silverton did not drink spirits of any kind, no matter how many bubbling glasses were set into her hands.

He smiled. Once at Notlund, he would have to explore that fact more deeply.

Only a week away. One week, and he could set his plan in motion.

He had hidden his prior knowledge from Rowen, but Sebastian already knew about the many suitors to visit Notlund—who was coming and when—as he had sunken to spying on his own best friend, rather than being upfront about his plan.

But he couldn't let Rowen be privy to his scheme just yet.

Not if his plan was to work.

~ ~ ~

Leaning back on the dark blue squabs of the open-air carriage, Brianna Silverton looked down at her younger sister. They had just escaped the final strained chords of the string quartet at the ball, and Brianna sighed in relief. She was almost—mercifully—done with the debacle that had become her life.

No longer filtered through the glow of candles in the ballroom, the bright morning sun burned through the London haze, showing just how foxed her sister truly was. Bleary blue eyes closing, Lily sank awkwardly into the corner of the carriage, dead to the world.

At least she wasn't throwing up this time.

Brianna reached over and shifted her sister's arm from the awkward angle it had landed, setting it gently across her sister's stomach.

She had been beyond mortified the first time Lily had thrown up in the Duke of Letson's carriage. The coachman had politely cleaned up after them and had continued to do so the three subsequent times it had happened.

After the fifth time, though, the duke had requested that Brianna take her sister to and from the soirées in the open-air carriage, as long as weather permitted. As polite as the duke had been in asking, it was in that moment that Brianna realized what true mortification really was.

Since then, Brianna had gotten adept at recognizing the moment before Lily upheaved. And she had also figured out how to drape her sister outside a moving carriage—safely—so Lily could retch in the cleanest manner possible.

The horses jerked forth, and Brianna removed her gloves, staring at her sister's mouth, waiting for the twisting lips and quickened breath—the surest sign the ride home would not be pleasant.

A few minutes passed, and Lily remained asleep, heart-shaped lips still. A small grace.

Brianna allowed herself to relax slightly, letting the muscles in her neck stretch back and forth as she let down her tight shoulders. Standing all night, vigilant over her sister, did nothing but put aches into her back and throbs down her left leg.

It had been a particularly trying night, this last ball of the season. The desperate had become exceptionally daring, fraying the edges of politeness. Brianna was a spinster—a companion—and it annoyed her to no end how often men thought they could still ask for an introduction—still talk to her.

She had enough running madcap through her mind to stop and converse with them.

But it was almost over—she just had to last another three months through the summer. Three more months of politeness, of watching her sister's every move.

Three months to determine which one of the final three suitors would be the appropriate one for her sister.

They hid it well, these men, but Brianna knew all of them drooled over Lily's dowry. She had thought to give her sister the best chance of finding a worthwhile husband when she had declared herself a spinster and combined her dowry with Lily's.

It had taken some machinations with the solicitor, but since she was in control of the Silverton estate, the man had done as

Brianna had asked. It had effectively doubled Lily's dowry, but now Brianna was second-guessing the wisdom of that decision.

Thank goodness the duke had convinced her not to add more into it, as she had planned.

The coachman turned left onto the block of the duke's townhouse.

Brianna poked her sister. A grumble, but no open eyes.

She poked her again. Nothing.

With a sigh, Brianna slid her arm behind Lily's back, the blue silk of her sister's gown soft on her forearm. She set her other arm in front of Lily, pulling her upright.

At least the next three months at Notlund, the Duke of Letson's estate in Yorkshire, would give her a slight reprieve from the constant hovering over Lily. Give her a chance to breathe.

In the two months they had spent at Notlund before the season began, Brianna had grown to love several of the young mares in the duke's expansive stables. Grown to love the far-reaching estate and the wide-open stretches where she could set her mounts to flying fast.

She had come to depend on those rides to keep her sane and had missed them bitterly in London.

Hopefully, the rides would allow her some precious quiet away from Lily to focus—focus on determining the right husband for her sister.

There wasn't anything more important.

For she wasn't about to ruin her sister's life. Not as she had done to her own.

Chapter 2

If Sebastian had any lingering doubts about his plan, they dissipated into the summer morning breeze the second he saw the vision in front of him.

He pulled up on the reins of his horse, leaving several rows of trees between him and the bank of the stream. He was well hidden, even if at that moment he wished he wasn't.

Caution held him back. Caution would be crucial to his success.

Hell-bent, her white horse thundering along an open field, Miss Silverton flew, half of her hair spilling from her bun and trailing her like a flag.

Skillfully guiding the horse, she slowed, the pair turning at the opposite bank of the stream, and the horse eased them down to the water.

At the stream's edge, Miss Silverton jumped from the sidesaddle, a laughing smile beaming across her face as she patted the horse's creamy neck. Miss Silverton's face was flush, and Sebastian could see she was panting through her smile, out of breath.

It was the first time Sebastian had seen a true smile grace her face, and it was a sight he was not likely to forget soon—or ever.

Sebastian could not make out the words, but he could hear her voice floating in the air above the running water as she rubbed the horse's nose. The horse whinnied, and Miss Silverton chuckled, stepping aside as the horse went to lap up water from the stream.

Stripping off the violet jacket of her riding habit, she tossed it back to the edge of the grasses further up the bank. She turned, walking to the edge of the stream as she pushed up the loose sleeves of her white shirt and then pulled several pins from her hair, fluffing her hair as she let all of her loose curls fall down her back.

Still in animated one-way discussion with the horse, she bent, balancing on her heels. Her skirts dipped into the stream, but she seemed to take no note as she scooped water into her cupped hands, first dousing her face, and then pulling her hair aside to splash water onto the back of her neck. She fished into a pocket in her skirts, producing a handkerchief and sinking it into the stream.

Everything about her was at ease. Completely relaxed. Her shoulders weren't high and tight. Her mouth wasn't set in its constant slight frown. Her brow wasn't furrowed in concentration. Her ice-blue eyes were aglow. She wasn't jabbing her own fingernails into the pads of her thumbs as she constantly did at parties.

Free. She was completely free, and Sebastian recognized it instantly.

Face upward to the sky, her words stopped as she closed her eyes. Holding the cloth to her neck, the water dripped, trailing onto the front of her chest as she stretched her neck, rubbing her own shoulder.

The dripping water soon began to take over her white linen shirt, her shift, and the top of her stays, and the darkness of a nipple started to show through the fabric.

Damn. She was beautiful. More beautiful than he had thought.

For all that he had planned, this—her true beauty—he had not expected. Sebastian could feel himself starting to harden.

He shifted in his saddle, frown setting on his mouth. He was going to have to go about his plan more delicately than he had thought. He had known she was beautiful, but he hadn't expected to physically react so instantaneously to her. The slightest show of a nipple, and he was gawking like a besotted whipper of eighteen.

He shook his head, irate at his own lack of restraint.

The white horse nudged Miss Silverton's shoulder, and Sebastian could hear a distinct groan come from her.

Hands on her knees, she rose, quickly yanking her hair backward and twisting it into a tight bun. Pins pushed in to hold the bun in place, she fetched her jacket from the bankside, quickly buttoning the front.

Sebastian's eyes stayed stubbornly trained on her ample chest until the violet cloth swallowed the view.

She sidled the horse, stretching her foot up into the stirrup and gripping the top pommel. A few hops, and she heaved herself upward into the sidesaddle. Awkward without a stump or a platform to step up upon, she managed the motion somewhat gracefully.

Settled on the white mare, her eyes went to the stream. She watched the rolling water for a few long moments, and Sebastian could see she was hesitant to leave the tranquility of the spot.

But then the set of her shoulders tightened and the smile slipped from her face. A few more moments, and her back straightened, somberness setting into her eyes.

The change was fascinating.

Fascinating. And unsettling.

Sebastian's head tilted, and he watched as she pushed the horse up the bank and disappeared from view.

He smiled to himself, clicking his horse into motion.

Maybe it was time Miss Silverton knew of his existence.

~ ~ ~

Brianna's eyes went to the sky, trying to make out the sun through the thick cover of the summer haze. Without the sun to guide her, she had ridden longer than she had intended, but it had felt so good to escape she couldn't quite bring herself to turn Moonlight back to the stables.

She set Moonlight to an easy walk. The way the horse had taken to the fields earlier, Brianna guessed that Moonlight had missed her just as much as she had missed the mare.

Grabbing the front of her form-fitting jacket, Brianna tried to fan a waft of air onto her chest. In only a few minutes, her wet shirt had matted to her skin, hot in the warm weather. It had been worth it, though, cooling off by the stream.

Her eyes flickered to the sky. Hopefully, she still had a few hours before Lily would be awake and moving about, and she could change and be ready before she needed to start trailing her sister.

The flurry of traveling here to Notlund and of their first guests arriving had consumed too much of the last week, and Brianna had far too much to do.

Of all of her sister's suitors, Lord Newdale was still the biggest mystery to her. She wished she had directed the bow street runner she had hired to investigate her sister's final three suitors to gather information on Newdale first, as society was very tight-lipped about him.

So far, Newdale was the biggest risk as a husband for her sister. And Brianna was not about to allow her sister a risky marriage.

Nonetheless, Newdale was now here at Notlund, arriving with his mother and two sisters the day before. Brianna would just have to be extra vigilant when Newdale was near Lily.

The sound of horse hooves broke through her thoughts, and Brianna turned just in time to see a man on a tall black horse slow and fall in line with Moonlight's gait.

Her spine instantly straightened.

No. This would not do.

"Hello. I do apologize for interrupting your thoughts, miss, but are you on your way to the Notlund stables?"

Brianna tried to ignore him, her eyes straight ahead while keeping Moonlight at a steady pace.

What was a strange man doing in this area of the Notlund estate? She had never encountered anyone on these grounds, save for the gamekeeper that once.

"Again, miss, I do apologize. Approaching a lady such as yourself is not done, but you are riding without a groom, and I warred between slowing to chat with you, or rudely moving past you without acknowledging your presence."

"You may still choose to move rudely past me, sir. That would do us both well." Brianna did not let her eyes even flicker in his general direction. The duke had always said the grounds were quite safe, and she had believed him until this man just appeared out of nowhere.

The man chuckled. "I am afraid it is too late for that, Miss Silverton."

Her face snapped to him. "You know who I am?"

The man smiled at her. Handsome. Dark brown hair. Warm chocolate eyes. A devil grin.

He nodded.

Brianna swallowed a groan, giving him her coldest eyes. "Then I am at a distinct disadvantage, sir, as I do not think I know you. And I am finding this conversation vastly ruder than it would have been to taste your horse's dust."

"Forgive me." His head bowed to her. "Since there is no one present to introduce us, I will have to do the honors. I am Sebastian Rallager, Earl of Luhaunt. I am a good friend of the duke's."

"Lord Luhaunt?" Brianna's panic at a rogue man appearing beside her subsided. She had been preparing to bolt, as she knew she could outride just about anyone on Moonlight if she needed to. So while she wasn't particularly worried about bodily harm from the man, she was unnerved—but then she recognized the name Luhaunt. At least this man was a known rogue, even if she had never met him.

She glanced at Lord Luhaunt again. He had settled his horse into Moonlight's easy pace quite comfortably. Too comfortably.

She gave him quick, flat smile. "I have heard your name, I believe. You are the one that produces the many fine horses for the stables?"

"Yes. Such as the very one you ride."

"Moonlight? You brought her here?"

"Yes." He shrugged. "Though the name is new to me."

"The duke asked me to name her since we have gotten on so well." Brianna glanced down at Moonlight's twitching ears then back to Luhaunt. "She is fine. And fast. Very fast. Where did she come from?"

"Hungary. The man who had her said she was displaced by the wars, but his character was suspect. I imagine she came to him through nefarious means."

"Did you question him?"

"No. I thought it most important to remove her from an owner that was ill-equipped to care for her. Questioning him would not have helped to that end."

Brianna offered the smallest nod. "The duke has said you have uncanny instincts when it comes to horses."

"I do not know about 'uncanny.' But when I do trust my instincts, there is more often than not, great reward."

His eyes did not leave her.

Brianna looked away, searching the trail along the stream for familiar foliage. Buggers. Still minutes away from the stables.

"Do you always ride without a groom, Miss Silverton? An unmarried lady such as yourself?"

"I am a spinster, Lord Luhaunt, and not in need of a companion." She didn't bother to hide the sharpness in her voice. "There is no danger here, and once the duke was convinced I knew the trails well enough, I have had his blessing to freely go about. I do prefer to ride alone."

She emphasized the word "alone" a little too harshly, and Moonlight reacted from her tone, springing an excited sidestep.

Brianna contemplated giving the horse rein to run again—it would remove her from this man's presence—but unfortunately, also be entirely rude. And she wasn't about to be rude to a good friend of the duke and duchess. Dismissive, yes, but not outright rude.

Luhaunt's eyes finally left her, and he looked ahead, his head bobbing in unison with his horse's steps. "Ahh, I had forgotten you had labeled yourself a spinster. I did hear mention of that in London. That has been vital to your sister's successful season, has it not?"

"You know of my sister?"

"I know of both you and your sister."

Of course. Of course he was here at Notlund for Lily. It made sense. But her sister had never mentioned this man. And Brianna truly did not want to deal with another admirer to investigate.

Her eyes narrowed on Luhaunt's profile. "I do not recall you meeting my sister. And I have kept a very watchful eye over her. Why are you truly here at Notlund, Lord Luhaunt?"

His gaze remained forward. "I will not lie to you, Miss Silverton. I am here for a wife."

Blast it. Her sister would look the fool if Luhaunt showed up, vying for Lily's attention in front of Lord Newdale. "Truly, Lord Luhaunt, you should have inquired about proper introductions to my sister in London. The season is over and she now has a very short list of men she will be considering."

"I was in London, but I thought Notlund would be a much better place for my strategy."

"Strategy? You have a strategy where my sister is concerned?" Brianna shook her head. "Lord Luhaunt, you will be disappointed if you think to get to my sister through me. I do not intend to let Lily anywhere near the likes of you—friend of the duke's or not."

"You do not think the duke might think differently?"

"No, I do not. He has no say in the matter."

"Your father is dead, correct? Is the duke not your guardian?"

"To the extent society needs us to have a guardian. The duke and duchess have been very generous in presenting us to society, and I am eternally grateful for my sister's sake. But we do not need a guardian, Lord Luhaunt. I control the estate." She looked pointedly at him. "And it is tied into trusts that are untouchable by any man my sister chooses to marry."

His look remained nonplussed by her words. "How did Rowe—the duke—become your guardian?"

"My father knew his uncle, the late Duke of Letson. Honorably, the duke wanted to fulfill his uncle's obligations."

She wasn't about to admit it to Luhaunt, but honestly, Brianna still could not believe her good fortune. She had never heard of the Duke of Letson, never read any mention of him in her father's papers. So when the duke had contacted her a year after her father's death, informing her of her father's wishes that the duke become their guardian, she had been more than suspicious.

Refusals were sent, but the duke invited her and Lily again and again to Notlund. Brianna had continued her polite refusals. But the weekly letters, always with an invitation, continued for months from both the duke and the duchess.

Brianna had resisted for months, but had finally caved to Lily's constant haranguing to visit Notlund.

Wary, Brianna had been preparing for a battle of control over the Silverton estate. But it never came. It took her months to trust that the duke and duchess just truly wanted to help them in any way they could. The duchess, Wynne, had become a grand friend to both her and Lily. And Brianna had grown to rely on the duke's wisdom when it came to managing her family's estate.

Luhaunt watched her, apparently waiting for more words from her.

Her guard spiked again, and Brianna realized she didn't care for his probing questions.

"But why ask me, Lord Luhaunt? If the duke is such a good friend to you, why not ask him? You are welcome to take your leave to go do so."

He shrugged, a soft smile playing on his lips. "Take no offense, Miss Silverton. I am just curious. I have known Rowe for many years, and had never heard of the Silverton sisters. Not until your sister became the darling of the ton."

She gave him a curt nod, her eyes going back to the trail. Only a few more minutes and she could escape this man. She would need to talk to Wynne right away when she got back to the castle to make sure Luhaunt was kept away from her sister.

He was far too handsome, and Lily would like that—which was exactly what Brianna needed to curtail. She had had a difficult enough time getting Lily to whittle her list of possible husbands to three.

"Tell me, Miss Silverton, I observed you in London and watched you treat a number of gentlemen with open and utter distaste. Why?"

Her eyes flew to Luhaunt, the question flustering her mind. Open distaste? Had she really been that rude in London? So rude a complete stranger could see it? But then, if she had been, did it matter? Spinster. She was a spinster.

The frown on her face deepened. "It is not my concern if those gentlemen did not understand the function a spinster companion serves at a ball. Their over-presumption was at fault. I never led a single one of them into, nor encouraged any conversation. They had no purpose with me, and I none with them."

"You do realize you are a beautiful woman, Miss Silverton?"

Her jaw dropped. She had absolutely no retort to the comment.

He smiled at her. Genuine. Warm. "I do not wish to offend. I just thought it needed to be spoken, Miss Silverton." He inclined his head. "As we are near the stables, I will leave you so we do not arrive together. I would not want any untoward words spoken of you."

He gave a low whistle, and the tall black stallion sprang into motion, trotting ahead of Brianna.

Staring after him, she did not close her mouth until Luhaunt and his horse disappeared over the crest of the hill in front of her.

She had not thought of herself in that manner in a long time.

Not since Gregory.

Not since her father died.

Not since the weight of her father's secrets had become hers.

She shook her head, clearing the air around her.

No. She was a spinster. And a spinster she needed to remain.

CHAPTER 3

Ears tuned to the conversation next to her, Brianna absent-mindedly plucked through the last few chords on the pedal harp before her.

Where she had once taken great pride in her musical ear, the notes had rung hollow, her fingers stiff over the strings for the past two years. But Wynne had convinced Lily to sing for their guests earlier in the evening, and Lily always sang better when Brianna accompanied her.

Before Lily was even done, Brianna realized the convenience of staying behind the harp. She could hover, monitoring Lily playing whist without being drawn into tedious conversation with Lord Newdale's mother or sisters.

So Brianna had plucked through every last sonata she could think of for the past several hours, fading into the background of the drawing room.

Lord Luhaunt's hearty chuckle caught her ear, warm and soft, and it was enough to make her glance across the card table at him. His charming smile was focused on Lady Rebecca, the younger Newdale sister, and he managed to keep his eyes well above the ample cleavage she was angling at him. Lady Rebecca's own high-pitched chuckle joined his, and she lightly touched his arm.

Apparently, Lady Rebecca was not heeding her sister's earlier advice.

Following dinner, and far from their mother's ears, Brianna had overheard the elder Newdale daughter corner her younger sister in the drawing room before the men had joined them.

"He is cursed, Rebecca," the elder sister, Beatrice, had said, her voice hissing out the side of her mouth.

The peculiar words had slowed Brianna's feet to a crawl as she passed behind them on the settee. She had turned, facing the wall to straighten one of Wynne's paintings—a stable boy at Notlund leaning against a pitchfork, a hidden smirk of shirking his duties curving his mouth. Brianna's head tilted slightly to the side, her ear straining to the settee.

"Lord Luhaunt?" Rebecca had smoothed the skirts of her teal gown, adjusting on the settee next to her sister. "Posh, do not be so dramatic, Bea. He was very charming while we were dining. And this whole stay is looking much less dull since he has arrived. We are in the middle of nowhere, for heaven's sake. Besides, how could Luhaunt possibly be cursed?"

"It is what they say. He uses the dark arts—it is how he knows the horses, his strange ability with them—and how he has gained his wealth," Beatrice continued, her words still a low hiss. "It is a well-known fact he traded his family's lives in exchange for his own gain. Both the title and the horses."

"But he is so dashing."

"Of course he is. He has the dark arts on his side, clouding his person. So set your eyes downward, Rebecca—mother would never allow it, so be done thinking on it."

Brianna had only heard Rebecca grumble something incoherent at her sister at that point, so she moved on past the settee, perplexed.

She was accustomed to hearing useless gossip, but the dark arts as a cautionary tale? That was new to her. And she wasn't so sure the elder sister hadn't concocted the whole of it as a ruse to keep Lord Luhaunt's attentions for herself.

But the words had stuck in Brianna's mind the entire night. Every time she ventured a look at Luhaunt, she tried to connect him in some way to a mind filled with sinister dark arts. And every time, she could not see it in him, no matter how hard she looked.

Then again, she did have a hard time seeing anything sinister in handsome men. That much was proven.

At the card table, Luhaunt glanced up at Brianna in the very second she was watching him, pondering once more the dark arts supposedly attached to the man.

Her head dropped instantly, hiding from his brown eyes that still crinkled at the corners in mirth. Brianna wondered fleetingly what the humor was about. It was the one thing she admitted to missing as a spinster—easy laughter over innocent nothingness.

"Are you positive, Lord Luhaunt, you did not just flip that card from your sleeve?" Lily leaned across the card table, her heart-shaped mouth in a teasing pout. "I do believe Lord Newdale and I were well on our way to winning. Dare I call trickery upon you?"

Brianna quickly plucked one last chord, cutting short the sonata, and stood. The way Lily elongated the word "dare" told Brianna that Lily was already two glasses of sherry past decorum. Not to mention she had just accused Lord Luhaunt of cheating.

It was going to be a long evening.

Biting her tongue, Brianna moved to stand behind Lily, ready to intervene. Her eyes flickered over Luhaunt's face. Men did not always respond well to Lily's bold assertions when things—be it a game of cards or a dance—were not going her way.

Lord Luhaunt gave Lily an easy smile. "I assure you, nothing of the sort. Cheating at cards is a skill I never acquired." He held his arms straight out, manically flipping his wrists up and down. "I have absolutely nothing to hide, Miss Lily." His eyes drifted up to Brianna.

Brianna exhaled a sigh of relief. At least Luhaunt was a gentleman where Lily was concerned. Though she was not entirely positive if his last words were directed to Lily or to her.

Lily laughed at his overblown antics, looking to Lord Newdale. "Do then shuffle the cards Lord Newdale. I would like to soundly beat Lord Luhaunt in the next round."

Lady Rebecca, the fourth in their game of whist, cleared her throat good-naturedly.

"And you as well, Lady Rebecca," Lily said, her head swinging to her other adversary. "The sound beating will be yours to own as well."

Brianna held her breath, but the whole table laughed. What her sister managed to get away with—merely by her sweet voice—never failed to boggle Brianna's mind.

Lord Newdale picked up the cards, shuffling them.

"Tell me, Miss Lily, about where you grew up," Luhaunt asked. "I understand from Rowe that you lived for many years with Viscount Friellway? That your father was his solicitor?"

"We did. But Papa was so much more than his solicitor."

"How so?"

Lily smiled with obvious pride. "Papa was the viscount's most trusted advisor and friend, and we lived at the viscount's estate in Norfolk for as long as I can remember. Papa guided the viscount's holdings into tripling their worth, and was rewarded thusly—which is how the Silverton estate grew. They were grand friends—one was rarely without the other. And the viscount was much more akin to a beloved uncle for Brianna and me."

"So a happy childhood?" Luhaunt asked.

"Yes. It was just the four of us—papa, the viscount, Brianna and I for many years." Lily picked up her glass, sipping the last of her sherry. "We have no other family. The viscount did marry a number of years back, but his wife died in childbirth soon after. A tragedy."

Brianna poked Lily in the back. Her mouth was running fast again.

Lily reached for the fresh sherry glass that had appeared by her hand. Brianna eyed the overzealous footman that had placed it there, silently cursing him.

"Incredibly sad," Lord Newdale said, shaking his head as he passed out the cards.

In one long sip, Lily drained a third of the sherry. "Yes. We were happy. So very happy." Her hand waved in the air. "Until everyone died, that is."

Brianna bent next to Lily, her voice a low hiss. "Close your mouth, Lils." She snatched the glass from Lily's hand, red liquid sloshing onto the table.

"Bree, you are making a scene." Lily looked up at her, miffed.

"Please, excuse us." Brianna set the glass on the table and grabbed Lily's elbow, looking around the table. "May I interrupt the game and steal my sister away for a moment? I have sudden need of her in the hallway."

Both men were to their feet in an instant.

"Of course, Miss Silverton." Lord Newdale gave a slight bow.

Brianna didn't give him a chance to say anything else as her fingernails dug into Lily's elbow and she dragged her to standing, then steered her out of the room.

She had hoped to make it down the corridor and into the library before Lily exploded.

They only made it halfway.

Lily tore from Brianna's grip in the hallway, her feet planted.

"How could you, Bree? You have embarrassed me beyond all decency in front of Lord Newdale—and his sister—and his mother—and his other sister. And this is only their first real evening here."

"Lils, you are overreacting." Brianna's palms went up, trying to sneak onto Lily's shoulders.

Lily slapped her hands away. "I am not. You cannot stand it that I have a man showering me with such attention—two men if Lord Luhaunt's actions tonight are included. You are jealous—jealous of the entire season and of what I can have and what you cannot."

"You know that is not true, Lils." Brianna fought to keep her voice calm. "You have just had too much wine tonight and you are not thinking well."

"Too much wine? You are to judge me? You?"

"Lils, I am only—"

"You are only what? Bitter?" Lily snorted a hard chuckle, her arm swinging wide. "That I already know, Bree. Ever since

Gregory, you will do anything to make sure I do not find happiness."

"Do not, Lily. Do not." Brianna's head shook, the words coming out hard. "I am doing all of this to make you happy. To get you what you want."

Lily scoffed. "What I want? What would you know about that? You have already ripped away every bit of happiness from me."

"I am doing all of this for you, Lils. For your happiness. The season. Being here at Notlund. Entertaining Lord Newdale and his family. All of it is for your happiness. This is what you wanted." Brianna stopped, taking a deep breath. She could tell not one of her words reached Lily. "What do you want me to do, Lils?"

"I want you to walk. Walk out of here. Leave me alone. For one blasted moment, just leave me alone." Lily's voice vicious, she spun away from Brianna, almost stumbling to the floor. She managed to catch herself on the stone wall before she went down. "Better yet, I will leave."

"Lils…" Brianna's voice faded as her sister staggered down the hall, veering back and forth.

Heart hurting, Brianna watched her, wanting to go after her sister, but confounded about what to do.

Lily disappeared around the corner at the end of the long corridor.

Brianna's hands came up to her face, both palms rubbing her eyes and forehead.

Loss. She was at a complete loss.

She had only been trying to stop Lily from embarrassing herself. And she had gone through this particular scene in the hallway too many times to count.

"You were overly generous with her."

Brianna whipped around, only to see Luhaunt with his arms crossed over his chest. He leaned against the stone wall under a hanging lantern, the candle-light flickering on his dark hair.

The absolute last thing she needed at the moment.

Swallowing a groan, her hands dropped to her sides, her chin going up as her spine straightened. "You do not know a thing about it, Lord Luhaunt."

Pushing off from the wall, he stepped from the light, moving toward her. "You are right. I do not know a thing about it, only what I overheard."

"And just what did you overhear?"

"Your sister apparently blames you for everything that is not right in her life." He stopped in front of Brianna, looking down at her. "And she likes her wine."

"Well then, you must know her quite well." Brianna did not bother to hide the sarcasm in her voice. "That should be advantageous for you while attempting to court her."

An odd smile crossed his face. "Your sister is upset. Do not be so sure it is you she is upset with."

"I am quite certain it is me." Brianna met his brown eyes, sighing. She did not have the energy for this. "What is it you came out here for, Lord Luhaunt?"

"Escape. It became somewhat awkward in the drawing room after you two exited. Wynne is scrambling to put cheer on, and Rowe is just sitting back, silently amused." He turned, motioning with his hand to the drawing room. "But now that you are free once more, maybe you can help to restore the balance inside? I will walk you back."

Brianna glanced over her shoulder to where Lily had disappeared. What she really wanted to do was sneak up to her own rooms and sit in the dark. But that was not an option for her—that was an option reserved for the drunk and dramatic.

She nodded in agreement, starting forth.

Luhaunt stepped in line with her, his hands clasped behind his back. "You play the harp exceptionally well, Miss Silverton."

The compliment caught her off-guard, and she glanced at him. "Thank you. I was happy to find the duke had a pedal harp in residence—my father always much preferred listening to me play the harp over the harpsichord, so it is what I am most comfortable with."

"But you do not sing?"

"I croak like a toad." She shook her head. "Lily is a true talent when it comes to voices. I am happy to merely be the accompaniment to her voice."

"In other words, you like to hide in the background?"

"It is easier for all involved."

"How is that?"

She looked at him, wry smile on her face. "Did you yourself not say I treat people with 'open and utter distaste' when forced to interact?"

He chuckled. "That I did. But I think I limited the comment to misguided gentlemen foolhardy enough to stand next to you."

He opened the door to the drawing room, stepping aside to let her in.

Her voice dropped to a whisper as she passed him. "So why, Lord Luhaunt, are you bothering to stand next to me?"

His chuckle, low and hearty, followed Brianna into the room.

~ ~ ~

The backs of her legs cramping from sitting on her heels for too long, Brianna slid backward, her bottom hitting the rocks lining the edge of the stream. She gingerly stretched her legs out in front of her, letting the blood flow back to her toes.

Lungs still on fire after the brutally exhausting ride she had just jumped from, she leaned forward to sink her handkerchief into the stream. The fabric sopping, she slapped it onto her forehead, trying to cool the throbbing skin.

Her jacket had come off hours ago, and she was still boiling. Thank goodness she had given up on wearing a stifling hat long ago—she had lost far too many of them over the years with her swift rides.

After escaping the castle just as the sunlight had broken through the sky, she had made it to and from the closest town, Pepperton, fast enough to afford herself a moment of quiet—a moment purely for herself.

But it was hotter than blazes—hotter today than Brianna had ever remembered it being. Maybe that was why the toads were loud this morning, croaking out loud grumbles every few seconds.

Still, it wasn't enough to break her concentration on what she had learned earlier.

Meeting her hired bow street runner by Pepperton had been her only option—she couldn't very well invite Mr. Flemming up to Notlund. The man had needed to deliver pressing news on one of the things she had him investigating, namely the discreet debts Lord Newdale had racked up at three gaming halls in London.

Brianna watched gurgling bubbles of water swirl behind a fat rock in the middle of the stream, her mind churning. By itself, the total sum of the debts reported by Mr. Flemming wasn't enough to remove Lord Newdale as a possibility for her sister. But Mr. Flemming also had several leads he was to follow next, the most interesting being Lord Newdale's ongoing visits to four separate brothels.

A mistress that was disposed of at marriage was one thing, but a man with a history of visiting random women at various brothels was an entirely different matter.

This exact information was why she particularly liked Mr. Flemming. Gruff and straightforward, he told her exactly what he discovered without trying to shield her female sensibilities. And if that meant reporting about brothels and mistresses to her, he did so in a matter-of-fact manner.

Unfortunately for Lily, if the leads were founded, Brianna was going to have to remove Lord Newdale as a marriage possibility. Brianna could already see that Lily favored Lord Newdale the most, but if she had to break Lily's heart over the matter, she would. She'd done it before.

Brianna picked up a rock, whipping it into the water.

Lily would forgive her. She always did.

Her hand holding the handkerchief to her forehead dropped. The wet cloth was now just as hot as her forehead.

She eyed the water, pondering the option of stripping down and plunking herself into it. She was filthy from the ride. And until Lord Newdale was truly eliminated as a suitor, she had to maintain the veneer of utmost propriety. That meant composing herself before she got back to the castle—not showing up drenched in sweat and trail dirt.

Plus—she had to admit—the water would be delicious.

She looked over at Moonlight nibbling on juicy grass a few paces downstream. The horse was content, and Brianna knew Moonlight wouldn't wander too far.

Without another thought, she removed her boots and stood, quickly unbuttoning her deep blue skirt and stripping off her white shirt and short stays, then tossing them away from the splash of the water. For a second, she thought to remove her shift as well, but then thought the better of it.

Wading into the stream, she was mid-thigh in the warm water before she found a spot where it cooled by her toes. She sank, going to her knees as the water rolled past her.

Heaven. Absolute heaven.

Her arms swung back and forth beneath the surface, letting the water reach all the nooks and crannies that she could feel still holding fast to heat. Pulling the pins from her knot, she tousled out her hair before taking a deep breath and sinking her head.

Breaking the surface, she leaned back to keep everything but her face submerged. She stared at the hazy blue sky for some time, only the sound of rushing water in her ears.

Her thoughts quieted for a moment, so she stayed in the position, lost in the blankness of her mind for as long as she dared—too long, and she knew it.

Reality drew her back, and she sighed, the air popping her ears under the water. Now she would have to contend with her wet hair when she returned to the castle. So much for primness.

Maybe if luck—for once—was on her side, she wouldn't encounter Lord Newdale or his mother or sisters along the way.

Brianna pulled her head out of the water, finding her feet and standing.

An instant scream yelped from her mouth.

Luck was not on her side.

Sitting streamside, forearms relaxed on his bent knees, Lord Luhaunt watched her with curious interest. His peculiar devil smirk sat obvious on his face.

Her eyes darted past his shoulder as she sank into the water, her arms covering the top part of her body the best she could. Her clothes lay five steps behind him.

In control before the second scream in her throat escaped, she forged the haughtiest face she could manage while being nearly naked and trapped in the middle of a stream. "This is grossly rude, Lord Luhaunt. How long have you been sitting there?"

"Long enough to make sure I am the only one stumbling upon you." He pointed to her horse downstream. "Where have you been all morning, Miss Silverton?"

"It is none of your business, Lord Luhaunt."

"No?"

"If you think to blackmail me to get close to my sister, you are sorely mistaken in your intentions, Lord Luhaunt. I have no regard for my reputation, and I believe the duke will look more unfavorably upon your grossly inappropriate ogling, than he will upon my taking an innocent swim on a hot day."

"That does not answer my question, Miss Silverton."

She shook her head, eyes to the sky. "Why do I imagine it is too much to ask you to remove yourself? That you clearly have no honor as a gentleman."

"Where have you been?"

Her look dropped to him, eyes narrowing. "I was on a long ride."

"You left before the break of dawn, and have been gone for five hours. Both you and your horse look like you have travelled hell-bent for days. So where did you go? I only caught your trail an hour past on the eastern border of the forest."

Jaw dropping, her eyes went wide. "You have been following me?" This earl was far, far too much.

"Yes. So where were you, Miss Silverton?"

"It is absolutely none of your business, you arse." She looked down at her chest. Even through the water, she could see her white—now transparent—shift did nothing to hide her skin. Blast it. She looked back to him, venom pouring from her eyes. "Remove yourself from my sight this instant."

His smile only widened. "You are a prickly one, Miss Silverton." His limbs languid, he stretched himself into standing. "But I am not about to leave you here alone, prey to any unscrupulous passerby."

"You are the only unscrupulous passerby, Lord Luhaunt, and you know full well you are purposely blocking my path to my clothes."

He glanced over his shoulder to her pile of clothes. "It would seem I am."

"You need to leave, Lord Luhaunt. Please, on all that is holy, leave."

Slowly, he turned from her, stepping away. Brianna sighed in relief. But then he stopped, picking up her clothes and spinning back to her.

Shaking her head in disbelief, Brianna set loose a vicious low growl.

"I do promise not to look." Arm outstretched, he held up her skirt, stays and shirt as a barrier between them, turning his head to the side.

"You are impossible, Lord Luhaunt. Cruelly impossible." She gave one last futile glance about the stream bank, praying for a boulder to appear and roll over him—or lightning to strike him—or his horse to trample him.

None of that seemed likely.

She was stuck.

Chest pounding, she angled one arm across her breasts, used her other hand to cover her pelvis, and Brianna moved out of the water, stepping up onto the slippery rocks.

"Why? Why do you insist on harassing me so, Lord Luhaunt? It gets you no closer to my sister."

"I do not want your sister, Miss Silverton." His head stayed turned to the side with nary a blink in her direction.

"No?" Her eyes squinted at him as she stumbled across the rocks. She shook her head. "No, I do not believe you."

Just as she reached out to grab her skirt, his head swung toward her, his brown eyes intense on her face.

Brianna froze, her fingers in mid-air.

"Quite simply, Miss Silverton, I want you. Only you."

She shook her head, forehead scrunched. "What?"

"I want you, Brianna."

~ ~ ~

Sebastian watched with amusement as it took several seconds for his words to sink into Brianna's brain. And then several more seconds before she managed to reach out and grab her skirt.

Clutching the dark blue cloth to her chest, it covered the front part of her, but Sebastian could still see the lean outline of her body through the thin shift.

He had been a cad, waiting, watching her from afar after following her for an hour. But she had looked exhausted, and then so utterly peaceful when she sank into the water, that he was entranced and could nothing except sit down to watch her. She would be his soon enough as it was.

Her face suddenly snapped into control, and she snatched her shirt from his hand. Her short stays dropped to the ground, but she didn't pick them up, instead stepping backward away from him. No matter that it sent her back into the stream, water rushing over her ankles.

"What madness are you talking about, Lord Luhaunt?" Still trying to shield herself with the skirt, she fumbled with her white silk shirt, trying to right it enough to get her head and arms into it. "Just because I am a spinster does not mean I am available for…for…" Her face turned red. "For your amusement."

"I am talking about marrying you, Brianna."

"Do not call me Brianna. You do not even know me, and whatever bedlam you have rolling around in your brain, I want no part of it."

Her fingers frantic, the shirt dropped, landing in the water. "Blast it. No part of it. Do you hear me? None."

She bent, snatching up her soaked shirt and half dropping her skirt with the motion. It slipped, dragging her shift down and exposing her very plump right breast to the open air.

Sebastian couldn't help an appreciative smile.

She growled, trying to right herself, only to slip on the rocks and fall, flailing, toward Sebastian.

He happily caught her.

"Brianna. What in the blazes are you doing?" A woman's voice cut into the air from above.

Holding Brianna in his arms, Sebastian looked up over his shoulder only to find the duchess standing at the crest of the bank.

Three more heads popped into view behind her. Lily, Lord Newdale, and his mother. The four of them spread out along the grassy bank, staring down at him and Brianna. Every mouth agape.

Fate.

Sebastian had a plan in mind when he came to Notlund, but plans could change. And fate had just granted him one entirely generous short-cut.

He was not one to pass upon what fate offered.

Sebastian quickly propped Brianna to her feet, hoping she was steady, and turned to the small crowd, shielding her from their view.

"Wynne. It seems as if you have stumbled upon a chance encounter."

"It looks like a hell of a lot more than that, Seb, and you damn well know it." Wynne's ire at him was instant. She jabbed her head to the side, trying to see past him. "Brianna, are you all right? Are you hurt?"

Sebastian could feel Brianna trying to scramble into her wet clothes behind him.

"Brianna, answer me. Are you all right?" Wynne's eyes darted to Sebastian. "So help me if you have laid a finger on her, Seb—"

"I am fine, Wynne." Brianna stepped from behind Sebastian, still righting her shirt. "It was as Lord Luhaunt said. A chance encounter. I was out for a ride and he happened upon me."

Wynne's arms crossed over her chest, eyebrows high to the sky. "He happened upon you naked?"

"Bree…" Lily's face was ashen, her eyes darting to Lord Newdale's mother.

The woman did not look pleased. Lady Newdale looked not only shocked, but horrified. Horrified to her very marrow that the sister of her possible daughter-in-law was a trollop. Her judging eyes did not move from Brianna.

Brianna's face burning red, her head went down and she shoved her feet into her boots and tied them as quickly as her shaking fingers allowed. She scampered down the streamside to her horse, and Sebastian wondered for a moment if she would just mount the mare and run.

She would have every right.

Instead, she fetched her jacket from where it was draped on the saddle. Jerking her arms into the sleeves, she walked back toward Sebastian, her eyes still hidden.

Her obvious humiliation did not sit well with him, especially when he knew full well he was the cause of it.

"What were you doing in the area, Wynne?" Sebastian asked, trying to draw the attention of the crowd above them away from Brianna.

"We were out for a ride," Wynne said. "I was showing them the estate and I thought I heard Brianna's voice. And do not try to change the subject, Seb."

"This particular subject is not one to be discussed right here, right now, Wynne." Sebastian looked pointedly around them. "No. This extremely serious subject is one to be discussed back at the castle, when we all have level heads about us."

"Duchess, this will not do," Lady Newdale said, finding her outraged voice. "This will not do at all."

With one last death glare at Sebastian, Wynne turned, stepping in front of Lady Newdale. "I agree entirely, Lady Newdale. But it is far too warm out here with nary a breeze. Let us move back to the castle, where we can discuss this at length. I am sure there is a reasonable explanation for all of this."

Lady Newdale harrumphed. "A reasonable explanation would be quite welcome at this very moment, Duchess."

Wynne lightly grabbed Lady Newdale's arm, gently turning her from the stream. "I am sure an explanation is forthcoming. I have never known another to hold propriety in such high regard as does Miss Silverton. But I am dreadfully hot out here, as I am sure you are as well, and this will be best discussed in the privacy of the castle confines. It will be much cooler there."

With one more judging glance at Brianna, Lady Newdale allowed Wynne to steer her away to her horse. Lord Newdale trailed them, an amused smirk on his face.

Lily remained rooted to her spot, staring at her sister.

When Brianna finally ventured a look upward, Lily shook her head at her, savage disappointment crinkling her eyes.

Brianna's mouth opened, but Lily spun, stomping away before Brianna could get a word out.

Sebastian watched Brianna's face crumple, watched the terror flash through her eyes at her sister's reaction.

For a moment, he regretted the pain it obviously caused her.
But the pain would be short-lived.
He would see to that.

CHAPTER 4

Shaking his head, the duke turned from the sideboard in his study, a glass of brandy in each hand—one with a polite amount of liquid, one filled nearly to the brim. He watched his wife exit the room, waiting until she closed the door to exhale a low whistle.

He looked at Sebastian, eyebrow arched. "Was Wynne's accounting of the scene accurate?"

Leaning against Rowen's desk, Sebastian shrugged. He had been silent through most of Wynne's tirade. "Yes. For the most part."

"All parts?"

"All the important parts."

Rowen walked across the study, handing Sebastian the nearly full glass of brandy. Good friend. Sebastian drained the top third of the glass.

"I have never seen Wynne that mad—at anyone aside from me, that is," Rowen said.

"It was extreme."

"She is worried about the sisters. She adores them and wants them to be happy. As do I."

"As do I, Rowe."

"Do you?" Rowen raised his glass, taking a sip and eyeing Sebastian over the rim. "You do know how this will go, Seb?"

"Yes."

"We can devise an alternate way out of this." Rowen traced the motif cut into the glass in his hands. "It will not be pretty, but it can be done. Your honor will take a beating."

"I accept what is coming."

"Truly?" Rowen's head cocked to the side. "Of all the idiotic moves, my friend. This tops them all. Naked ladies in streams are always to be avoided. Ride on past, Seb. Not that hard to do."

"It was in this instance."

"Why?" Rowen took another sip of the brandy.

"I planned this."

Rowen sputtered, brandy catching in his throat. "You what?"

Sebastian tipped his glass, taking a healthy swallow of the amber liquid. Best to just confess all at this point. "I planned this. Since you pointed out the Silverton sisters at the Thorton ball, I have been planning this. Planning to marry Brianna."

"What? And you did not think to tell me? Outside of last night, I have never even seen you talk to Brianna. And you think you want to marry her?"

"I do." Sebastian fingered the rim of his glass patiently. He could see Rowen was having difficulty coming to terms with Sebastian's words.

"That was why you stayed in London?" Rowen rubbed his forehead. "That is why you are here? But Brianna? Lily, I would understand, she is beautiful—"

"Brianna is beautiful."

Rowen tilted his head, thinking. "True. I guess I never thought on the matter as she is so set on being a spinster. But she is so...rigid."

"She does not bother to show her beauty off. She would prefer everyone to be looking at her sister."

Rowen frowned at him. "But why? After all these many years, you have done nothing but dance away from the merest thought of marriage. You have been running at breakneck speed from one place to the next for the last seven years. So why her? Why now?" Rowen stopped, clearing his throat, his voice going low. "You should know that Brianna can be...controlling. It is in her nature."

"I am aware."

"So why her?"

"You will think me fanciful."

"Fanciful?" Rowen scoffed a chuckle. "The word has never even been bandied near you, much less been attached to you. I have known you for too long, my friend, to ever think you fanciful."

Sebastian pushed himself from the desk, standing straight. "Do you recall that time, a bit more than a year ago, when we talked of marriage, talked of women, and I told you I would know her when I saw her—the woman that is meant for me? Just like I do with the horses—I know the best ones when I see them?"

"Yes. I recall."

"It was merely bravado at the time. Putting off any discussion on the matter." Sebastian's words slowed with unyielding disbelief. "But then it happened. Out of nowhere. It happened. When I saw Brianna at that ball in London, even from across the room, I knew it. I knew it instantly, and I almost did not believe it myself. It is why I hovered about for weeks there. I was trying to convince myself it was not true."

Sebastian shrugged, shaking his head. "But she is it. I want her, Rowe—no doubt in my mind. She is it. She is the one."

"When were you planning to tell me?"

"Eventually."

"So you have been scheming this? Scheming to trap her?"

"No. I had planned to woo her properly here at Notlund. I realized quite early that she has erected a fortress around herself like no other. So it would take time. Time that I would not be afforded in a London ballroom—but time I would be afforded here at Notlund." Sebastian smiled. "But then fate decided to intervene today. And I could not let the opportunity pass by. I had truly only stopped to talk to her, but then Wynne appeared."

Rowen gave another low whistle and then drained his glass. He shook his head, grabbing Sebastian's glass from his hand and then drained that one as well.

"Anyone but you, Seb, I would have deposited with a broken jaw onto the front lawn." Rowen sighed. "But if this is what you want, you know I am not one to ignore fate. You should know, however, that Brianna has become dear to me, and you had best not wreck her. Do remember, a broken jaw can be delivered at any moment."

"I will remember."

Rowen's head tilted to the door. "Shall we enter the fray in the drawing room? Best to get this done as quickly as possible."

~ ~ ~

All that time spent.

She had never once let her sister out of her sight in London.

It had taken the utmost vigilance, keeping Lily's reputation above reproach. Keeping Lily free from the grasp of any scoundrel. Not letting her fall prey to an unscrupulous snare. Sequestering her from anyone with the slightest notion to besmirch her reputation.

All that time.

All that time and Brianna hadn't recognized that very thing coming for her. Hadn't seen the importance of protecting herself with the same vigilance. Hadn't seen her own reputation as valuable.

Hadn't understood any of it, until the very moment she saw Lady Newdale's face by the riverbank.

The judgement. The scorn. The destruction of everything she had worked so hard to give Lily.

Brianna yanked a fresh shift over her head.

Lord Luhaunt. The complete and utter ass. He had set her up. And she had fallen for it.

Want her indeed.

The man wanted nothing more than to ruin her reputation, watch Lily's suitors beg off, and then ease himself right along a cleared path to Lily. For who else would want the sister of an openly ruined woman? No respectable man, that was obvious.

Not bothering to wait for the maid that she knew would eventually appear to help her, Brianna pulled a mud-brown dress from the wardrobe, slipping into it. The muslin dress had short, capped sleeves, perfect for the hot day—but a high neckline, not so perfect for the hot day.

Damn the hot day.

She was so stupid. Idiotic not to see this coming. Not to see the plotting of the earl. He had said he had a strategy here at Notlund, and she had taken his words far too lightly. She wouldn't be surprised if the man had invited the group to that very spot to catch them.

What had she been thinking, going for a blasted dip in the river? Nearly naked for all the world to see. All she had wanted was to not have to think for one moment. One blasted moment of reprieve. One moment in the water. A moment in the middle of everything speeding around her so her mind could sit still. One moment when she wasn't worried about absolutely everything.

"So very easy to fool, you little wench—your simple brain is not large enough to think beyond what is in the mirror."

Fingers tightening around her slippers, Brianna's eyes shut tight, forcing sneered words from long ago gone—banishing them as they ruthlessly tried to take over her mind.

She sank to her bed, her body gone to jelly. Long seconds passed before she could lift her feet high enough to slide on her slippers.

If only her father were still alive. If only he hadn't counted on her finishing what he had started. If only she could tell Lily the truth. If only she could take back what she had done to her sister.

If only.

Her sudden tornado of wallowing complete, Brianna took a deep breath and gave herself a slight shake, popping to her feet and straightening her spine.

All of those "if onlys" were not possible, so she needed to not dwell.

She needed to harden.

She needed to go down to the drawing room and devise a
way for her reputation to not be so fully shattered that Lily lost all
three of her suitors. And the longer Brianna stayed hiding away in
her room, the guiltier she looked.

She went over to the mirror, quickly pulling her hair into a
tight knot. Adjusting the lace that curved up her neck, she sighed.
She had chosen the dourest dress she owned, and she hoped she
looked enough the unmarriageable spinster that no one could
question her innocence in the scene by the stream.

Her slippers soft on the stone floor, she silently made her
way through the ancient castle's halls. Approaching the Celeste
drawing room, she slowed. She could already hear the awkward
murmurs from within.

A deep breath, and she turned the corner, walking into the
elegant room.

Wynne was cloistered with Lady Newdale on the settee, and
Brianna could see she was trying to placate the woman as best she
could. Lily, still in her prettiest mauve riding habit, stood next to
the duke and Lord Newdale by the fireplace.

Lily's eyes kept jumping nervously from Lord Newdale to
his mother. Lord Newdale wouldn't be the problem—Brianna
had already seen that by the stream. Newdale found the situation
amusing, nothing more dire than a discreet summer dalliance
near the water.

His mother was a completely different matter, and in all
the information Brianna had gathered about their family, Lady
Newdale ruled her clan with a harsh fist. She was the one that
would allow or break any sort of relationship between Lily and
Lord Newdale.

Brianna could not blame Lady Newdale for her harsh
judgement. The woman had two other daughters she needed to
marry off. And if she had any chance of that, she needed a proper
match for her son. Not one attached to scandal.

And then there was the last person in the room—the one
Brianna had purposefully avoided looking at. Her eyes flashed to

Lord Luhaunt. He was opposite her, standing by himself near the wide windows that looked out over the newly planted gardens on the east side of the castle.

He was the only one that had noticed her enter the room, and the side of his mouth lifted when her eyes met his. Not a smirk. More of a comforting, everything-will-be-fine half smile. Even apologetic.

She almost believed it.

The man had a strategy, she had to remember. He most certainly was not an ally.

Brianna gave a small cough. Instant silence fell upon the room, all eyes landing on her.

Her throat went dry. How did one even begin a discussion such as this? How to explain the innocence of what was seen?

"Brianna, thank you for your haste in joining us." The duke stepped forward, saving her from bumbling words. "I understand there was an incident by the eastern stream?"

Brianna nodded. She was not about to hide from the truth. "It is true. I had stopped—"

"I would not call it an 'incident,' your grace." Lady Newdale pushed herself between Brianna and the duke. "Indecent is a much more appropriate term for what we witnessed. Your charge, naked with this man." Her forefinger flew out at Lord Luhaunt.

"Come now, Lady Newdale, we must not rush to conclusions," the duke said. "Your accusations skirt a fine line upon destroying both Miss Silverton and Lord Luhaunt's honor."

"Do not patronize me, your grace. I am far too old for that nonsense." Lady Newdale's fists went to her hips. "I know very well what I saw, your grace. We all know what we saw. It cannot be overlooked. I cannot allow my son to be involved with your charge, if this is the type of nonsense you allow. Repercussions must be applied after what we witnessed. And if you will not do so, I will see to it myself—one way or another."

The duke's jaw visibly flexed. "Lady Newdale, as you are a guest in my home, I say this as politely as possible…do not dare to threaten my charges."

Lady Newdale's jaw clamped shut, her breath seething through flared nostrils.

"This is a matter that is best discussed with the primary parties," the duke said. "I am sure the resolution will sufficiently assuage your morals, Lady Newdale. To that end, I would appreciate you and your son to take your leave." His eyes did not leave Lady Newdale. "Lily, please excuse yourself as well."

Lady Newdale spun with an exaggerated sigh, stomping out of the room. Her son silently followed.

The duke's eyes swung to Lily, still standing by the fireplace. "Lily?"

"But I need to stay," Lily said, her hands wringing. "Brianna does not know the damage she has done."

"I am sure Brianna grasps the seriousness of the situation, Lily. And you have too much at stake. Wynne will stay, if it helps your concerns."

Lily's eyes dropped from the duke to Brianna. The sheer disappointment in Lily's eyes cut straight through Brianna's pounding heart.

Her head bowing, Lily turned, disappearing out of the room.

The door closed, and aside from the shuffle of Wynne moving from the settee to stand next to her husband, the silence thickened in the room. Lord Luhaunt stayed in his place by the window, oddly silent.

Wynne cleared her throat, clasping her hands together. "I am aware that I am the American in the room, so I understand the nuances of this the least, but we have a very dire situation here, do we not?"

"To put it mildly, yes," the duke said.

"Thank you for handling Lady Newdale, your grace," Brianna said. "I appreciate your words. And I do appreciate the awkward position this has caused everyone. But truly, you must believe me—what happened by the stream is of no concern. I was hot and I waded into the water, and Lord Luhaunt happened upon me. I had my shift on the entire time. I was extracting myself from the situation when Wynne and the rest of the party happened upon us. There was no misconduct."

"You can remove the worry from your face, Brianna. I do believe you," the duke said. "Seb has also assured me of the innocence of the situation."

Relief flooded Brianna. The last thing she wanted was the duke and duchess to think her wanton. Now they could go about fixing this. "Is there any way out of this that will ensure the mishap does not taint Lily's marriage options?"

Brianna watched as a deep frown set onto Wynne's face as she looked from Brianna up to her husband.

"What? What is it?" Brianna asked.

"They have to get married, do they not?" Wynne asked.

The duke heaved a sigh, nodding.

"What? No." Brianna took several steps backwards, hands up in front of her, waving. "No—no, no, no. I was hoping for suggestions to help clear the situation. Not a marriage. No."

"Brianna, a marriage is the only thing that will clear you of this." The duke's face was gentle empathy. "Scandal is sure to attach itself to you, no matter what. There is nothing we can do about that. The best we can do is to mitigate the scandal with a marriage. There will be chatter, but a full scandal will not haunt you. Will not haunt your sister and her prospects."

"But…but only we know," Brianna stuttered. "We cannot control this? There must be something we can do. We are just not thinking hard enough."

The duke shook his head. "If it were just the four of us in this room—all would be well. But it is not. Both Lord Newdale and his mother saw you—to be blunt—near to naked with Lord Luhaunt. There is no avoiding the scandal. A marriage is the only way we can save your reputation and quiet the scandal before it can harm your sister. If you were thinking...objectively, you would already know this. Seb has already agreed to the marriage."

"He what? He has?" Mouth agape, Brianna's head swung to Lord Luhaunt. He gave her a slight nod, the same half smile from earlier on his face. She whipped back to the duke. "Well, I will not. Absolutely not. I will take the scandal fully, then. I will not marry him."

The door to the drawing room crashed open.

"You will." Lily stalked into the room, slamming the door closed behind her. "On all that is holy, Bree, you will marry him."

Brianna's hands flew up in front of her. "Lily, I know that would be easiest, but I will not—you know I cannot."

Not slowing, Lily came at her, and Brianna thought for a moment that her sister was going strike her. But then Lily stopped, only a breath away.

"How could you do this to me, Bree? You know I am hoping for a proposal from Lord Newdale—but now his mother—how could you? He will never marry me if you do not do this."

"Lily, this is my scandal, not yours. This need not affect you."

"You know that is not true."

Brianna looked desperately around the room for help.

None came.

Her eyes went back to Lily's, a mirror of her own. "My reputation has nothing to do with you, Lily. I am sure after a few days, if I just disappear, Lady Newdale will forget everything that happened by the stream. I do not think Lord Newdale cares a whit about what happened—it is just his mother. So if I go away, you can continue on with him. It will be like it never happened."

"Blast it, Brianna—she will not forget, and you know it." Lily's voice turned vicious. "You have ruined my life, Bree. Again. You have done it again."

Brianna grabbed Lily's arms, trying to get her to see reason. "I have not. This is an overreaction. All of it is. Your life is not ruined, and there is no need for me to marry."

"How could you do this to me, Bree?" Lily's vicious tone spun into desperation. "You promised—you swore you would make it up to me—and now this? I finally have a chance to be happy, and you rip it from me like this?"

"No, Lils, this is just a misunderstanding. It can still be fixed."

"You owe me this, Bree. You owe me."

Brianna's hands dropped heavily from Lily's arms.

Lily was right. She did owe her sister this.

Numb, she turned from Lily.

Not about to let her escape, Lily jumped in front of Brianna. "You will do it? You will marry Lord Luhaunt? Tell me you will do it, Bree."

Brianna could not look at her. Could not look at the duke or duchess. Could not look at Lord Luhaunt. Slowly, she nodded, her chin falling to her chest. "Yes."

"Thank you." The two words, and her sister flew back out the door.

The door quietly clicked closed.

"I would presume she is off to report the resolution to Lady Newdale?" Wynne asked in a whisper.

"I imagine." The duke grabbed his wife's hand, setting it in the crook of his elbow. "We should follow. There will be questions."

Eyes on the patterned maroon edge of the rug covering the wood floor, Brianna listened as the footsteps of the duke and duchess exited the drawing room.

What had she just done?

What the hell had just happened?

When, in all of that, had she so completely lost control of everything?

A hand wrapping over her shoulder from behind made her jump, and she realized Lord Luhaunt was still in the room.

He had been silent through it all. So silent, she had forgotten he was even present.

For the merest second, there was something so kind, so comforting about his warm hand near her neck. But then Brianna revolted, stumbling out of his grasp.

"What do you think on that, Brianna? We are to be married."

She turned to him, looking up, meeting his brown eyes.

His smile had widened, still soft, reassuring, but now there was a twinkle behind it.

If she didn't know better, she would say the devil in his smile had planned this whole thing.

~ ~ ~

"You are shaking."

Sebastian had seen it right in the middle of Brianna's argument with her sister. Saw the moment Brianna had started to shake. The exact moment when she lost all control of the situation.

And she was still shaking.

She shrugged, twisting to avoid his hand going to her shoulder again. "I am not."

"Look at your hands, Brianna."

Her quivering hands came up as her eyes dropped to them. She held them suspended in the air, staring at them trembling for a long second.

"Oh."

She crossed her arms, tucking her hands into her body, hidden. But it didn't hide the quaking in her shoulders.

Of all that he had seen and done that day, it was this—her body out of control—that cut to his conscience and had Sebastian truly questioning his tactics.

Not able to stop himself, he pounced before she could avoid him, setting both of his hands on her shoulders, hoping to still the trembling. He stared down at the top of her head, searching for words to make this easier for her. "Brianna...what is done is done. It is the right course."

Her eyes whipped up to him. "Did you plan this, Lord Luhaunt?

"What?"

"Did you plan this? Plan to ruin me?"

"How could I have possibly planned what happened by the stream?"

"Did you invite Wynne to catch us?"

"You question my honor?"

She glared at him, accusation plain in her clear blue eyes.

A soft chuckle escaped from his lips, his hands tightening on her shoulders. "Do you honestly think I somehow knew I would find you near to naked in a stream, and miraculously, I had thought ahead and asked Wynne to meet us in that very spot? You truly must think me magical if I could have possibly done any of those things."

Her bottom lip disappeared under her teeth as she stared at him. "No. I apologize. It was wrong to question your honor." Her eyes narrowed at him. "But your actions by the stream—all of this could have been avoided if you had just left. Left instead of sitting there a cad, antagonizing me. And to what end? Look at where we are now."

"You blame me?"

"Yes."

His hands dropped from her shoulders. She was angry again. Angry, but the shaking had stopped. He would take the anger well over the shaking shell she had just been.

"I cannot change what happened, Brianna. And I am not going to fight what is to come."

Her eyes lit up. "But you could. You could leave. Disappear. Sneak off. Jilt me. I would be ever so grateful if you would. And you need not worry—I would only speak kind words of you."

"I am not about to do that, Brianna."

"I do not...I do not know what to do." Her hand went to her forehead, rubbing it. "I do not know how to extract us from this situation. And you—you vex me, Lord Luhaunt. You. This situation. Everything. All I wanted to do was to find a suitable husband for Lily, the only reason we even came to Notlund, and now this...now this."

She sank onto a side chair, her fingers going back and forth under the brown lace crawling up her neck as if it was choking her. Sebastian could see her start to crumble again.

He moved to sit on the chair next to her, leaning forward so she was forced to look at him. "All of this will be easier, Brianna, if you just accept the inevitable."

"That easy?" Her head shook, her gaze going to the ceiling. With a deep breath, her blue eyes dropped to him. "What do you want from me, Lord Luhaunt?"

"Foremost, Brianna, I would like you to not look repulsed at the very thought of marrying me."

Her head jerked to a tilt. "I look repulsed?"

"Slightly."

"Oh...I fear I have lost all politeness."

"It is understandable. Second, and most importantly, I wish to marry you. You will recall I did come here for a wife."

"And it does not matter to you who that wife is?"

"I want you, Brianna. I have made no secret of that."

Frown deepening on her face, Sebastian could see the suspicion in her eyes only heighten. As many times as he had told her that, not once had she believed him.

Not once.

Sebastian stared at her, attempting to see past her eyes, past her wall.

Not once had she looked at him without suspicion.

And he needed to figure out why.

CHAPTER 5

She only had two days left.

Two days before the marriage, and as much as she had tried to convince the duke, Wynne, and her sister that the marriage wasn't necessary, Brianna had made no progress. True, she had agreed to the marriage, but that didn't mean she wouldn't try to escape it until the very moment she said "I do."

Her sister avoided her at every turn, and Wynne would merely turn the conversation to wedding preparations. The duke had been scarce, Brianna only saw him at dinners. But at least he was still at Notlund—unlike Lord Luhaunt, who had disappeared altogether.

Brianna hadn't talked to Luhaunt since the day of the scandal. He had left Notlund for a few days, presumably to prepare things for the wedding—arrange the special license—but she wasn't sure. She had hoped against hope that he maybe just wouldn't return. That he would disappear, fleeing the need to marry her.

But then Luhaunt had returned. And Brianna had become desperate. So desperate, that she was about to trade one secret in order to keep an even more precious one.

Pacing the wooden boards on the porch of Wynne's painting studio, situated just up the hill from the expansive stables, Brianna's eyes scanned the rolling pastures. She had been waiting for two hours for Lord Luhaunt to appear, jittery and watching the workers that were busy constructing the fourth, and grandest, stable at Notlund.

One of the stableboys had reported that Luhaunt had taken out a new young mare to test her stamina. But how long did it really take to test a horse's stamina?

Brianna stopped, rocking back on her heels as she looked at the horizon above the forest canopy. The sun's rays were beginning to wane. If Luhaunt did not appear soon, she would miss her chance to talk to him in private today.

Thundering hooves from her right made her jump, and a cloud of dust preceded a lean brown horse coming to a sudden halt in front of her. Brianna looked up.

Lord Luhaunt. Of course. The man was not bashful.

"Brianna. You are waiting for me?"

Brianna's arms crossed over her belly. Was she that obvious? She nodded.

A quick smile crossed his face. "Had I known the pleasure awaited me, I would have returned much earlier. Let me get this one settled to her stall. You will wait?"

Brianna nodded again, her arms tightening against her belly. She hadn't realized how twisted her stomach had gotten during the past several days, but there it was, a spiked rock ravaging her belly at the mere sight of Luhaunt.

Within minutes, Brianna was watching Luhaunt walk up from the second stable. In a simple white linen shirt with sleeves rolled back, buckskin breeches, and well-worn, tall black Hessians, Lord Luhaunt looked entirely comfortable, entirely at ease with dirt and sweat covering his tall frame.

He ran a hand through his dark brown hair, mussing even more the tousle of it. She took a deep breath. If she did end up having to marry the man, at least he was easy to look at. Too easy, truth be told.

"Have you been waiting long?" Luhaunt asked halfway up the hill.

Brianna stepped from the porch onto the scrubby grass splotching the dirt. "Yes. But it was fine to wait. I wished to speak to you in private." She met him a few paces from the studio.

He stopped, eyeing her for a quick second, then looked around. "Walk with me to the castle?"

Brianna nodded, her arms dropping from her stomach. She didn't trust being alone with him, but she also couldn't risk having this conversation anywhere near prying ears.

They walked in silence to the start of the path that ran through the forest up to the castle. Her eyes on the trail in front of her, she could feel Luhaunt's curious glances her way.

Once they were secluded in the quiet of the trees, Luhaunt cleared his throat. "What was it you wanted to discuss, Brianna?"

The hairs on the back of her neck prickled. That he continued to call her by her first name put her on guard—far too intimate. But she wasn't about to fight that battle. She had much bigger problems—like extracting herself from getting married.

She glanced up at him. "To my dismay, this wedding appears to be moving forth. I had hoped that with a few days' time, the duke and my sister would see that it is not necessary, but they have not budged in their opinions."

"Nor have I."

"Yes, well, you may think differently after I tell you what I need to. And in which case, I will be more than happy to absolve you from any entanglement with me."

"What is it you need to tell me?"

"The money, the Silverton estate. I am sure you know that it is vast and healthy."

"I do."

"I was not lying when I told you days ago that all of it is tied into trusts that are only accessible by me, and limitedly, by my sister. A husband for either of us would have no access to the fortune. I have had three separate solicitors working to make it so, and the trusts are unbreakable. I would be happy to show you the documents."

He shrugged. "I do not need to see the documents, Brianna. I believe you."

"Do you understand? You will not gain anything by marrying me, Lord Luhaunt."

"I disagree."

"You do?"

"I will gain a wife."

Brianna gritted her teeth, taking a controlling breath. "In no uncertain terms, Lord Luhaunt, if we are forced to marry—and I emphasize forced—you will not be able to take control of any assets, and you will not be able to make me choose to give you anything." Her voice went hard. "No matter what you think you can do to me, I will give you nothing. If you think you can break my will, you cannot."

His eyebrow cocked up at her, curious. "I believe you misinterpret every intention I have, Brianna. I do not want your money—I never did. The earldom eclipses anything I could ever desire, and then some."

Brianna's feet stopped. "But you work so hard for this stud farm—all of your travels. Wynne has talked about all you have done to make these stables, this business, successful—you work on it like you need it to be prosperous."

Luhaunt halted, turning fully to her. "I do not have to do anything, Brianna. I work with the duke on the herd because I am good at it. I am good at discovering the best horses. Good at convincing people to part with them. Good at breeding matches." His left hand went up, fingers running through his hair and then scratching the back of his neck. "I do all of it because it is worth my time. Something I can contribute to the world. Something more than sitting in London and gambling and drinking."

He pointed back in the direction of the stables. "What Rowen and I started here—what we are creating is something truly special. These horses—we are creating new breeds—new lines that are nothing but a gift to the world."

Following to where his finger pointed, Brianna stared at the trees that now blocked the stables from view.

She suddenly realized she knew absolutely nothing about this man. She had been fighting so hard to extract herself from marrying him, that she hadn't even considered learning anything about him.

She looked up at him, meeting his brown eyes that were squarely on her. "It is just not usual, an earl that has more to do with his time than gambling and hunting and politics."

Luhaunt shrugged and turned, resuming the walk. "Yes, well, I was a spare—a second son—for most of my life. My purpose had never been the earldom, and I should not be vilified for having aspirations outside of it."

Brianna followed, falling into step beside him. "I apologize. I did not intend to disparage your work. I made assumptions."

"Do not give it another thought."

"Are you cursed, Lord Luhaunt?" Brianna glanced at his profile, the question flying out of her mouth before she could control it. Annoyed with herself, the fingernail of her ring finger jabbed into the pad of her thumb—her control over her own tongue seemed to particularly lack around Luhaunt.

A few steps passed without him looking her way, and then he chuckled, his eyes on a low branch in front of them. "Cursed? That is the latest the tongues wag about me?"

"The Newdale sisters, yes. The elder mentioned that you are cursed and that you practice the dark arts. Especially with the horses. It is how you are able to see things with them that others do not." Brianna cleared her throat. As the words escaped, she realized how utterly silly they sounded. "I am, of course, keenly aware she is not the most credible of sources. So I thought to ask you on the matter."

"Do I see things that others do not?"

"Is that the curse?"

"I do not know if one would call it a curse, but yes, I do recognize nuances with the horses that others do not. I did not understand how different, or useful, the skill was until we were immersed in the wars on the continent."

"The duke has mentioned time and again how crucial you were to saving some of the very best horses to ever walk the earth."

"He is too kind."

"He is also honest and not given to exaggeration."

Luhaunt shrugged.

They continued in silence for several more steps. Her boots crunching on twigs, Brianna's eyes fell to the forest floor.

She was moving in the exact opposite direction she had intended. She hadn't waited for hours just to speak to Luhaunt to get to know him better—no, she was supposed to be trying to convince him to call off the wedding. She had hoped reminding him of the money he would not have access to would be enough. That he would realize there would be no benefit to marrying her.

She had been a fool to pin her hopes on that.

Swallowing the lump in her throat, her fingernails started to, one by one and back and forth, dig into the pads of her thumbs.

She would have to tell him. It was the last thing she could think of. The last chance for escape.

"There is one more thing I need to tell you, Lord Luhaunt, and again, I give you free rein to put a stop to this marriage when you hear it. In fact, I encourage it."

He gave her a sideways glance, sudden smirk on his face. "Yes, I imagine you do encourage it. There is nothing that will change my mind on the matter, Brianna."

"I am not a virgin."

His stride froze instantly, and it took Brianna another two steps to stop. By then, he already had her elbow in his hand, pulling her backward. She turned to look at him, finding his smirk had vanished and his eyes had turned deadly serious.

Brianna's throat constricted, cutting her breath as her body went stiff. She hadn't thought Luhaunt a violent man, but then, she had been wrong before. Very wrong.

Trying to wedge her arm from his grasp, her head swiveled around, looking for escape into the trees.

He didn't let her go. "You are not a virgin?"

She shook her head, leaning into his arm, trying to use her weight to break his hold.

"Brianna, stop. Did something happen to you? Did some man—"

"No. No. It is not what you are thinking. I was willing."

He dropped her elbow, staring at her. She didn't move from her spot, accepting his stare. Accepting his judgement. If it got her out of the marriage, then she would take it—anything he had to dole out.

It took him a long moment to form words. "You loved this man, then?"

Brianna sucked in a gasp, blood draining from her face.

"You loved him?"

She fought the dizziness setting in.

But what did it matter now, the truth?

"I…I did. I thought I did."

"When?"

"Years ago."

"What happened?"

Her head whipped to the side and she turned to walk away from Luhaunt. She had to move or she was going to faint. She had thought it would be easy, speaking these words, speaking of the past. But it wasn't—far from it. Chin at her chest, words mumbled out. "I loved the wrong person."

His hand went to her elbow again, halting her steps. Luhaunt planted himself in front of her. "Your face is ashen, Brianna. And your eyes tell me it was not as simple as that—that it was traumatic. Did he die? Did he abandon you?"

She glanced up at his face for the smallest moment, and then her head dropped and she stared at the dust on his black boots.

Seconds ticked by before she gained enough control to lift her head and force her eyes to meet and stay on his. "Lord Luhaunt, I have told you what you were owed to know before you married me. I am a fallen woman. Beyond that, I do not wish to speak of that time."

She inhaled a deep breath, her left hand flat on her stomach. "Will you talk to the duke about the broken engagement by yourself, or do you wish me to accompany you?"

His answer was instant, his brow furrowed at her. "This does not change a thing, Brianna. I still want you."

"But…but you cannot. I am a fallen woman."

"I can, and I do. I want you as my wife."

Brianna swallowed a frustrated growl. This man was impossible to escape. "Lord Luhaunt, I do understand that you came here for my sister, and that I am—"

"Why is it, Brianna, that you continue to insist I came to Notlund for your sister?"

"The first day we met, you said you were here for a wife."

"Yes." Luhaunt's grip on her elbow tightened, and he leaned in, heat in his brown eyes. Unmistakable heat. Heat that was directed, full force, at her. "A wife is exactly why I came here."

Dumbstruck, unable to deny what he insinuated, Brianna leaned slightly away from him. His heat was too much.

"But why me? I am not interesting, not a painter like Wynne, not light and bubbly and charming like Lily. I have offered you nothing but frowns, and yet you still insist on saying you want me." She wedged a foot backward to gain some space. "Why? I do not understand it."

His intentions sufficiently expressed, Luhaunt dropped his grip on her arm, letting her escape him. She pounced on the opportunity and continued walking up the path. He stayed right next to her, his arm brushing hers.

"Honestly, Brianna, I do not fully understand it either. But it is true. I want you. It is just like with the horses—I see something in you that others do not."

"What could you possibly see in me?"

"Aside from your beauty you try so hard to hide? Maybe I see that there is more to you than you are willing to let the world see. Maybe that is what I am marrying."

"Then you are the most optimistic dreamer that I have ever encountered." She looked at him out of the corner of her eye. "Are you truly willing to chance your whole life on something you do not understand?"

Luhaunt looked at her, watching her closely. His voice went low. "Just because I do not understand it, Brianna, does not mean I do not trust it."

"And if you are disappointed with what you have married— with what you uncover of me? What then? You will be shackled to a woman you do not care for."

He smiled, but did not break stride. "I am willing to take that chance."

~ ~ ~

Sebastian walked slowly down the long stone hallway. He had just parted ways with Rowen and Lord Newdale in the study, and hadn't bothered to bring a candle with him.

He knew the path to his rooms well enough, even if they were set far back in the castle away from all the other guest chambers. He liked the silence in this part of the keep, and Rowen had offered to outfit Sebastian with his own suite of rooms a year ago when the castle was being renovated.

"Wait, Lord Luhaunt, please, a moment."

Sebastian turned, only to see Brianna's sister scampering toward him, the lantern in her hand sending swaying shadows on the grey stone.

Of all things, this was one he hadn't expected. Brianna's sister had been so enamored with Lord Newdale during the past week—and quite often, foxed—that Sebastian had questioned if she even remembered her sister was getting married the next day.

"Miss Lily, what can I do for you?"

"Forgive the intrusion." Slightly out of breath, she stopped in front of him, holding the lantern up so she could illuminate his face. She still wore the pretty peach silk dress she had dined in earlier, though the back half of her brown hair had been let down. "I just wanted to ask you a question."

He offered a nod. "Feel free."

"It is about Brianna—after you two are wed, you will treat her well?"

Sebastian's eyebrow arched. "That is what you have come to ask me? Do you not think it a bit too late to be putting forth that question?"

She shook her head, his barb not giving her pause. "No. I do not think so. I think I could go to Brianna right now and tell her she does not have to marry you, and she would be perfectly happy to cry off. It is why I am even here talking to you. I had thought once she got accustomed to the idea, she might grow to like it— even be excited about marrying you. But she is not."

Sebastian's head tilted, perplexed. Brianna's sister was much cannier than he had given her credit for. Apparently, just because Brianna controlled so much of her sister's life, he had begun to think of Lily as somewhat of a simpleton. Not so.

"I do not think your sister would allow herself to get excited about anything, much less a forced marriage."

"Maybe not. Not now. But there was a time when she would have." The shadows played on Lily's face. "A time when she would have looked upon marriage with happiness and plans of babes."

"But not now?"

"Not since our father died. Not since then. Not since she has been working to find me a proper match. It has consumed her." Lily paused, her eyes dropping. "You do not know what she has gone through."

"So tell me. It has something to do with the man she loved, does it not?"

Lily's eyes snapped sharply to him. "She told you of him?"

"Only that a past love existed for her. That was all. What happened to him?"

She shook her head, her eyes darting around. "Brianna is the only one that can tell you. I swore to her long ago that I would never speak of that time. It is not my place."

"She had been treated poorly?"

"I will not answer that. But it is the reason I need to be assured you will treat her well." Her jaw hard, Lily stepped closer to him, lifting her lantern even higher. "Make no mistake, Lord Luhaunt, if it means my sister's happiness, I will happily accept the scandal that would ensue were you two not to marry. While I do not wish to lose the possibility of Lord Newdale as a husband—or the other two—I will accept it if my sister's ultimate happiness is on the line."

She went to her toes, leaning in even closer, her voice sharp. "So I am asking you, Lord Luhaunt, on your honor, will you treat my sister well?"

Sebastian didn't think it possible, but he was suddenly the tiniest bit afraid of Brianna's sprite of a sister. He nodded. "Yes. On that, you do not have to worry."

"Excellent." She dropped to flat feet, apparently taking him at his word. "Then I will tell you this. There are those of us that will live with lies—live with not knowing things that might hurt us. But Brianna is not one of them. She needs honesty. Brutal honesty in her life. But she also needs kindness—she needs that more than anyone I know."

"Thank you. I will remember that."

"Good. Do not disappoint me, Lord Luhaunt."

With that, Lily spun from him, her silk slippers silent on the stone as she disappeared down the long dark hallway.

Sebastian stood as still as a rock, watching the light of the lantern until it whittled down to nothingness.

Imagine that. Lily was fiercely loyal to Brianna.

Apparently, Brianna wasn't the only Silverton sister with hidden layers.

CHAPTER 6

Brianna stood naked, or nearly so, with what little bit of modesty the sheer, deep red nightdress draped over her shoulders afforded her. Sleeveless and long, almost to the wooden floorboards, the transparent fabric clasped together between her breasts and down her belly with a row of five thin ribbons.

The wedding had come and gone, the whole day, really, without drama, without crying. Just flat acceptance. She wasn't about to allow tears to fall over something she had no recourse to change.

Two polite "I dos" and that was it. She was married.

Lily, Wynne—even the duke—had tried to make the occasion as jovial as possible. But Brianna could not even pretend for their sakes.

She had married—something she had promised herself she would never do. Never allow herself to be that vulnerable to a man. To what a man could do to her.

So now she stood, waiting for her new husband to appear, painfully aware that she was now his property. She may have been able to secure the Silverton fortune away from the greedy hands of husbands—but that was all. If only she could have done that with her body as well.

Brianna looked around Luhaunt's bedroom. A large four-post bed with no canopy centered the room. The bed was set high with a silk grey coverlet draping over plushness. She would have to hop up just to get into the bed. Two matching walnut wardrobes sat on opposite sides of the bed, but Brianna hadn't bothered to snoop in them. She had also discovered a dressing room through one of the side doors, and a sitting room lined with bookcases through the other.

The drapes open, she looked out through the arched windows that lined the wall across from the fireplace. A long, skinny cloud slid in front of the half moon, tempering most of the light.

The windows faced the forest that led to the stables, surprising, because Brianna's general sense of direction had gotten twisted as she moved through the castle to Luhaunt's rooms. They were set far into the keep through a maze of hallways, and Brianna had spent very little time in this area of the castle.

It was quiet—achingly so—compared to the bustle of where her and Lily's chambers were, and Brianna doubted anyone along these hallways could hear a sound from Luhaunt's rooms.

Palms rubbing her bare arms, Brianna's eyes shifted from the moon to the fireplace. She had thought to approach this outright. Put on the nightdress that Wynne had produced for her and just be ready for Lord Luhaunt without preamble. Do what was necessary, and then she could escape back to the comfort of her own room.

But the thought to approach this forthright had only stuck in Brianna's head for so long before she began to waver.

Walking over to the fireplace in her new husband's room, she reached for the robe that she had set on the arm of the leather wing chair. Only a small fire blazed, just enough to fight off the chill that had crept in with the setting sun.

Shrugging into the robe, she overlapped the fabric as far as she could across the front of her. Just as she tied the belt snuggly around her belly and pulled her loose hair free from the robe, the door opened behind her.

Brianna spun, crossing her arms in front of her chest. "Lord Luhaunt."

He closed the door as his gaze ran from her toes peeking out from under the cloth of the simple tan robe, up her body until it rested on the point where the cloth ended, just below her chin.

"I must be honest, Brianna, I had hoped for the slightest bit more skin." He stepped into the room, stopping in front of her, his brown eyes scanning her face. "But if I only have your face to look at, that will do. I do appreciate the lines of it."

He took a step closer and his hand moved up, fingers entwining along a soft curl of her loose hair. "And this is welcome. I like your hair down. Free."

Brianna could not help the frown on her face from deepening. "I did dress appropriately. I merely caught a chill."

His eyebrow arched as his devil smile played on his lips. He continued to play with her hair, wrapping a strand around his forefinger. "Appropriately? Now I am entirely curious as to what is under that robe."

"As prickly as you may see me, Lord Luhaunt, I am very conscious of appropriate dress for this act."

His hand instantly dropped from her hair. "You do not need to remind me that you have been another's, Brianna. I am well aware. And while I am choosing to overlook the fact that another has your heart, I do not wish to be reminded of it at every turn."

She blinked, stung at his words. She had not even been thinking of the past—she tried very hard to not do so—but memories bubbled from her gut, chasing up her chest to land in a lump in her throat.

Taking a step backward from him, her thighs hit the wingback chair as she unwittingly went rigid. "I...I was not speaking of the past."

Lord Luhaunt stared at her, flames from the fire flickering in his brown eyes as he watched her intensely.

Brianna's gaze dropped from him, finding the black marble threshold of the fireplace to concentrate on. What did he want from her? She had been trying. Trying as hard as she was capable of to get through this with the utmost pleasantness. But now. Now with thoughts of Gregory invading her mind...

"Stop."

The fierceness of the word made her eyes jerk up to him.

He grabbed her left hand, wedging his thumb into her palm and lifting her hand. His voice went low, soft. "Stop thinking.

Stop the frown. Stop your nails from attacking your thumb. You are dwelling upon things that hurt you. I can see it."

Startled, Brianna looked at her hand, now being held still by Lord Luhaunt.

"Wherever you are in your mind, Brianna, you need to stop. You are here with me. And whatever happened in the past is not what is happening here, happening now."

His other hand came up, his fingers slipping under her hair, curling around her neck. "You were hurt. I can see that. You did not enjoy it."

He leaned in, his lips by her ear, his voice a smooth rumble. "You will enjoy it with me, Brianna. I will ensure it. My hands on your body. My mouth on yours. You will writhe under me, and your body will arch into everything I have planned for you, Brianna. You just need to let me."

His words filling her head, he touched his lips to her skin, fire on the spot. Moving down her neck, his tongue trailed along her skin. He dropped her hand, his fingers sliding inward along the edge of her robe, tugging at the fabric to gain access to her skin.

Brianna lost herself in it for a moment, lost herself in the sensation of his mouth adoring her skin, the shivers down her spine, her speeding breath tightening her chest. Heaven. Heaven on her neck, her nerves turned to flame.

The exact thing she felt in the past.

She fell too quickly into it. The exact thing that she had felt years ago, body and soul. The burning in her core. The aching. Her body begging for more.

Lord Luhaunt was wrong in his assumption. So very wrong. She did enjoy it—she had enjoyed it immensely. Too much so.

And it was the exact thing she was betrayed by.

She stiffened under his touch.

The robe slipped off her body, and she froze in place. Unable to respond. To talk. To move. Yet still, Luhaunt continued his assault on her skin.

His lips moved against her collarbone. "You do know, Brianna. You know quite well what to wear."

His hand went onto the base of her neck, his fingers wrapping into her hair as his mouth dropped further on her body, and he loosened the top tie of ribbon on her sheer nightdress. It dropped open, exposing her left breast.

His mouth descended upon her nipple, sucking, teasing.

She tightened even further, leaning away from him. Leaning away from what her body craved. Away from how she wanted to arch her breast into him.

He was right. He could make her body want it.

And it was exactly what she wasn't about to let happen.

Brianna closed her eyes, her arms going rigid at her sides.

Luhaunt's mouth left her nipple. She could feel him straighten in front of her, his breath heavy, the hot air wispy on her cheek.

She cracked her eyes.

He was watching her, his face only a breath away with a speculative look in his eyes. She could see she was a puzzle he was determined to solve.

"I do not want you like this, Brianna."

Her eyes opened fully to him. "I am trying, Lord Luhaunt. My sister—you—forced me into this marriage. I am doing what is necessary. And I am attempting to do so with the least amount of foolish spectacle."

"Unacceptable." He shook his head, sighing, then took a step away from her. "This is not necessary. This cannot be an obligation—a duty, Brianna. I will not accept that from you."

"But it is what you wanted—the obligation of a wife. That is what you said."

"I wanted you, Brianna. The wife part was merely the preceding formality."

"Oh."

No matter how many times Luhaunt said he wanted her, Brianna could not bring herself to believe him. She doubted she ever would.

"You are not ready. I had hoped the week without seeing me would have helped, but it has not." He reached forward, grabbing the top ribbon of her nightdress. With more delicacy from his large hands than she would have expected, he retied the ribbon into a perfect bow. "So I give you time."

He bent to pick up her robe, wrapping it around her shoulders.

"You do?" Brianna eyed him suspiciously.

"Yes. I only ask two things in return."

Of course. This was when the demands would appear. She pulled her robe tighter around her torso. "Which are?"

"The first thing I ask is that you call me Seb. Or Sebastian. No Lord Luhaunt. It is grating from you. That was my father, not me."

Brianna's head tilted, disbelief in her eyes. That request was too easy. "I can do as you ask. What is the second?"

"The second thing—you will sleep in bed with me." He pointed at his enormous bed. "I will not touch you. Not until you ask me to. But you sleep in my bed with me."

"Tonight?"

"Every night."

Brianna glanced across the room at Sebastian's bed. It was large enough. She could wiggle herself to an edge, and never be anywhere near him.

She looked back to him, meeting his dark brown eyes, knowing she shouldn't trust him. But these were simple things. Simple things for a husband to request of a wife. She took a deep breath.

"All I have to do is change what I call you and sleep in your bed? And you will not touch me?"

He gave her one nod.

"Before I agree, I have one request of you."

"I would expect no less."

"May we remain at Notlund throughout the summer? I had meant to ask you before today, but I was holding out hope…" Her voice petered out awkwardly.

"Hope that the marriage would not happen?"

She met his eyes, nodding. "Yes. But it has, so I cannot worry upon that anymore. But I cannot curb my worry over my sister. I do not want her to be left without guidance as she contemplates the worth of her suitors. I need to be here to protect her."

"She has Rowe and Wynne."

"Yes. And they are wonderful. But she needs me. She will not make a good decision without me."

"Are you sure? Your sister seems like an intelligent young lady. One that is perfectly capable of deciding upon a husband."

"She is not."

"No?"

"No. So may we stay at Notlund? Just through the summer. Just through the visits from Lord Bepton and Lord Rallager and their respective parties. Lily needs my guidance."

A half smile crossed Sebastian's mouth. One Brianna couldn't quite place.

"I will agree to your request if you will agree to mine," he said.

Brianna nodded, relieved. "I do."

It was the second "I do" she said that day, and it struck her that for as much trepidation as had accompanied the first one, the second one had managed to ease much of her anxiety.

Her eyes flickered to her husband.

The man was clever.

Had he planned this as well?

CHAPTER 7

Brianna's eyes opened to see an elaborately carved coffered ceiling. The pre-dawn glow sneaking in from around the heavy draperies sent an orange hue onto the dark mahogany. The ceiling startled her, and for a second, she panicked. But then her mind slowly caught up to all the realities of the day before.

Married. She was married.

Still stunned at the very thought, she noticed the rock in her gut from the night before had only expanded overnight.

Except it wasn't a rock in her gut. It was a forearm draped over her belly.

Brianna turned her head on the pillow. His face turned away from her, Sebastian was sprawled on his stomach, his bare arm capturing her, heavy on her waist.

Not touch her indeed.

Pinkies in the air, she grabbed his forearm with both hands, fingertips sliding along the silky dark hair on his skin. Gently, she lifted his arm and then slipped sideways off the edge of the bed.

Holding the dead weight of his arm in one hand, she grabbed the pillow and wedged it into the spot where her belly had been.

He didn't move. Didn't rustle. Perfect.

Still in her robe from the previous night, she cracked the door and tiptoed out of the room, quickly making her way through the maze of hallways to get to her chambers. No matter that it was the first day after her wedding, she was already late and she needed to get out of the castle and down to the stables before dawn fully broke.

Three hours later, Brianna was pacing in the abandoned gristmill outside of Pepperton, her boots softly thudding on the rotting wood floor. She stopped in front of the enormous round millstones, flicking loose a piece of rock from the top cracked stone that had been bothering her. Mr. Flemming was already an hour past their appointed meeting time, and Brianna had gone from merely annoyed, to irate.

She needed to start back to Notlund within a half hour if she was to avoid questions about her whereabouts. She was never out on rides for more than four hours, so being gone for too long, especially on the first morning of her marriage, would be highly suspect.

She went back to pacing, scattering dust as she twisted her lambskin gloves in her hands.

It was another ten minutes before the wooden door, half askew on its hinges, creaked open. Mr. Flemming stepped into the damp darkness of the stone structure.

"I expected you sooner, Mr. Flemming." Brianna stopped her pacing, smoothing her hair into her tight bun.

"You are in Yorkshire, Miss Silverton. It is a distance." Mr. Flemming opened up the worn leather satchel he always carried strapped across his body. "And it has given me very little time to investigate in between these appointments with you."

"Then I will pay you to ride faster. And hire another investigator. What have you learned of Lord Newdale?"

Mr. Flemming pulled a set of papers, folded in thirds, from his bag. "I have discovered nothing as of yet about the brothels he has frequented. But I have discovered this about his financial affairs."

He handed the papers to Brianna. She unfolded them and quickly scanned the contents.

"These are output numbers—Lord Newdale has a copper mine that is failing?" Brianna flipped to the second page.

"He does. The mine has been supporting the rest of the estate for years. As you know, his lands, although vast, barely support themselves."

Brianna nodded, refolding the papers. "How long does it have?"

"Two years, maybe more."

"So if one was planning for the future…"

"One would be lining up an infusion of cash," Mr. Flemming said. "Or another means of supporting the estate."

"And he has not done so?"

"He has not diversified his funds into anything else that would help long term. Trading, manufacturing—I have found nothing, as of yet."

"You will keep these safe?" She handed him the papers. "I do need to be absolutely assured on any information about Lord Newdale, Mr. Flemming."

"I understand. I will get you the answers you need. And do remember, there is the possibility that new deposits in the mine will be discovered."

Brianna nodded. "Why do you know nothing yet about the brothels? I have begun to wonder if he may have a stake in them of some sort, instead of just frequenting them for base needs."

Mr. Flemming shrugged. "I would presume it is the base needs. But as I have said before, I would prefer to see true evidence, instead of conjecture, before I vilify the man."

"I trust you are working on that matter?"

"I am."

"Good. Lord Newdale is only at Notlund for another fortnight, possibly a few days past that. I hope to have answers before his departure so I know how to proceed with Lord Bepton and Lord Rallager. We will meet here the second Monday from today, the same time?"

"That will be fine, Miss Silverton."

"Excellent. Please do be on time." Brianna's hands tightened on her gloves. "And your associate, Mr. Welbury, did he send word on the other matter?"

"He did not. But he did tell me to assure you he is making progress."

"I do hope that is so." She motioned to the door. "Do make haste, Mr. Flemming. There is much to do."

With a short nod, Mr. Flemming disappeared out the rickety door.

Brianna stood in the dim room, staring at the dust floating in the rays of sunlight streaming in through slit openings scattered along stone walls.

She knew every day that passed, Lily was more and more enamored with Lord Newdale. So much so, that Brianna was afraid Lily had already made up her mind amongst her suitors.

That wouldn't do. Not with the nagging questions still lending suspect to Newdale's character. Brianna would need to start curbing Lily's time with him before they went down a path it would be hard to dissuade Lily from.

With a sigh, Brianna pulled on her gloves and walked to the crooked door of the mill, muscling it open. Stepping into the sunlight, she looked around, her eyes adjusting. The chill of last night had already flipped into steamy, oppressive heat. And she still had a long, hot ride back to Notlund in front of her.

Unbuttoning and stripping off the black jacket of her habit, Brianna rounded the back corner of the mill. There would be no time for stopping at the stream, so if nothing else, she was going to be comfortable with air flowing through her tailored white linen shirt.

She had tied Moonlight loose enough to a branch so the horse could reach what little water still trickled by in the near-dry creek bed, and now the mare was nibbling on tall grass at the base of an oak tree. It wasn't until she reached Moonlight, setting her jacket on the saddle, that she could see past her horse.

Brianna froze.

Right behind the mare, leaning back onto a tree with one foot propped against the trunk and arms crossed over his chest, Sebastian watched her, calm on his face.

"You followed me."

Sebastian pushed off from the tree. "I was not about to lose my new wife on our first full day of marriage."

He walked around Moonlight to stand in front of her. "Is this where you have been disappearing to? To meet with Mr. Flemming?"

"You listened in on my discussion?" Brianna could feel her face turning red, indignation exploding. She stomped past him, her shaking fingers trying to jerk loose Moonlight's reins from the branch.

Sebastian grabbed her elbow, spinning her to him.

"Should I have charged in, instead, Brianna? My new wife sneaks off before dawn to meet a strange man in an abandoned mill, and you chastise me for listening in? I believe I have shown incredible restraint with the situation."

Her eyes went to the sky. "Yes. Incredible restraint. I applaud you."

His eyebrow cocked at her.

She heaved a sigh. "If you spied upon me, then you must full well have figured out Mr. Flemming is a bow street runner I hired to investigate Lord Newdale. This is only the second time I have met with him here in Yorkshire."

His hand dropped from her elbow. "You thought to do this on the first day of our marriage?"

"My meeting with Mr. Flemming was planned well before our wedding was. I could not change the timing of it."

"You also could have told me of it. I would have accompanied you here."

Brianna blinked hard at his words. The thought had never even occurred to her to tell Sebastian about the meeting. "Yes, well, this is my business. I did not think to drag you into it."

He nodded slowly, and Brianna watched his ire evaporate from his face. "So you are investigating your sister's suitors?"

"Of course I am—I am not about to let my sister marry a wastrel. I discovered most of what I needed to know of Lord Bepton and Lord Rallager while we were in London. Lord Newdale was a late addition to the mix, so I had little time to discover much about him while we were still in London."

"And Mr. Flemming speaks to you about brothels? That is part of the investigation? You think discussion of brothels is appropriate for a gentle bred lady?"

"Of course it is not." She met his eyes. "But we are both well-aware that I am a not-so-innocent spinster, so appropriateness passed me by long ago."

"I would disagree with that. Do I need to remind you that you are no longer a spinster, Brianna?"

"No. No you do not. I am painfully aware of my new status." She waved her hand, dismissing his concerns. "Be that as it may, Mr. Flemming has had little luck discovering what business Lord Newdale has in the brothels."

"I would imagine his business in a brothel is the same as any other man's."

"Yes, but I need to be certain." Brianna took a deep breath for patience. She didn't care to have to defend her actions. She was doing what she knew was right. "You may think I am going to an extreme, investigating Lily's suitors, but I am not. I have to be certain of them. And that also means I have to be fair. I cannot scratch Lord Newdale from the list on conjecture alone."

"And you get to make that decision for your sister—who gets scratched?"

"Yes." Brianna's arms crossed over her ribs.

"What about your sister's feelings?"

"Feelings should not be a part of her decision to marry."

Sebastian's head cocked. He was staring at her with extreme curiosity again. "I have been around your sister. I imagine she would have a different opinion on that."

"Yes, well, that is why I am making the decision."

"Does she know that?"

"I can see your judgement, Seb. Judgement you have no right to make. You know nothing of why I do what I do."

"No." His lips pursed, contemplating. "Though I do see that you love her dearly. But you give her no margin to control her own fate. To control what her own heart desires."

"You do not understand." Brianna's eyes closed, her head shaking. "The heart lies, Seb. It is ignorant." She could not help the lump that forced its way into her throat.

Turning from him, her arms dropped to her sides as she went once more to untangle Moonlight's reins. "But this—the intentions of men—this I can control, or at least know about. If I know about intent, I can control how it is dealt with. I can control how I protect Lily."

Sebastian followed her, moving in close, straddling her side, both touching and not touching her with every breath. "That is what you need most, control?"

She paused, her eyes far from him, solid on the reins over the tree branch. Her voice went soft. She wasn't about to deny it. "Yes."

"No room for spontaneity?" He leaned down, his mouth near her ear, his breath tickling the skin on her neck. "No room for a heart that speeds? No room for a tingle down your spine?"

He bent even closer, his lips brushing her earlobe. The heat that came with his body should have suffocated her, but it didn't. It only enveloped her, sending her heart thudding out of control.

Damn that he could make her body react like that. He did it the previous night, and he was doing it again. She had to remember to listen to her mind and not her body.

Her chin dropped to her chest as she tried to even her breath. "No."

"Again, I disagree."

Her hands dropping from the branch, Brianna turned to him, looking up at his eyes. The comforting brown eyes that were constantly on her. She swallowed hard. "Why? How? In all of this, Seb—in marrying me. You have convinced yourself you think you see something in me. But why? Why me?"

Without breaking eye contact, Sebastian lifted his hand, his fingers slowly capturing a loose tendril of her hair and tucking it behind her ear. His hand dropped, curling around the back of her neck. "Because of the first time I saw you, Brianna. That first time, the whole world dropped away. Everyone. And you, you were the only person left."

"You talk gibberish, Seb—you met me by the stream at Notlund."

"No." His fingers danced slow circles along the back of her neck. "I saw you in London, Bree. I watched you for two weeks."

Her head jerked back from his touch, shock shaking her core. He had watched her? She had to forcibly keep her feet from turning and running, terrorized, from him.

Running at this point would do her no good.

She had already married the man.

She swallowed hard. "For weeks? You watched me? Why?"

His smile spread slowly. "That first time I saw you, I knew. Just like I do with the horses—the curse, you called it. It was at the Thorton ball. Rowe had pointed out you and Lily to me. You were talking to your sister with that indulgent-scolding look you get on your face whenever she is getting her way and you are begrudgingly letting her."

His thumb came up to her bottom lip, tracing the edge of it. "And I do not exaggerate. The moment you turned in my direction—the ball, the music, the people—all of it dropped away and there you stood. My eyes did not leave you that night. And they have not since that moment."

For a long second, Brianna stared into his eyes, allowing herself to believe him. Allowing herself to believe it truly was her he wanted. Allowing her body to want his—to want him to kiss her, to strip off her shirt.

But then her mind clicked in.

Words. They were just words. And she had fallen for sweet words before.

This was no different.

She took a step backward, almost falling over. Sebastian grabbed her upper arm, steadying her.

She gave him a weak smile and spun from him, successfully loosening Moonlight's reins from the branch. "We should get back. Lily will be wondering as to my whereabouts."

~ ~ ~

"Bree. Bree."

Brianna squinted in the midday sun, her eyes slowly adjusting to the light after stepping out of the far right stable. Her eyes acclimated and she spotted Lily running down the hillside from the forest trail to the castle.

She panicked for a second and then realized Lily was yelling her name in excitement, not in distress.

Brianna looked over her shoulder at Sebastian. He was talking to one of the stable boys but glanced her way with a smile and motioned for her to go ahead.

She resisted a curious shake of her head. Much to her surprise, Sebastian let her ride mostly in silence during the long ride back to Notlund from the mill outside of Pepperton. If he was upset at her reaction to his words, he didn't show it.

Instead, he proved himself to be an easy riding companion. They ran the horses hard in some stretches. Languidly moving along in others. If anything, he made the ride fun, and Brianna had even found herself laughing at times.

All of how he had conducted himself that morning, she appreciated, if nothing else. She knew full well a different man— most men—would have had a very different reaction to his new wife sneaking off in the dawn to meet a strange man.

Brianna turned back to Lily, now almost down the length of the hill and past Wynne's painting studio. Brianna hurried to her.

"Bree. Bree. It has happened. I am so excited." Her sister didn't slow when she reached Brianna, instead, nearly knocking Brianna over as she grabbed her in a hug, swinging her around.

Brianna grabbed Lily's shoulders, wrangling her backward so
she could see her sister's face. "What? What has happened?"

"Lord Newdale—he proposed." The squeal in Lily's voice
echoed into the forest.

Brianna stilled. "He has proposed?"

"Yes. It is wonderful." Lily's cheeks glowed, her light blue
eyes sparkling. "He has proposed and I am so excited."

"Did you answer him?" Brianna's grip on her sister's
shoulders tightened.

"No. Not directly. I hugged him. I was so happy. But I told
him I had to talk to you first."

Brianna nodded. "Good. Thank you for respecting my wishes
to not answer without talking to me first."

"Of course." Lily wiggled out Brianna's grasp, giving her
another throat-choking hug with happy hops. "When can I tell
him?"

"Tell him what?"

Lily pulled away. "Tell him yes, silly. When?"

Brianna cleared her throat, stalling for a moment. "I think
you need to wait a spell. Think about what you truly want. This is
a lifetime you are committing to, Lily."

"But I do not need to think on it." Lily's hands fell away
from Brianna, clasping in front of her. "I want Lord Newdale. He
is the one. I am positive."

"But what about Lord Bepton and Lord Rallager?"

"Lord Bepton is doable, but a bit stuffy. And I do not feel
for Lord Rallager nearly as much as I do Lord Newdale." She
squashed Brianna in another hug. "This is all so wonderful, Bree."

"No."

Lily drew back sharply. "No? What?"

"No. You need to wait to answer him, Lily. At least until the
end of summer."

"But I just told you. I want to say yes. I will write letters to
Lord Bepton and Lord Rallager to cancel their trips." Lily's hands
went frantic in front of her. "Or we could get married right away

and leave Notlund, and you can still entertain both of them here—it will not be overly awkward if I am gone."

"No, Lily. I cannot allow it."

"No?" Lily shook her head slowly, angst taking over the confusion. "No? What? You cannot mean that, Bree. I need to tell him yes. Immediately. There is no need to wait."

"No, Lily. I am demanding it. You will wait until the end of summer."

Lily's hand clasped to her mouth, her face horrified. "No, Bree. How can you do this to me?"

"I am not doing this to you, Lily, I am doing this for you," Brianna said, her voice even. "I just want to make sure you make a good decision in a husband."

"But I have already made the decision."

"You are right in the throes of this, Lily, and I know it is very exciting. But you need to spend time with Lord Bepton and Lord Rallager before a decision is made. That is the only way."

Lily's eyes narrowed at Brianna, her hand dropping from her mouth. Brianna braced herself.

"Why are you doing this to me, Bree? Again? How could you?"

"Lily—"

"No." Birds scattered through the trees at the screech of the one word. Lily sneered, her mouth turning to spite. "You are only doing this because you have no heart left, Bree. None. No heart—you cannot even see what is in front of you."

Lily's finger pointed over Brianna's shoulder. "This man—he adores you for no reason. No reason. You have done nothing to deserve it. Nothing."

Brianna glanced back over her shoulder to see Sebastian standing behind her. She hadn't even heard him approach. Her eyes swung back to her ranting sister.

"You got to marry him. It is not fair. You got to marry and I do not. I have someone that wants to adore me. Me. And now you are trying to take away what little happiness I am managing to scrape out after what you did to me. It is not fair, Bree. You are being cruel."

Brianna's palms went up, trying to reason. "Lily, my life has nothing to do with this—"

Lily swung, her arm knocking Brianna's hands out of the air. "It has everything to do with it, Bree. You cannot love, and you know it, so you do not want me to have love—to have happiness."

"You know that is not true, Lily."

"It is. You are cold, Bree. Nothing but a cold stone that no one can touch, and I hate you for it. You refuse to let me live my life. You refuse to let me go and you are determined to drag me into your cold world. Make me like you."

Lily stepped into Brianna, nose to nose, her voice vicious in bitterness. "Well, I will not become you, Bree. I will not. I will not become the sour, controlling woman you have collapsed into. You can have your cold heart, Bree. Just keep it away from my warm one."

Lily whipped around, running off before Brianna could even react. Before she could even make sense of her sister's words.

And then they hit her.

Every word.

Every truth she spewed.

They hit Brianna and doubled her over. She curled into herself, holding her stomach. If her sister had punched her in the gut, it would have hurt far less.

As much as she tried to hold them in, tears filled her eyes, spilling over, dropping to the ground in front of her.

"Brianna…" Sebastian's hand landed gently on her shoulder.

She jerked away from him, hiding her face in her hands. "I have to go to her…I have to…" Her words choked off, her feet stumbling.

Sebastian did not let her go far, grabbing both of her shoulders from behind. His hands solid against the shaking of her body.

"Let me." His fingers tightened on her shoulders. "I will go after her."

Brianna could not answer him at first. She tried. She tried to lift one leg and then the other. But they were dead weight. She thought she could regain enough control to go after Lily, to make her feet move, but she could not.

Not at the moment.

Someone had to go after Lily.

Slow in defeat, she nodded.

Sebastian's hands moved along her shoulders, and with one final squeeze to her neck, he left her standing by the stables.

~~~

Sebastian found Lily in a quiet alcove of the new gardens Wynne had designed alongside the castle's east side. Not yet mature, the evergreens that denoted the paths and garden rooms only reached to Sebastian's forehead, which had made it much easier to pinpoint the soft crying.

He stepped through the opening along an evergreen wall to find Lily sitting on a wrought iron bench with delicate scrolls curving in an elaborate dance along the back of it.

"I have noticed Brianna does like to make your decisions for you." Sebastian dropped a white handkerchief in front of Lily's downcast head. "But I do think she has your best interest at heart, Lily. It is something that I find curious about her."

Startled, Lily looked up at him, her eyes red rimmed. She took the cloth.

"May I sit?"

Lily nodded.

Sebastian sat next to her, leaning forward to balance his forearms on his thighs, his eyes on the bright green grass. "I do not think Brianna makes these demands to hurt you, Lily." He glanced at her. "She wants to keep you safe. Even in my limited time with her, I recognize that."

"Yes, safe—too safe. It is just so frustrating how she now acts." Lily wiped her eyes with the cloth, her breath quivering. She looked over to Sebastian. "She has not always been like this."

"No? I imagined her cutting your food until you were sixteen."

Lily chuckled through her frown. "You are so very wrong. Brianna would have been the very first person to be excited about my engagement. She would have been planning the wedding even before it was something to be planned."

"I find that hard to believe."

She nodded. "It is true. Bree used to be the exact opposite of what she is now. She always took care of me, of course, she is my older sister after all and our mother was dead. But we had the best times—so much fun, so much laughter. Our papa was the kindest man—he could weave the most incredible, funny, inappropriate stories for us. Our family, our life—with the viscount and his son, and Brianna and my father—the five of us were incredibly happy before the viscount died, and then…"

She shook her head, her chin dropping. Sebastian let her take a moment to wipe her eyes again.

"What happened to your father?"

Even with a view only of her profile, Sebastian could see Lily's face darken considerably.

"He died," she said, her head down.

"How?"

"He was killed. I do not know what happened. I only saw the aftermath."

"Aftermath?"

Lily took several deep breaths before she had steadied herself enough to look up to him. But her voice still shook. "I swore to Bree I would never speak of that time again."

"You do not have to tell me, Lily."

"But I do. You are her husband. So I do. Someone needs to." She paused, wiping her eyes once more. "I found them…in the abandoned abbey on the viscount's estate. Papa was dead, his throat slashed. Brianna was tied to a chair. Blood all over her. I thought she was dead as well. She lived."

Lily took a shuddered breath, twisting the handkerchief in her hands. "But what happened…it killed her. Who she was. Who she had always been. Easy and bright and spontaneous and funny—someone you just wanted to be around because she shined. She would have been the darling in London…she would have. She truly shined." Lily's eyes glassed over with fresh tears.

Instant rage at the scene Lily described flooded Sebastian's veins. That someone had dared to hurt Brianna. That she had watched her father die.

He swallowed the fury in his throat. "Who did it? What happened to Brianna in that abbey?"

"I do not know. I have asked her a hundred times over, but she has never told me." Lily's blue eyes, exact replicas of Brianna's, saddened even further. "And then I just stopped asking."

"You know nothing?"

Lily shrugged, her head shaking. "Only the horror of what I saw. And the only word I heard her say in that bloody room was 'Gregory.' And just once. I could have misheard her, for all the terror in those moments. Papa was dead, she was fighting for life, I was screaming—panicked—I do not know."

"Who is Gregory?"

Her eyes snapped to him, instant distress invading her features. "I have said too much."

Lily turned from him, starting to her feet.

Sebastian grabbed her forearm, stopping her. "No, please, tell me. I need to know. Who is Gregory?"

She shook her head.

"Please, Lily. I am her husband. I need to know."

Lily looked at him for a hard moment and then sat on the bench with a heavy sigh. "I do not wish to be rude or cause offense to your current situation…but she loved him, Gregory. He was the one I spoke of. She was so different then—she knew how to love once—she truly did. She was set on marrying

Gregory. They were engaged—weeks away from the wedding. But then he just disappeared."

"Right after your father died?"

Lily tilted her head, thinking. "I believe so. Maybe he felt guilty for not saving her from what happened—maybe he could not face her—I do not know. I am trying to remember if he was at the funeral…it was all such a blur. Brianna was in so much pain, and then the funeral, and then her wounds gave her a fever—she almost died twice after that first day."

Tears escaped Lily's eyes. Her head dropped, and she quickly wiped away fat droplets. "I apologize. I try not to think of those times. So when I do…they make me sad, that is all. All that was lost on that day."

"I understand. It could not have been easy for Brianna. Nor for you." His hand went lightly to her shoulder. "All wounds are not physical, Lily."

Lily nodded softly, her head down, eyes closed. It took several moments before her breathing evened and she looked to him. "It is why I let Brianna control everything. She needs the control more than I need her not to have it. So I let her be and love her, because I will always see her exactly as she used to be. Warm and kind and funny and adoring me. Not just my sister— my mother, my confidante, my dearest friend—my everything. And she will always be that person. I refuse to give up that filter. Because I know—I saw how what happened that day stripped her of everything she was and left her as she is now."

A warm smile spread across her face. "I hope one day I will not need the filter. That she will be all those things to me again. I truly think she can be."

"Yet just now, you were harsh with her."

The smile evaporated from Lily's face, her voice turning somber. "Yes, I was. Sometimes I think that is the only way I can reach her. She will forgive me."

"Will she? Is it that easy?"

"Yes. She always does. As I will forgive her." Lily wiped her cheeks once more, then began to offer the handkerchief back to Sebastian before thinking the better of it and crumbling it into her fist. She stood from the bench. "We are sisters, brother-in-law—do not underestimate that bond."

Lily walked out of the evergreen alcove, leaving Sebastian on the bench.

He leaned back, eyes going to the puffy clouds dotting the sky.

A name. Now he had a name. Gregory.

But more importantly, now he had proof that the beliefs he had about Brianna—about who she really was—were founded.

Proof that he hadn't just made the biggest mistake in his life.

~ ~ ~

"So easy it was. You believe, deep down, that you deserve love. That it was coming for you. That it was yours by right. Such a silly girl. I did not even have to work at making you believe I loved you. But you are unlovable, Brianna. Completely unlovable. Absolutely nothing special about you. There is not one word you uttered to me that did not bore me. It is a wonder your very own family can stand you."

The creak of the door made Brianna look up, yanking her from the cruelty filling her head.

"Brianna, I apologize. I was looking for Wynne." The duke stood in the open doorway of the painting studio by the stables. "Have you seen her?"

Lily and Sebastian had only been gone a few minutes and Brianna couldn't speak, not yet. She had come into the studio for refuge, to cry, hidden. Shaking her head in answer to the duke's question, she hoped it would be enough to make him leave.

"What are you doing in the studio? It is unnaturally stuffy in here—suffocating." He walked in, going to the side windows to pull the drapes wide and open the windows. "At least open a window and let some light and air in here."

He turned back to her and then stopped. "Have you been crying, Brianna?"

Quickly wiping her cheeks, Brianna shrugged, averting her eyes as she leaned on the arm of the wooden chair she sat in. "It is nothing."

The duke walked over to her, planting himself in front of her and leaning casually back on Wynne's large wooden working table. His eyes studied her for a moment. "What is it? Seb?"

Brianna forced a breath down deep into her lungs. "No. Lily. Lord Newdale has asked for her hand in marriage."

"But that is good news, no? Lily is quite enamored with him—more so than the other two—or so Wynne tells me."

"I told her no."

"You what? Why?"

"I do not know if he is the right man for my sister."

The duke didn't answer right away, instead, crossing his arms over his chest as he contemplated her. "Forgive me if I say this bluntly, Brianna, but do you get to make that decision?"

"I do if it means saving Lily from a wastrel of a husband."

"Do you know something of Lord Newdale, Brianna? If so, you need to tell me, and I will ensure the man exits Notlund immediately. With a harsh kick in the backside, if necessary."

Brianna waved her hand. "No—I do not want to overreact—I just wanted to give Lily more time with Lord Bepton and Lord Rallager. More time to make a decision this momentous. I did not mean to ban her from Lord Newdale completely—I just need to discover more about him."

The duke's shoulders relaxed. "What do you mean, discover?"

She shrugged, sighing. "You may as well be informed—now that Seb knows, I imagine he will tell you regardless. I hired a bow street runner to investigate Lord Newdale—all of Lily's suitors, actually. The other two do not concern me, but Lord Newdale, he is the one I still have questions about. So I told Lily she could not commit to him right away, merely to gain some time."

The duke nodded slowly, hand on his chin, and Brianna could see his mind working. "And what is it in particular that gives you pause for concern?"

"His revenue comes from a failing mine, so I am, of course, concerned he sees Lily more as a bank than a wife." Brianna frowned, wondering if she should continue. But again, Sebastian already knew, so he would tell the duke regardless. "And the man visits brothels. A number of them."

The duke coughed, rubbing his forehead until he stumbled out some words. "What…why…why would you need to know more about that?"

And now the duke knew of her depravity. Brianna eyed him, her voice beaten. "I did not wish to investigate him in this particular area, but I need to know if his…intentions in that realm of life include vices he cannot control. That he does not have unusual tastes that may harm Lily."

The duke shook his head, his mouth opening and closing several times with no words escaping.

Brianna would not have thought him the skittish type when it came to the topic of sex. But one never knew what was really going on in another's mind. Which was exactly why she needed to investigate Lord Newdale so thoroughly.

The duke found his voice. "I can help you with the mine. Learn how viable it is long term, or what other options he has for his land. And the brothel part—I cannot believe I am even saying this, but I will make some discreet inquiries. I want as much as you to find Lily a good match. And if your concerns are warranted, I will back you in dissuading her from Lord Newdale. I will also see if Wynne can dissuade Lily from hastily answering Lord Newdale's proposal. That should give us some time to get proper answers."

Brianna knew she had been handling the investigation as well as anyone could have, but a mountain of relief still lifted from her shoulders. That the duke had the same information and could also wield his influence over Lily—it would be a tremendous help.

"Thank you, your grace. I appreciate anything you can discover of Lord Newdale."

He nodded. "Now tell me about this runner you hired. How did Seb discover him?"

"I met with the man this morning near Pepperton. Seb followed me."

The duke chuckled. "So that is where you have been disappearing to in the mornings?"

Brianna blinked hard at him, surprised. "You know I am gone in the mornings?"

"I know every single horse that comes and goes from the stables."

"But you have never asked about it."

"I did not think I needed to," the duke said. "You could have asked for my help earlier, Brianna. I would have been happy to assist you. And it would have saved you from sneaking about. It is no wonder Seb went out after you."

"To invade my privacy? He cannot respect me as you do?"

"I have never asked you where you went because you return safely, and I trust you will not put yourself in harm's way, Brianna. But that does not mean it has not taken me a while to get used to the idea of your solitary morning jaunts."

The duke relaxed his arms, resting his palms on the table. "Seb, on the other hand, is new at this. He is now your husband. So of course he followed you. Which is actually a relief to me—I do not have to worry about you if I know he is following."

"You were worried about me?"

"Of course. How could I not be?"

"I apologize, your grace. I did not intend to worry you."

The duke shrugged. "It was my choice to worry instead of trail you. But Seb is learning to trust you as well. He wants to know you, Brianna. Wants to make a life with you."

"He told you that?"

"He does not need to. I know him. We have been friends for a very long time."

Brianna's eyes dropped, resting on the duke's dark boots. Apparently, everyone but her had recognized Sebastian's obvious sentiment for her.

So why had she missed it? Why did she not believe it?

A lump formed in her chest. She knew exactly why she did not believe it. The very thing that would continue to keep her from believing it.

Her eyes crinkled as she pinned the duke with a solemn look. "Do you trust him—Sebastian?"

"Yes. With my life." Without hesitation the words came, genuine, from the duke.

Brianna stared at him, searching for something to make her believe what seemed to come so easily to everyone around her. "How can you say that?"

"What do you mean?"

"How can you trust someone that unequivocally?" Brianna shook her head, attempting to manifest words that could explain. "You say something like that, and there is no question in your voice. But how can you really know what is in another's mind? For what someone puts forth to the world can be very different from what true intentions are."

He nodded, an understanding smile crinkling his face. "That is true. But it is not only instinct that informs my belief, it is history as well. Never once have I questioned Seb's honor. His integrity—although his actions next to the stream with you were highly suspect."

Brianna could not help a small smile from crossing her face.

"You will recall, we were in the wars together," the duke said. "And through all of the death and injury that surrounded us—when sane men would have run and not have been called cowards, Seb was loyal—to his own detriment—to me, to the mission. He is loyal to a fault. Quite simply, I trust him because he deserves it."

"I did not realize that about him."

"You have only known him for a week, Brianna, so it is forgivable," the duke said. His fingers tapped the table as he watched at her. "Here is what I know about Seb, Brianna. He has never once failed me. His intentions are pure. But he is also always moving. This past month—between London and Notlund—is the longest I have ever seen him stay in one place. He runs. From one location to another. Since the wars, he has always been like that. Nothing makes him stay in one place for more than a few days. But not now. It has been fascinating to witness."

The duke stood from the table, stopping in front of her. "And quite honestly, Brianna, there is only one reason he is here, feet planted at Notlund."

Brianna looked up to him, her voice tiny. "Me?"

He gave one crisp nod. "Yes. So that is how I know he wants to make a life with you. He would already be gone, were that not true."

CHAPTER 8

The pounding hooves sidled Brianna, appearing out of nowhere. Halfway down the open border of the south woods where she could really let Moonlight fly in the morning mist, she looked at the snorting black nostrils next to her.

Her head craned back. Sebastian.

She yanked up on the reins.

Moonlight slowed, then pranced in a circle, upset that the run had been interrupted. Brianna tried to control the horse's fidgeting while glaring at Sebastian. "I was the only one in the stables—how did you catch up to me so quickly?"

Sebastian's mouth curled up, the devil smile appearing with his shrug. "Seven days' worth of you slipping from under my arm in the morning and making me trail you from far behind, and Little Tommy is now under orders to ready a horse for me the second you step foot in the stables."

"Tommy? He was asleep in the hay when I went by him."

"You must have woken him."

"Yes, well, next time I will be sure to kick him awake so I do not have to saddle Moonlight myself. Apparently, the little bugger was bamboozling me with his fake snores."

Sebastian chuckled. "Quite possible. He is not the most enthusiastic worker."

Brianna tugged on the reins, finally stilling Moonlight's excited steps. "Well, there is no need for you to follow me. I am just out for a ride, as I have been every other day this past week. You need not worry about a clandestine meeting for me this morning."

"Or I could simply accompany you."

"Or you could make your way back to the stables."

"Are you afraid I will put your riding skills to shame?" He smiled at her, charm oozing. Damn if it didn't make him look even more attractive. And he full well knew it.

Her frown deepened. She was completely aware he was baiting her. She had just spent the past week successfully avoiding her new husband, or at least ensuring she had the barrier of other people in the same room with them.

That, combined with retiring early every night and feigning sleep when he entered his bedroom, and Brianna had managed to have very little real conversation with Sebastian.

She knew she couldn't continue it forever, but she had hoped the avoidance could go on for a long stretch. But now he was right in front of her, no buffer available. No buffer except to keep the horses moving.

Brianna didn't want company—she never did when out riding, but what did it matter if he rode along with her? If he became too bothersome, she could unleash Moonlight and be free of him.

She gave him a curt nod. "If you can keep up, I will not resist your presence."

She turned Moonlight, nudging her into motion. The mare was only too happy to oblige, and sprang forward, back up to her interrupted pace in seconds.

Brianna had the jump on Sebastian, but within two minutes, he was next to her, his black horse going stride for stride with hers. She pushed Moonlight harder, taking the lead, and turned inward to a trail that snaked through the woods.

Stuck behind her on the skinny path, Sebastian grumbled a laugh, and the second the trail widened, he attacked, passing her and sticking her with the dust.

Back and forth they traded the lead, mud flying as they crossed over the stream five times, weaving along the forest trails, clearing fallen trees, and bolting through two wide-open pastures. By the time they had raced down the last grassy knoll, far from

Notlund, Brianna was gasping for breath, her muscles screaming for her to stop.

She looked over at Sebastian. He was watching her, smiling—not winded—but she could see the sweat on his brow.

Back near the bank of the stream, Sebastian pulled up, slowing his black horse. Even exhausted, Brianna wasn't about to give in and stop first, so she was silently ecstatic when he halted and she was able to follow suit. As, she imagined, was Moonlight.

Sebastian was off his horse, removing his gloves and to her side before Moonlight's feet had stopped.

His hand came up to help her down. Brianna grabbed it, her thigh slipping off the pommel of the saddle. Instantly, his free arm came up around her waist, and he slid her downward along his body. Unexpected, but she had to admit it was easier than jumping down from the saddle in her riding habit.

Sebastian didn't release her right away, instead, holding her captive between him and her horse.

Busy energy still coursing through her body, she looked up at him, smiling. "That was fun."

A half smile caught his face as his thumb came up, wiping a splotch of mud from her temple. "You say it like you are surprised you could actually have fun with me."

"Well…" Her head tilted back and forth noncommittally.

He squeezed her waist, bringing her tight to his body.

She laughed, pushing off from his chest and grabbing Moonlight's reins. "I just was not expecting it. I have never ridden with anyone like that. Usually I am anxious, waiting impatiently when I ride with another."

She patted Moonlight's white neck and then started to walk her horse down the grassy bank to the stream. "I did not realize you had such skill with a horse, but I suppose I should have guessed."

"Why is that?" Sebastian joined her, bringing his black stallion to the water's edge.

"Your work with the horses. You must know just how to push them to get the best from them in order to choose the right ones. The duke has said there is no one better than you at recognizing horses of great worth."

"Then I owe him a thank you if he informed your opinion thusly." Sebastian tied back his reins to his saddle, letting the horse wander along the bank of the stream, nosing about for the juiciest grass.

"The duke's opinion only verified what I just witnessed." Taking off her gloves and dark blue riding jacket, now splattered with mud, Brianna knelt by the stream, dipping her hands into the water. "I do realize you could have gone on much longer than me."

"I cannot believe you just uttered those words." His feet stopped next to her and he bent, balancing on one knee. He cupped water to splash his face and then the back of his neck.

Brianna looked at him, chuckling, watching the water drip down his neck and soak the top of his white linen shirt. He had foregone a jacket this morning—probably in too much of a rush to catch her. Again, like every morning this week, she had been forced to slip out from under his arm over her belly that morning. She would have to become more skilled at not waking him.

He looked over to her, smirk on his face.

She rolled her eyes, splashing a spray of water his way. "Do not think it was easy for me to admit to such a thing. Do you ever enter races with your horses?"

"Occasionally—minor ones, but only when we are trying to convince an owner or investor of the worth of our breeding lines. We have jockeys for the major races like the Derby and Oaks at Epsom Downs."

Sebastian sat back on the edge of the stream, crunching small, smooth pebbles as he stretched his legs out in front of him and leaned back on his palms. "And then we have a number of other riders throughout England and the continent that race our horses."

"They are successful?"

"Our horses do have an admirable winning percentage behind them."

Brianna pulled a handkerchief from the pocket in her skirt, dipping it into the water and wiping away the other splotches of mud she could feel on her face.

"I apologize for the mud splatters," Sebastian said, pointing at her face.

"It is nothing. Mud only signifies a good ride." Brianna looked over her shoulder at him. "And I am not the only one with a splotch or two."

Smirking, she turned, leaning back to him to wipe clear two mud spots that remained on the side of his cheek, mixing with the dark stubble.

She went back to the stream, dipping the cloth and rinsing it in the water, then wrapped it around the back of her neck before she sat down next to Sebastian.

"Water?" Sebastian handed her a leather-wrapped flask.

Brianna sipped from it, relaxing for a few moments in comfortable silence, letting her eyes rest on the rolling water and her mind wander into nothingness.

Sebastian sat just as easily in the silence, gazing at the ground rising from the stream opposite them where the rocks and pebbles transitioned into a hill covered with long, flowing grasses.

He nodded to the view across from them, his voice breaking through the crackle of the water and the birds chirping. "That—I have always loved when the fields come alive—when the wind hits the grasses, waking them up, making them dance in green waves. So free, so much space. Just like the fields we went flying through."

Brianna watched his profile. He was handsome, and each and every time she looked at him, she was reminded of it. His full dark hair with streaks of light brown in it, a finely cut jaw and hard cheekbones.

If she had thought to actually gain a husband, he would have been very much what she would have been attracted to. And for all she didn't trust him, she was having a hard time not liking this man, liking his depth of character. Liking that no matter how many frowns she threw his way, he was unaffected—seeing right through them.

Maybe he truly did have an unnatural ability to see things others could not. At least with her.

She picked up a pebble, rubbing the smoothness of it on the pads of her fingers. "Is that why you spend so little time in London—you like the open lands? The duke told me you rarely stayed there for long. You must like the freedom?"

"Too much so. I have never been one for the close quarters of London. Nor for being pinned down in one place. I know Rowe thinks I am a wanderer."

"Are you?"

He smiled his devil grin, his eyes still watching the grasses play. "Possibly." His look swung to Brianna, the brown in his eyes particularly warm in the dappled sunlight. "But I am finding wandering less and less appealing."

Transfixed by his gaze for a long moment, Brianna knew exactly what he implied.

It caught her off-guard, as all those moments did when he looked at her like that—the look that silently screamed he wanted to grab her, kiss her, tug the shirt off her shoulder, slide her skirts up...

Brianna yanked back on her wandering thoughts, clearing her throat and setting the flask down as she forced her eyes to the stream. It would not do to look at him in those moments. Though she was highly suspicious of his attentions, she was finding it harder and harder to resist them.

She flipped the smooth pebble in her fingers, tossing it into the stream and watching the rings float away with the slow-moving water.

"Where are your lands, Seb? I never hear you speak of them."

"You have never asked. Most of them are scattered throughout Suffolk and Essex. We also have a few swathes in Lancashire."

"What are they like?" Brianna pointed at the field across from them. "Do they look like this? Do you have stables and pastures like here at Notlund?"

"No. My family never cared for horses past the coaches they pulled, even though there are pockets devoted to horse racing near our lands. Most of the Suffolk land has rich dirt for crops. And in Lancashire we are devoted to sheep and we have several textile mills."

Brianna nodded, tossing another pebble before looking at him. "Your family? Do you have brothers or sisters?"

"My father and older brother are dead. I have no other siblings. My mother lives mostly at our main estate in Suffolk."

"Your mother is alive?" Brianna sat straight, turning toward him.

"Yes. Why?"

"I did…I did not think she was alive. I am surprised she has not been invited to Notlund, what with our marriage. It is not done that I have not met her. Will she be coming soon—has she been invited to Notlund?"

A deep frown settled on Sebastian's face. "I doubt she would come." He looked away from her. "Nor is she awaiting a visit from her son."

The way he said it, sharp, with a note of closure, clamped Brianna's mouth shut.

For all that she hid from him, he wasn't exactly forthcoming about information of his own family.

Before she could explore the topic of his mother further, Sebastian's frowned eased, and he pinned her with his eyes.

"Speaking of family, Brianna, I have been curious about something."

Brianna's guard flew up. "Yes?"

"Tell me what your sister refers to when she says you are doing something to her again. I have heard Lily say that more than once to you. So what is it that you are doing to her again?"

A quick glance to his face, and Brianna picked up the flask for a slow sip before setting it down and leaning forward, resting her forearms on her knees.

Sebastian grabbed the flask, swallowing a healthy gulp as he waited for her to answer.

She stared at the water tumbling past a mound of rocks at the edge of the stream, weighing her response.

While she had never shied from taking responsibility for what she did, she hesitated. For some reason, she didn't want to have to highlight her flaws in front of Sebastian. But if he wanted to learn of the real her—what she was capable of—he may as well hear it from her lips.

Brianna's eyes stayed on the water as she swallowed sigh. "About a year ago, Lily was in love and wanted to marry a man, Garek Harrison. He was not good enough for her, so I paid him to leave her alone. To leave the country."

Sebastian sputtered out the water he was drinking. "You what?"

"I paid him to leave, to disappear." Brianna refused to look in his direction. "The very fact that he took the money proved he was not worthy of Lily. No one is who can be bought so easily."

"So you manipulated the situation? Took away someone Lily loved?"

Her head whipped to him, her eyes meeting his. "I am not proud of what I did, Seb—of how I went about it. I could have done it in a more delicate way, but I panicked, and that is what happened. I cannot change my actions."

"And Lily found out?"

"Yes."

"So why do you even think to interfere with her and Lord Newdale?"

"I am still going to protect her, Seb. And the past is exactly why I need to investigate Lord Newdale so thoroughly. I cannot be wrong about him. If I interfere again—if I block anything between the two of them, I have to be absolutely certain of his intentions where Lily is concerned."

"You were not certain of the man you paid off?"

"Yes…No. Not certain enough. There was a possibility I was wrong, but I did it anyway."

"Do you regret it?"

"Yes. At least that I acted without knowing all of the facts as actual facts. And that is why Lily continues to remind me of my past actions—she has never fully forgiven me for it. Not that she should." She shook her head, her voice trailing. A pause, and then her eyes snapped to Sebastian. "But I do not apologize for keeping him away from Lily. Whether or not I was certain of him, of the facts, there were lies and he was not to be trusted."

"So it is back to that. Trust." Sebastian set the flask down, grinding the leather wrap into the pebbles. "Is there anyone you trust, Brianna?"

"Lily." She shrugged. "Wynne and the duke, partially."

"That is your list?"

"Yes."

"What about me? What about your husband?"

"I have only known you for a fortnight, Seb. I have no reason to trust you."

"I married you. Married you without any gain for myself. Does my faith, my trust in you not count for anything?"

"You trust in your own instinct, Seb, not in me." Her look went back to the stream. "Do not confuse the two."

The rocks clinked beside her as Sebastian sat upright. He grabbed her chin, forcing her gaze to his face. A face that looked more intense than she had ever seen it. Heat pulsated through his fingers, throbbing against her skin.

"No, Brianna you are wrong. I trust you. Do not question it. And do not think to dismiss it."

Taken aback, she nodded silently.

His fingers slipped from her chin, but his eyes stayed on hers. "What can I do to make you trust me, Brianna?" His voice was earnest, truly wanting an answer from her.

"I know it is not what you want to hear, Seb. But there is nothing. I cannot trust."

He nodded, slowly. "I understand. But is it a cannot, or a will not?"

"Does it matter?"

"Yes. A cannot means there is no hope, Brianna." He grabbed her right hand, clasping it between his palms. "But a will not means I have a chance to alter your mind. Alter your will. You trust Lily, and you trust—even if only partially—Wynne and Rowe. So I think that means there is hope. That you are capable of trusting me."

Brianna took a deep breath, trying to steady her racing heart. "Why do you continue to push this, Seb? I know I cannot be what you want me to be."

"I think differently. I think you know what you are today. But today is not tomorrow. And tomorrow can be very different."

The fingers of his top hand slid onto her wrist, pushing the cuff of her sleeve upward as he traced the fine bone in her forearm. "I think I have a wife that wants, somewhere deep inside, to have a life with a marriage and children and laughter and fun. I have seen glimpses of it—you, unbridled. I saw it today. I think you are capable of doing anything you decide you truly want to, including trusting me."

Brianna closed her eyes, her chin dropping as her head shook, fighting. Fighting Seb's words. Fighting thoughts and dreams that she had long since killed. "Do not do this to me, Seb. I cannot. You do not know what you ask of me."

His hand went to her chin, slipping along her jaw and tilting her face to him. "I only ask that you open your eyes, Brianna. Open them."

Brianna let her eyes open a sliver to him, her breath held.

"Do not trust me today, Brianna. Do not trust me tomorrow. I am willing to accept that. But give me a crack. The slightest way into you."

Her breath exhaled, shaking her voice. "What do you want of me?"

"If your mind will not trust me, maybe your body can." His fingers tightened along her jaw. "I have seen how your mind pulls away from me, while your body leans in. How your skin vibrates under my touch. How your muscles ache to awaken."

Her eyes went wide. "You said you would not touch me. Not until…"

"You were ready. I did say that." He leaned in, his lips to her ear, voice soft. "I think you are ready. You can tell me no, Brianna, but I think you are ready. You hide everything from the world, but you cannot hide how your body reacts to my touch. Not from me."

Brianna's eyes slipped closed as his breath sent shivers down her neck. Her body a statue, she could neither lean in nor pull away from him.

"Trust in this very moment, instead of the past, instead of the future." His lips brushed her neck right below her earlobe. "Just trust in right here, right now. Trust what your body wants."

Her chest tightened, sending her breath shallow. She could only afford a whisper. "You are trying to seduce me?"

His face moved from her neck so he could meet her eyes, and he smiled, slow and lascivious. His other hand came up, cradling her face. "Yes. I am trying to seduce my wife. My beautiful wife. No apologies. I want you, Brianna, and I am not going anywhere. I am your husband, and I am not leaving your side. Not going to disappear."

Words abandoned Brianna. She had no logic against this. No defenses to call upon. He was her husband—he had every right.

And not only her husband, a man that wanted her in the most basic way. A man that had already sent her stomach plummeting, lighting the fire burning deep within her. A man that found her beautiful and desirable. Her husband.

"Let me kiss you, Bree."

Trepidation swamped her mind, but she slowly gave him one nod.

His lips met hers, gentle, exploring. Warm lips that sent tingles along her skin. His hand slid from her jaw, moving to the base of her neck, his fingers entwining into her hair.

Her upsweep only precariously held together after the breakneck ride, it fell almost immediately with a few tugs from Sebastian. Her hair free, he dug his hand deep, weaving strands along his fingers, tightening his hold until he could tilt her head, deepening the kiss.

His tongue parted her lips, brushing inside, and at the very touch, her core sparked, aching, wanting very much what he was doing to her body.

Her mind railed against the pleasure consuming her, fighting to the surface, but she forced it to blankness. Forced it to shove all reason—all thoughts of everything except what Sebastian was doing to her—into the abyss.

At least for this moment. She could do it for this moment.

Her mouth ravaged, his head dropped, tasting the skin on her neck as he unbuttoned her shirt, tugging wide the fabric and tracing his teeth along the lines of her shoulder. Hungry, he made his way back up her neck until his mouth was against hers once more.

One hand holding the back of her head, the other moving down her ribcage, he pulled slightly away, his forehead on hers, and took a deep breath.

"I want nothing more than to strip you down and take you so hard, you are screaming for release, Bree." His voice went low, gravelly. "But it is not what you need."

Her mind foggy from his onslaught, his words sifted, floating erratically through her brain. She opened her eyes to him. "No?"

"No. You need to be in charge, Bree." His fingers pushed back the loose hair on her temple. "I will touch you where you want me to touch you. Kiss you where you want me to. Move how you need me to. Every demand is yours to make, Bree."

Her heart swelled, thudding in her chest. She had been lost in what he was making her feel. And now he wanted her to tell him...she swallowed hard.

True, she was no innocent, but she was far from experienced.

But that she could control him—that he would give her that—it awakened something deep and raw in her soul.

"Tell me where to start, Bree. I am yours," he said, voice rough.

She took a deep breath, her eyes going downward and stopping at the first thing she saw. "Your shirt."

He silently nodded, then gave himself enough space to yank his white linen shirt off his torso.

Her eyes ran down his body.

Every muscle along his chest, along his stomach was taut, hard. She had recognized he wasn't flabby beneath the usual dark jackets she saw him in, but the sight forced a sharp intake of breath. The man was molded as finely as a Greek statue. Her eyes stopped just short of his buckskin breeches, flipping up to his face.

Her voice shook, nearly failing her. "My shirt."

He silently nodded, his fingers going to the rest of the pearl buttons lining her silk shirt. Slowly, his fingers dragged along her skin, teasing as he slipped the shirt down one arm and then the other.

She leaned her head back, exposing her neck. Her hand came up, trembling, landing at the junction of her neck and shoulder. "Here. Your lips. And the rest of it. The shift, the stays."

He nodded silently, his mouth going to her neck, setting fire to her skin as he unlaced her short stays and slipped her shift down.

Unnaturally bared to the wide-open air, Brianna took solace in the fact that Sebastian's torso shrouded hers, his hard chest pressing against her breasts. She set her hands on his shoulders, letting them slip down his back, pulling him closer to her.

His breath heavy, his lips did not leave her as his words came out guttural. "Tell me I can go downward, Bree. Give me permission."

"Yes."

With a half growl, Sebastian moved downwards, his hands going up her ribcage, fingers moving to cup her breasts. He took her right nipple into his mouth, rolling it around his tongue before sucking until it strained into his mouth.

Brianna gasped, her head falling back as he moved on to her left breast.

The onslaught to her senses continued until Brianna could no longer take it, her body demanding so much more. She grabbed his face, pulling him from her chest. Her palms scratched on the stubble lining his jaw as she brought his eyes into view. "I want this, Seb. The rest of it. Your clothes, my skirt. You under me."

A heated smile came to his face, and he nodded silently, his hands going down to her waist, fingers sliding underneath the wool fabric of her skirt. Within a minute, he had disposed of both of their clothes and was pulling her onto his lap.

Brianna kept her eyes on his face, both wanting to look down but refusing to do so. Her hands tightened on his shoulders. It had been so long since she had last touched a man—since a man had touched her. And the last time this had happened—

"Stop. Do not leave me, Bree." His hands captured her face, his brown eyes right before hers. "Stay with me. Stay right here. This moment. You are in charge. I will not do anything you do not want me to."

She inhaled with a nod, the intensity of him overtaking her senses, overtaking her sudden panic.

He searched her face until satisfied with what he saw and then slipped his palm alongside the back of her hand, entwining his fingers with hers. "Feel me, Bree. Feel how much I want you." Before she could resist, he moved her hand downward from his shoulder, wrapping her fingers around his member.

A guttural intake of breath, and he groaned, his eyes closed. "You do this to me, Bree. You."

His free hand went to her leg, moving along her inner thigh until he reached her core. "And this is what I can do to you, Bree. Make you feel." His fingers dove, caressing. Exploring. Teasing her into a pitch.

She did want this. He was right. In this moment, she wanted this. Desperately. Wanted to feel like a woman. Wanted to be desired. Wanted to give satisfaction.

She shifted her legs, straddling his lap fully, moving forward until her chest touched his.

Her hand squeezing the lean muscle of his hardness, she dragged her fingers slowly up the smooth skin, and then abandoned it to settle both of her forearms on his shoulders, her palms solid on his back.

She had to force the words, thick, from her throat. "I do want this, Seb. Lift me. Put me on you. You in me."

His hands were on her hips in an instant, lifting her, and then he set her gently down, his shaft sliding into her tightness. He dropped her painstakingly slow, letting her body open completely to him before lowering her further.

Fully filled, her body meeting his, Brianna exhaled a quivering breath, her nails digging into his back. "Again."

He nodded, silent, lifting her just as slowly, and repeating.

"Again. Faster. And do not stop."

This time his nod was not silent. A tortured groan rumbled from his chest. But Sebastian continued on, bringing her up and down, his muscles straining, his breath heavy.

He grimaced, battling against his own body as he looked up at her, desperate. "Tell me not to come, Bree. Tell me you are close."

Her right hand curled into the back of his hair. "I want you to, Seb. Do it now. I want to feel you deep inside me. Feel you fill me. Feel you shudder. Now."

"Dammit, Bree."

"Do it, Seb." She pushed downward, fighting his hands on her hips that held her high. "Do it."

Growling, he let her slide down on him, his body violently quaking with the last stroke. He buried his face into her chest, his mouth on her skin. Brianna could feel him expand wide within her, the waves ripping through his body and emptying into hers.

Still pulsating deep inside her, he tore his head backward, looking up at her. "Hell, Bree. I am not about to accept that. You did not join me." His hands ran up from her hips, his fingers going to her breasts. "Give me permission, Bree."

"Permission for what?"

"To do to you what I want. What you need me to do. Give me the control. If only for a few minutes. I will stop if you demand it." He grabbed the back of her head, pushing her mouth down to his, his voice a low rumble. "But you will not demand to stop, Bree. I will make sure of it. Just give up control, Bree. Let it go. Let me have it."

Her eyes went wide, watching his face, staring into the brown eyes that she knew, quite honestly, had only comforted her.

She could do this. She had to. For the very need he had awakened, but she had not allowed to be satisfied. She had to. Her soul needed this.

"You have my permission."

"I will only do this if you swear you will not hold back, Bree."

She nodded.

"Swear it."

"I do."

He attacked her lips, his mouth demanding, taking control of her, nipping her skin as his tongue consumed. Her mouth battered, sated, he yanked away, grabbing her around her lower back and flipping them. She landed on the cool pebbles, the smooth stones clinking underneath her backside.

He moved his legs between hers, sending her thighs apart. For a second, his body left her as he went upright on his knees. He looked down, his eyes travelling over her body, and Brianna could see quite clearly that he wanted to attack every line of her skin.

His left hand went down, slipping beneath her right knee and bending it upward. He bent, his eyes not leaving hers, and set his mouth on her calf. Leisurely—agonizingly so—he moved upward along her leg, each touch of his mouth only a hair away from the last touch of his mouth. Past her knee, he continued the assault, teasing the curve of her inner thigh.

By the time he reached the top of her thigh, Brianna could barely breathe. And then he advanced.

Spreading her legs wide, he set his mouth to her core, his tongue sliding into the folds. Brianna buckled instantly at the touch, a breathless scream ripping from her mouth.

Circling, his tongue explored her, sending her body to pitch hard against him, her fingers going into his hair, grasping for stability. He sucked. He teased with his teeth. He thrust her body into writhing with the onslaught of his tongue delving deep into her.

And just when Brianna's scream turned into pleading, demanding for release, he pulled up.

His lips left her for only a second until they landed on her belly, and he travelled up her body to take control of her left nipple.

Within seconds, his face was above her, hovering as unsatisfied frustration boiled in her.

Then realization hit Brianna. Her eyes went huge. "Again? You are…"

"Hell yes, I am ready, Bree. And you are too this time."

He smiled as he plunged into her, no hesitation, and brought her back to the edge within three strokes.

Brianna screamed, nails ripping across his back. "Seb."

He did not slow. "I am doing this to you, Bree. You will come for me."

His words, a hard thrust, and Brianna crashed, her body vibrating, exploding in all directions. He continued through her tremors, pulling more out of her with each stroke. At the second she could take no more, he slammed into her, exploding and filling her again.

He dropped onto her and rolled, gripping her and pulling her with him, his body still connected with hers.

The movement made little sense in Brianna's haze. Nothing made sense in her haze. The only thing in her head was wave after wave of release pounding through her brain.

Only one thought managed to make its way clear into her mind. This, what Sebastian had just done to her, was something she had never felt before.

And it scared her to the bottom of her soul.

CHAPTER 9

Sebastian watched the long strand of hair, brown with a streak of blond in it, untwirl from his forefinger and drop onto his chest above Brianna's head.

This, he could do all day. Brianna sprawled on top of him. Her head resting on the divot along his chest. The stream gurgling by. Summer sun warming his skin.

He picked up the strand again, threading it through his fingers.

Brianna shifted on top of him, their skin, sticky hot between them, pulling. No matter. He had his wife in his arms. A wife that surprised him at every turn.

He had always sensed the depth in her, the passion being suffocated. But once she had committed, she had no reservations about how their bodies should meet, how Sebastian could touch her.

His hips moved under her, pebbles clinking as he readjusted. He didn't think he could be ready again so soon, but he was quickly thinking himself to that point.

Distraction. He needed a distraction, lest his new wife think this was all her life was to become.

"What is in your mind right now, my wife?"

Her face toward the stream, her voice came out soft, lazy. "I was wondering why I always seem to end up naked or near-naked with you by a stream."

Sebastian chuckled.

"Yes. And how unfair it was the last time when it was so innocent, but the repercussions were so enormous."

"And this time?"

He could feel her smile against his skin. "So much more deserving of a forced marriage, as I had better be married to any man that is going to do what you just did to me."

She shifted her head, her chin resting on his chest as her crystal blue eyes found his face.

"And if anyone caught us now, it would be awkward—a few red faces—but nothing more, no repercussions. It is freeing. I had not thought on how much freedom being married would actually afford me."

"You thought you were to be captured?"

"Yes. And I am captured. I am no longer my own property." She shrugged. "But I am not in a cage. This—at least today, has not been the worst day ever."

"That is a compliment, I presume?" He freed a strand of hair that had matted onto her cheek, tucking it behind her ear. "And I doubt I could ever keep you in a cage, Bree. You have far too much will for that."

His finger traced her cheekbone as he hid a sigh. She still resisted him. For all her body had given over to him, she still resisted their marriage—him. It had been too much to ask for, that this would change anything in her mind.

Patience. One moment at a time, he reminded himself.

He forced a grin onto his face. "Plus, Bree, you out in the world—free, riding a horse, pleasuring your husband in broad daylight by a stream—is far more enjoyable to my tastes then having you at Notlund."

"You find the castle suffocating? But your rooms there are exquisite—not to mention, hidden well away from the mix of the other rooms and activity."

"True, Rowe did do a commendable job with my suite, but I still find most things inside suffocating."

She tapped his chest in front of her nose with her forefinger. "You do appear to be in your element outside, riding a horse— oh—the horses."

She pushed herself upright, untangling her body from his as her head swiveled up and down the bank of the stream.

Sebastian sat up. "There."

He pointed downstream a stretch. Moonlight was standing under the shade of a large willow tree, and he could see the tail of his horse just past the branches. "They have not wandered too far."

"As long as we do not have to walk back to the castle, I am happy." Brianna spun to sit on her behind, stretching out her legs to dip her toes into the water. "It appears as though it will be beastly hot again today. This is the oddest weather."

Sebastian could not resist joining her, moving forward to the water to sink his own feet and legs into the stream. He leaned forward, sliding his hand along the inside of Brianna's left knee, bent up to the sky, and pressed it to his own leg. So smooth. He missed having the blanket of her on his body already.

Just as he was about to let his hand slip down her inner thigh, he spotted the end of a white scar wrapping around her left calf.

He scooted forward, lifting her leg so he could see the back of her calf.

How had he missed this earlier? Five separate scars, long and white with time, cut across her calf.

"Hell, Brianna…"

His mind raced. He could think of no instrument, no piece of machinery that could have possibly accidently cut her in such a manner. Not for how evenly they were spaced down her leg.

He glanced up to her face, only to see all color drain from her cheeks.

"How?" Sebastian's fingers ran up from her ankle, pausing at each line bumping from her skin. "Tell me about these."

"No." She jerked her leg away. "No. Do not ask me about them, Seb."

Tucking her leg under her, she glared at him, mouth tight.

Sebastian could not stop himself. "Then tell me about Gregory."

Stung as though he had just thrown fire on her, she jumped to her feet, rushing away from him as she yanked up her shift from the pile of clothes on the rocks. She jabbed her head and arms into the cloth. "What do you know? What did my sister tell you?"

"Nothing." Sebastian followed her. "Just that you loved a man named Gregory. You were to marry him, but he disappeared."

Brianna froze at his words, her hands gripping the shift she had half down her body. It only took a second before her body began to shake, instant anger pouring from her. "That is something. She had no right. No right at all."

"Lily did not tell me in order to hurt you."

"She still had no right to speak his name." Ignoring her stays, she picked up her silk shirt and shoved her arms into the sleeves.

"Why?" Sebastian grabbed his breeches and slipped them on as he moved to stand in front of her. "What about him makes you this mad?"

"I am not mad." Her hands trembling, she attempted to button her shirt. She failed.

"No?" Sebastian grabbed both of her quaking hands, pulling them from the fabric. "Then what about him makes you this scared, Brianna?"

Her eyes snapped up and she stared at him, her mouth pulled tight, fury pouring from her. The shaking left her hands and travelled up her arms to her shoulders. The trembling invaded her body, and the longer she stared at Sebastian, the more she shook.

Holding her hands captive, he stepped closer to her, slowly, gently. "What did he do to you, Bree?"

Her head swung back and forth, her mouth tight.

He dropped her hands and bent over, his fingers slipping under her shift to lift it and expose her left calf.

"Did he do this to you? Did he ruin you like this?"

She stared down at him, tears springing to her eyes, her head shaking. "No. Do not."

"You loved him, Brianna. You were going to marry him."

Her hands balled into fists. "Lily should not have told you that."

Sebastian dropped the skirt of her shift, standing straight. "But she did, Bree. Is this why you have fought me at every turn? Refused to acknowledge the very willing man that is in front of you? Refused to acknowledge that I want you? And not just your body. This has never been about your body. It is about you, Brianna. All of you."

She spun, trying to escape him.

He snatched her wrist, shaking it. "You would rather live with your heart tethered to a lost love than look at the man in front of you?"

Brianna jerked her arm, trying to free herself while refusing to look at him.

Sebastian rounded her, grabbing both of her shoulders. She kept her head turned, avoiding his eyes.

Sebastian leaned in, his hard words in her ear. "Or is it that he did this to you and you have never admitted it to yourself?"

Her eyes whipped to him, on fire. "Admitted it to myself?"

She scoffed a forced laugh, her eyes to the sky. Shaking her head, her look dropped to him, pinning him with ferocity.

"I live with this every single damn day, Seb, every single damn second. So do not venture to think you know what is in my mind. Do not think you know what happened. I damn well know exactly what he did. What he did to me. What he did to my father."

"And you still love him."

Her fists came up, shoving hard enough at his chest that she broke his hold. Several desperate steps backward and she stumbled, turning from him. "Dammit, Seb, shut the hell up. You do not know what you speak of."

Palms up, he stepped cautiously toward her. "So tell me, Brianna. Tell me that you do not still love him."

"I hate him." She spun back to Sebastian, barreling past his hands to hit his chest, shoving him away. "I hate him with every breath I take. With every step. With every thought. I hate him. Is that what you need to hear, Seb? You need to make me speak of him? Think of him?"

In an instant, the exploding fire in her vanished and she crumpled to her knees.

Her arms wrapping her own body, she huddled into herself, gasping for breath.

Crushed. She was utterly crushed. On her knees, her entire being broken.

He had wanted to know—but not like this. Not with the pain he saw coursing through her body. He bent, his hand spreading wide on her back. "Brianna—"

She jerked around, smacking his arm away from her body. "Just leave. Leave me the hell alone, Seb."

"Brianna, I am—"

"Leave me alone, Seb." Her eyes came up to him, her words vicious. "I hate that you are daring to ask me these questions. I hate that I had to marry you. I hate what you are making me do."

"Bree, what am I making you do?"

His hands came forward, but she slapped him away before he even touched her.

"Just leave me the hell alone, Seb." She looked up at him, her head shaking, her voice a mere whisper. "Do not make me hate you as well. I will. I will hate you. If you do not leave me, Seb, I will hate you."

Sebastian looked down at his wife. Huddled, shaking, wanting—yearning—to hate him.

He couldn't afford to give her a reason to do so.

With one nod, he stepped away from her.

Picking up his shirt and boots, he walked downstream to collect his horse.

And he vanished.

~ ~ ~

Brianna didn't want to have to sink to the level of asking the duke about her husband's whereabouts, but she was desperate.

Desperate to unleash her anger at him, but Sebastian was not at Notlund. And her annoyance was starting to unjustly bleed out at the people around her.

Sebastian had been gone for a full fortnight—two very long weeks—and not a single soul had questioned his disappearance. No one—except Brianna.

It was quite possible that everyone around her knew where Sebastian was, and wouldn't that be a cruel joke? Everyone but his wife knowing where he was, what he was doing.

Brianna knew she had been overly harsh with him at the stream. She had known it almost immediately. But he had pushed—dug too deep into memories that she could not let see the light of day. Not if she was to remain strong. Remain sane.

She had been so close to breaking in front of Sebastian, and she couldn't let that happen.

Ruined. His word for what happened to her. And that was exactly what she was—ruined—not whole. She had been hiding that fact for years.

She wasn't about to let Sebastian see how broken she truly was. No. She would refuse it to her last breath.

But now he was gone. He had left her, just like that. Used her body and then disappeared. And Brianna wasn't about to let another man do that to her.

A deep breath to swallow her pride, and Brianna stepped into the open doorway of the duke's study, her knuckles rapping on the wood frame.

Sans a jacket, the sleeves of his white linen shirt rolled up to his elbows, the duke looked up from the papers on the desk in front of him. A genuine smile crossed his face.

"Brianna, come in."

"I am not interrupting your work?"

"You are more important than a few pieces of paper. Come, sit." He motioned to the leather chair across from the desk.

"You have a more serious look about you than usual. Was there something amiss about Lord Newdale and his family's departure? Lily did not commit to him—answer his proposal, did she?"

"No, nothing of the sort." Brianna sat. "They have departed and Lily has done as I asked and promised him an answer at the end of summer."

"And you met with your runner the other day—did he have any news?"

"Unfortunately, no. But he now has until the end of summer to investigate, which should help."

"Good. So why the concern in your brow? What is it you need from me?"

"Where did Seb go?" The words blurted out.

The duke leaned back in his chair, finger tapping the desk as his eyebrow cocked at her. "I assumed you knew. He headed up to Clavenshire for their annual local races. There is a studhorse in the area we would like to match with one of our mares, but we first have to convince the owner of the match."

"Oh."

"Seb did not tell you?"

Brianna shook her head, heat flooding her cheeks. She had no idea this would be so mortifying, having to ask the duke as to where her husband had run off.

His head cocked. "Seb left you without a word?"

"Yes." Brianna bit her tongue, stopping further words. She didn't want Sebastian to look the cad, but the duke also didn't need to know that she had demanded Sebastian leave her alone.

"Bizarre. I thought it odd that he left so abruptly..." The duke shook his head, dismissing whatever thought he was having. "And he did not tell you he was leaving or when he would be back?"

"No." Brianna's fingernails started digging into her thumbs. "How far is Clavenshire from Notlund? I would like to go there."

"I imagine Seb will be back within a week—a fortnight at most. The racing starts in a few days and takes place over two days—three or four if the weather is bad. And then he is due back."

"I would still like to go there. I need to see him. I can take a maid in the Silverton carriage—how long will it take to travel?"

"Clavenshire is two days away on horseback. But by carriage, it will take you at minimum four if the roads are good."

Brianna nodded, understanding. "But then I may miss him. Do you know of an appropriate maid or groom that could accompany me? One that can ride a horse well enough to keep pace and not slow me?"

"I cannot allow that, Brianna."

"But—"

His hand came up, halting her. "So I will accompany you. I do believe I am one of the few people that will not slow you on a horse."

Stunned that he would offer so generously, Brianna nodded, relief lifting her sour mood.

Now she just needed to keep her ill temper at bay another two days—at least long enough not to offend the duke.

CHAPTER 10

"Rowe, I did not expect you. You look like you have been riding hard." Sebastian opened wide the door to his double room at the Twisted Oak Tavern. "Is something amiss, or did you decide to attend the races?"

The duke stepped into the room, waiting for Sebastian to close the door before he spoke. "No, I am headed back to Notlund. I am only here to deliver something you forgot."

"What?"

"Your wife."

"What? Brianna? You brought her here?" Sebastian's head cocked, his mouth tightening.

"She is down the hall." The duke thumbed over his shoulder and glanced about the room. "I wanted to make sure there were no…guests…with you. It would not have been appropriate for her to see such a thing."

"I know damn well what you are implying, Rowe, but I have not touched another woman since I saw Brianna in London." Sebastian glared at Rowen as his arms crossed over his chest. "And you, friend, are interfering in things you should not be interfering with. Brianna does not want to see me. Does not want me near her."

"On the contrary, she is the one that wanted to come to you, Seb. I am merely the courier."

"Brianna left her sister unchaperoned?"

"Yes, if you can believe it." The duke shrugged. "Lord Newdale has departed—without an answer from Lily on his proposal—but will return at the end of the summer. Lord Bepton has arrived, and is currently settling into his visit, I imagine.

Wynne is at Notlund and can serve as an overzealous mama if needed. Brianna trusts her to chaperone appropriately."

"At least she trusts someone," Sebastian muttered half under his breath.

"What?"

"Nothing."

The duke sighed, tapping his gloves on his thigh. "Seb, I do not know what is between the two of you at the moment— Brianna has been very tight-lipped around all of us—Wynne, me, even Lily. I have just spent two very silent days on the roads with her. And it was painful to watch her have to approach me to find out where you were." He shook his head. "You left without a word to her, Seb."

Sebastian took his glare and returned his own. "She wanted me to leave, Rowe."

"Did she? Is that why I just travelled all the way up here to deliver her to you?"

Sebastian shrugged, sighing, but not answering.

"All that said, I trust that you will take care of what needs to be taken care of, Seb? Or do I need to stay and wait to escort her back to Notlund?"

"No." The word came out as a grumble.

"Good." The duke slapped his gloves on his thigh once more and inclined his head as he turned, opening the door. "I will see you at Notlund after the races."

"You do not wish to stay for the night?"

"No. Wynne was already at her limit with Newdale's mother—trying to convince her we are respectable." The duke stepped into the hall, turning back to Sebastian. "So she was none too pleased that I had to leave with Brianna right when Lord Bepton arrived."

"Send her my apologies."

"Fix this. That is all the apology I need." With a pointed tilt of his head, the duke turned to leave.

Sebastian followed him into the hallway, watching as he walked down the distance to the stairs and stopped where Brianna was waiting. With a quick goodbye to her, the duke disappeared down the narrow staircase.

Sebastian waited until the duke's head was out of view before his eyes went to Brianna.

She stood at the end of the hall, a deep blue riding habit wrapping the curves of her body. Her hair was pulled back in an upsweep, but much looser than usual with several tendrils escaping to curl around her face. A little matching blue hat sat jauntily on her head, something he had never seen her wear.

She fidgeted under his scrutiny, unsure. It was out of character for his wife, as she usually tried to strike first and control every encounter they had.

Not moving from her spot by the stairs, she opened her mouth, but no sound came from her lips. She clamped her mouth closed, clearing her throat, then tried again.

"You told me you were not going to disappear."

Dammit. Sebastian could hear the anger vibrating in her words.

"Brianna. Come into the room. I do not want to discuss this in a hallway with you."

Her eyes narrowed at him.

"Please, Bree. Come into the room."

She glanced over her shoulder to the stairs, then looked to him. With an audible sigh, she started down the hall toward him.

A cold breeze walking past him through the open door to his room, Brianna avoided looking at his face.

Sebastian steeled himself, closing the door behind him as he followed her.

She looked around at the surroundings. "This is pleasant."

"It is. I have these rooms kept for me as I travel through here frequently." He watched her in silence for a moment, her gaze fixed on a window and avoiding him. "Why did you come here, Brianna?"

Turning, her crystal blue eyes centered on him. "To yell at you."

He waited, but her voice didn't rise, words didn't follow. "And?"

Her head shaking, she shrugged. "Somewhere in the past two days…I do not know. I lost it. Lost my anger. Most of it, at least. Though I am still mad."

"Mad at me for my questions about your past?"

"No." Brianna took a deep breath, her eyes going down and her voice softening. "You said you would not leave my side, Seb." She looked up to him. "That you were not going to disappear."

Sebastian nodded, acknowledging the truth. "I did."

"And I believed you. Fool that I am, in that moment, I believed you."

"You are not—"

Her hand flew up, waving to stop him. "So I am only here for one thing, Seb, and then I will part. I was furious—bitter—for days, but I am past all of that now. Now I only need to hear the truth from you, even though I already know it. And then I will leave."

"Brianna, Rowe is already gone."

"I can catch up to him."

"Bri—"

"One thing Seb, from your lips." Her mouth went tight. "You said those things to me so I would let you touch my body, did you not?"

Sebastian blinked hard at her words. Words he was not expecting. "Brianna—no. No. Nothing of the kind."

"But you obviously did not mean your words—that you would not disappear—so why even say them, then? Why lie? You wasted no time in leaving me."

"Brianna, you wanted me to leave. You demanded it of me."

"You pushed me too far, Seb, and yes, I wanted you to leave me at the stream." Her leather-gloved hands balled into fists. "But for you to leave Notlund without a word, Seb? To humiliate me—

to leave for weeks without any indication of where you went or when you would be back?"

Sebastian ran a hand through his hair. "You said you would hate me, Brianna. What was I supposed to do with that?"

"Not abandon me? Not have sex with me and then disappear?"

"No. That thought is nothing but false—that I took you by the stream had nothing to do with why I left."

Her right fist slammed into her thigh. "Did you use me, Seb?"

"No. God, no, Bree. I married you. Do you remember that? Married you. Happily. Willingly."

Her chest rose in a heavy breath, her words shaking. "You should not have been so stupid."

"It was not stupid, Brianna. It was a leap of faith. A bow to fate." He stepped closer to her. "I married you because it was what was meant to happen."

"You like to say it was fate, Seb, but what about now, what about this?" Her arm swung wide about her. "Is it fate that you use me and then leave? You play with me for a few weeks and then disappear when it suits you?"

"No, Bree, that is not what happened and you know it." Sebastian could not stifle his own ire. "By the stream—you wanted to hate me. You were looking for a reason—any reason— to hate me. You have been from the beginning."

Her arms crossed over her chest and she stared at him, blue eyes narrowing. "I may have been looking for a reason to hate you, Seb, but you were looking for a reason to escape me."

"What?"

"You ran, Seb. You pushed me too far and then ran so fast from me I did not even know what happened."

Sebastian heaved a sigh. "I could not risk you hating me, Brianna."

Her face went to the ceiling, her head shaking. Sebastian watched as her gaze waned from cold anger to sadness.

It took long seconds, and then her eyes dropped to him, her words creeping out, soft, barely audible. "What did you think leaving me would do?"

The sheer vulnerability in her voice startled him. He had seen snippets of it, unguarded moments when the slightest vulnerability had surfaced.

But this. This reached straight into his heart, gripping it, squeezing it, forcing him to really look at her.

Look at what his actions had done to her.

He suddenly realized that he had risked far more by actually leaving her. And he had no excuse for it.

"I do not know what I can tell you, Brianna." He moved to stand in front of her, daring to slide his palm along the side of her jaw. "But I did not intend to hurt you. Never that."

His voice dipped low. "I could not have you hate me, Bree. Not you."

He watched as her body deflated, her arms dropping to her sides as she searched his face. Searched for the honesty that Lily had said she needed more than anything. Sebastian hoped against hope that she saw the trueness in his eyes.

Her head bowed. "By the stream, I should not have said...I just needed you to leave, Seb. I would have said anything to make you leave in that moment." The light in the room made her blue eyes drift to aquamarine, to the blue of a deep swathe of sea. They ventured up to him. "You ask of me things I cannot give you. Things I cannot tell you. Things I cannot relive. You push me too far, Seb—and I do not know if I should hate you or..."

"Or what?"

She sighed, her head tilting. "You just ask too much of me Seb. I cannot visit the past."

His hand dropped from her face. "And I do not want you to hate me, Bree."

"I do not." She took a deep breath, her eyes leaving his face to look around his room. Her gaze stopped at the four-post bed by the fireplace. "I missed..." She gave him a tentative glance before nodding to the bed with her head. "I missed your arm over my belly while I slept."

"You still slept in my bed?"

She shrugged, embarrassed. "It was our deal. As was staying at Notlund—you promised me that we could stay at Notlund through the summer. But then you left."

"I will not risk your hatred if I return?"

She shook her head. "No. Not unless you do something worthy of it." The smallest smile touched her lips.

"Then I will return after the races tomorrow."

A nod and she smoothed her skirt as she stepped around him. "I will be on my way, then. I am sure the duke has not made it too far."

Sebastian threw an arm in front of her, catching her around the waist. "You are not leaving, Brianna."

"No?"

He dropped his arm, as he could see her already bristling at his demand. "No. I want you here, if you will stay, Bree. Or if you do want to go back to Notlund with the duke, then I will accompany you to him. But I hope you will stay. There are a few more races today, and the main race—the reason I am here—is tomorrow. We can eat and walk about the festivities."

She blinked hard at his words, a hesitant smile coming to her face. "I will stay, if I will not get in the way of your dealings here?"

The relief that swept through Sebastian was unexpected. He smiled, wanting to touch Brianna, to wrap his arms around her and carry her to the bed.

But he stayed still.

Patience, he reminded himself. That was how he was going to finally crack his way into Brianna. Patience.

"You will be the furthest thing from in the way." He went to pick up his boots by the door, holding them up as he turned to her. "Shall we go and find ourselves food?"

Brianna nodded, her smile widening.

Sebastian returned the grin. Patience.

~ ~ ~

"Aye, ye fine lady, ye be lookin' to see what fate has fer ye? Only three shillings fer yer palm. Five fer yer cards."

A tiny wisp of an ancient woman, necklaces piled high and swinging upon her chest, leaned out from the back of a ruby red traveler's wagon. Lanterns with a rainbow of colored glass hung, lit, all around her. Her grey hair trapped in long braids down to her hips, the top of her head was hidden under a red handkerchief. "Ye be a-wonderin' 'bout yer future, lass? I can spy it from twenty paces."

"A fortune teller? Please, Seb, please—so delightful," Brianna squealed. One arm already entwined in his, she wrapped herself in front of Sebastian, grabbing him as she stumbled with a skip to a stop. A skip with such gleeful abandon that he had to laugh.

One mystery solved.

Up until three hours ago, Sebastian had never seen Brianna touch alcohol—not a drop, not even the slightest sip of claret with dinner.

But a red wine-fortified blackberry punch was the only thing handy from a vendor close to the stables where they settled Moonlight. Brianna had been parched, so she had hesitantly accepted a full mug.

Sebastian knew she hadn't eaten anything that day, for within half the mug, Brianna was foxed.

He had stuffed several small hot pies and a turkey leg down her throat, but she had also insisted on several more filled-to-the-brim mugs of punch with them.

And with that, the answer as to why she so strictly avoided alcohol—his wife could not hold her liquor. Not even a bit.

"Please, Seb? Please?" Brianna looked up at him, and even in the darkness of the eve, he could see overblown excitement sparking her face as she hopped, both hands tugging on the lapels of his jacket.

"It will be so much fun—and she can truly tell the future—look at her—you can see it in her face. She is mystical—magical—I can almost see the spirits about her. Please, Seb? Please, please, please?"

Sebastian had a hard time keeping a straight face. He nodded. "Let us see what fortunes your palm unfolds."

She jumped, giving him a quick peck on the cheek with a giggle, and spun to the fortune teller, bounding up the few rickety steps into the traveler's wagon.

Sebastian followed, squeezing into the tight space behind the chair Brianna sat down in. Lit with a slew of sputtering candles, the space in the wagon glowed dimly and Sebastian had to bend slightly so his head didn't touch the colorful strips of ribbon lining the ceiling.

He wedged himself at an angle to Brianna so he could watch her profile. The last few hours were the first time Sebastian had ever seen Brianna truly unrestrained—relaxed both in body and mind—and he didn't want to miss a second of it. No matter that it had taken a healthy amount of spirits to make it so. He was just happy to see that this side of his wife—the one Lily had alluded to—truly did exist.

It turned out Brianna had an amazing ability to laugh quickly—with others and at herself—and to immerse herself with insatiable curiosity into all humanity had to offer. From the vendors selling meat and drink, to the acrobats, to the hawkers of ballads, to the puppet shows, to the dancing—she met everything they saw with enthusiasm, including the feverish bartering she did with a silversmith for a finely crafted bracelet she wanted for Lily.

His wife could chat as easily with a pedlar hawking wares, as she could with the business acquaintances of Sebastian's that they passed while wandering the festivities. All of them instantly responded to Brianna's inquisitiveness, which was followed by a genuine ability to listen with interest in all they would talk about.

Holding her palm out, the ancient fortune teller waited until Sebastian pressed the coins into it before she sat across from Brianna, leaning on the little table between them.

Brianna looked up at Sebastian, giddy with a grin as the woman took her right hand. The fortune teller examined it under the flickering candle flames, the tips of her boney fingers running paths along the lines on Brianna's palm and then up and down each of Brianna's fingers.

"There be somethin' particular ye want to know 'bout, child?" The fortune teller's voice crackled.

Brianna shrugged, smile on her face. "No, anything you see is fine."

She nodded, humming a scratchy tune as she studied Brianna's palm. "Yer head and heart—strange, might strange— they struggle—war with each other. One is in charge 'til they twist, fight. And then the other takes over." The woman nodded, dropping her face, her nose almost touching Brianna's wrist. "Ye are conflicted. Yer heart pulls to yer thumb, yer desires—yer head pulls to yer forefinger, your responsibilities."

Moments passed until the fortune teller grunted, lifting her head and straightening. "Lucky child. Born under the curve of protection. Ye have known happiness. Smooth waters in yer life. But then the curve ends."

The teller shook her head, grunting again as her fingers froze on Brianna's palm.

"A mar—a wall. One life stopped. Disappeared." She coughed, dropping Brianna's right hand and grabbing her left. Her gnarled fingers ran over Brianna's palm, and then she dropped the left hand, going back to Brianna's right. "That be what it is. One life stopped. A new one started—they are very different, child. Yer lifeline is solid, but it be marred. There be darkness afoot. Darkness in the past. In yer future."

Sebastian could see Brianna try to pull her hand away, but the fortune teller gripped tight, her wrinkled fingers holding Brianna in place.

Panicked, Brianna looked up to him, terror creeping into her eyes. Just as Sebastian was about to tear the woman from his wife, the fortune teller flashed her palm up, stopping his movement.

"Ye survive it child." Her crackly voice filled the wagon. "Yer lifeline tells me that."

Brianna's look dropped from Sebastian to the fortune teller. "I do?"

"Yes."

"But…but what do I become?" Brianna asked, her voice trembling.

The woman shook her head, staring at Brianna's hand. The heavy wrinkles along her forehead scrunched, darkening the lines. It took her long seconds to answer. "Yer fate line. It leans to yer heart, to happiness, but I warn ye, child, it has not decided yet. Fate has not set her mind on a path. There be times when yer mind must rule. Then there be others when yer heart must take the lead."

The fortune teller's face lifted, her clear dark eyes that belittled her age, fervid, piercing Brianna. "Choose wise, child. That be what I can tell ye."

The woman folded up Brianna's hand, setting it onto Brianna's lap. An awkward silence filled the wagon.

The fortune teller looked to Sebastian. "Ye be wanting a reading as well?"

Brianna glanced up at him, a wobbly smile crossing her face. "Yes, how about one for you, Seb?"

He shook his head. "I already know what my future holds, Brianna."

Her eyes went wide at him. "You do?"

Arms crossing over his chest, he nodded.

Brianna chuckled, leaning toward the fortune teller, cupping her hand next to her mouth to shelter her words, but her whisper went impossibly loud. "He already has the gift—my husband does. He is good friends with fate."

The fortune teller took in Sebastian, eyeing him critically from foot to head. "Aye. This one be lookin' as if fate favors him. And maybe she does."

The woman stood, ushering them out of the wagon. "Just be rememberin' fate be a fickle mistress, if ye ain't be respecting her."

Sebastian stepped down from the wagon, grabbing Brianna around the waist and lifting her down to the ground. He inclined his head to the woman. "I will remember that, kind lady. Thank you for your time."

"Good luck to ye both." The woman turned from them, already searching through the throngs of people for her next client.

Sebastian kept his arm solid around Brianna's waist as he steered them through the throngs of people down the dirt road to the Twisted Oak Tavern. Vendors and tents lined the road in every possible space, their lanterns shedding just enough light upon the crowds for people to not step on toes.

Brianna craned her face backward to the wagon, then leaned into Sebastian, her hand going to his chest as her head tilted up to him. "I had not anticipated that—it was much more creepy than fun."

He smiled down at her. "What did you expect from an old woman in a ramshackle wagon? Did you want her to speak of butterflies?"

"That would have been nice." She ruffled her shoulders, a shiver running through her. "I had not expected her to actually see into my being."

Brianna lifted her hand, staring at her own palm. "It is enough to make me want to lock myself deep into Notlund castle and never come out."

"Fate always finds a way, Bree, whether you lock yourself away from life or not."

"Now you sound like a fortune teller." She stepped lightly over a gnarled mess of tree roots as they squeezed past a large, immovable mass of people. She looked up at him. "Do you truly believe that, that fate will find a way?"

Sebastian took a step in front of her, stopping and turning to fully face her. His free arm joined his other around her waist. She made no motion to stop him, to wiggle from his hold. Progress. A smile filled his chest. "I trusted fate to find me you. And she did. Why would I start doubting her now?"

Brianna frowned.

"No, Bree. You will not go to a dark place because an old woman in a rickety wagon scared you. You do not hide from life. Whatever it is she thinks you will survive—you will survive—that is the point. That is the butterfly you were hoping for."

Brianna's bottom lip slipped under her teeth. She looked up to him, her eyes somber. "But do I survive as a butterfly or become a decrepit moth? That is my worry."

Sebastian could resist no more, and he bent, his lips meeting hers. His hand travelled up the side of her body as he moved her backward until she was tight to the tree.

His tongue slipped out, tasting her, parting her lips as he deepened the kiss. No resistance. She opened her mouth to him, her chest rising against his as her fingers came up, circling his neck and curling to find his skin beneath his cravat.

Under his hands, he could feel the worry ease from her body, feel her melt into him.

He pulled up slightly, his knuckles tracing down the side of her face. "You already are a butterfly, Bree. Nothing is going to change that."

She opened her eyes, the glow of twinkling lanterns reflecting in the blue as she looked at him. Her fingers twitched on his neck. "I am afraid to want this life, Seb."

"A life with me?"

She nodded. "With you. With happy. With feeling."

"Why?"

"I do not want to have it, only to lose it."

"I am not going to let anyone harm you, Bree."

She closed her eyes, nodding as she inhaled. Her dark lashes cracked open to him. "Kiss me again, Seb. I do not worry when you are kissing me."

He met her lips before her words finished, and let the night take them over.

CHAPTER 11

Brianna's eyes popped open, searching in the darkness to take in the strange place that surrounded her.

And then she felt it. Sebastian's warm arm heavy on top of her belly. Right where it should be. Her eyes closed, the seconds of instant worry forgotten as she drifted back into the abyss.

"Wake up, Brianna. Wake up."

Her shoulder jostled. An instant pounding in her head followed it. Her belly was cold—Sebastian's arm was gone.

Brianna groaned, rolling over to her side on the bed. It took her several seconds to convince herself to open her eyes against the knives of pain slicing into her brain.

Her left eye buried in the pillow, her right eye opened.

Still in the strange place, and she could see Sebastian moving across the room, shrugging himself into a white linen shirt. It all flooded back to her. She was in the Twisted Oak Tavern in Clavenshire. With Sebastian. And she was naked under the sheet.

She had drunk far too much last night. Far, far too much.

Her left eye opened.

Sebastian saw her movement and came to the side of the bed, his fingers brushing aside a chunk of hair that hung haphazard across her cheek into her face.

"You are awake—finally."

"It is late?" The words croaked out, fighting her dry throat and swollen tongue.

"It is."

"I do not usually sleep so long."

"I am aware. I do believe this is the first time I have woken before you." He stepped away from her, pulling on his dark waistcoat and coat.

The insistent hammering in her head unyielding, Brianna could not move from the position on her side she had landed on. She watched Sebastian quickly tie his cravat. He was in a hurry. In a hurry to escape her?

"Seb?"

He turned to her. "Yes?"

"Last night—was I a twit? Embarrassing? There is a reason I do not touch wine."

An easy smile came to his face. "No, and no. You were… energetic."

Her eyebrows arched.

"You do not believe me?" He came across the room to her and sat on the edge of the bed, his hip snugged next to her thigh. "Do you not remember?"

"I remember most of it." Her arm went up, her fingers scratching the hair just above her forehead. "Until we got back here."

"You dropped—fell asleep." His easy smile turned into his devil smirk.

"I did? But the tree—I thought we…"

His hand went on her hip, rubbing it, his fingers slipping across her backside. "Apparently, my romantic wiles are no match for your weak belly. We were only up three stairs before you collapsed on me."

"You had to carry me?"

He shrugged. "You are not the first woman I have had to carry."

She reached back, grunting, and grabbed a pillow behind her, throwing it at him. He caught it, but it still nicked his head, mussing his brown hair. He tossed it back onto the bed.

"But you are the last, Bree—whenever and wherever you may need carrying." He bent forward, kissing her bare arm, and then stood.

Brianna watched as he went over to his boots by the door and sat on the wooden chair next to the fireplace to put them on.

His brown eyes came up to her. "Speaking of your belly, I am going down to get you some food for your stomach before we move on to the race course." He stood, walking over to her and then bent to kiss her forehead. "I think that will help your head."

She grumbled a few words that didn't make any sense, and she knew it, but didn't bother to try again.

He chuckled. "In a different development, my jockey broke his wrist last night."

"How?"

"Something about a bet and a tree and a rope that was on its last threads."

She stared up at him, trying to make sense of his words. "So your horse will not be racing today?"

"The jockey will not be. The horse will. I will be riding it."

"You? But are you not far too large?"

"Thank you, I think, for the compliment. But this is a much more informal local race, and not bound by the likes of the Jockey Club. I only need to show the horse in the best possible light to Lord Bayton. It is the race he wanted to see Red Swallow in, so see her he shall."

Sebastian pointed to the second chair by the fireplace. "I took the liberty of laying out your riding habit. We do need to make it to the course soon."

"So you are rushing me?"

"Yes." He winked.

With that, he was out the door, and Brianna flopped onto her back, trying to still her throbbing head. What had happened to all of her control? One mug of wine, and she had bandied about all night like a lovesick chit.

She groaned to herself. Sebastian was making her ponder too many fanciful notions. Notions of a normal life, of no responsibility. Notions that she had no right to entertain—not if she was to protect what needed to be protected.

Her head fell to the side, sinking into the deep pillow as she looked out the window. Sebastian had pulled wide the heavy

curtains and opened the windows. A breeze wafted in, and
Brianna could smell cooking meat—probably from the kitchens
behind the tavern. Her stomach turned. She wasn't sure she could
keep down anything Sebastian did bring to her.

Taking a deep breath to steady her stomach, she watched
the teardrop leaves on the branches outside the window rustle
in the wind, somewhat at a loss of what to think about. She was
days away from Notlund, so there was nothing to manage at the
moment.

Only Sebastian in front of her.

Him, she could think about, even though her mind screamed
at her to be cautious. To not feel too deeply.

But maybe she could enjoy him for just these few days. No
harm could come of it. Enjoy his company. She couldn't deny
he was refreshing to be around—he was witty, and he made her
laugh with every other comment he made. Her whole soul felt
lighter when she was next to him.

Not to mention he was a handsome man to look at.

And when he looked at her with his devil grin, she could do
little to slow her racing heart.

Her hand went to her forehead, rubbing it, trying to banish
the ache in her head. If she was going to give herself this margin
to relax, she didn't want it ruined by a foggy brain.

Relax. She could do it.

Just until they got back to Notlund.

Enjoy the day. The journey home.

Then she would refocus.

~ ~ ~

Brianna leaned out from the high, but rickety, platform, her
gloved hands gripping the wood railing so she didn't topple over
into the crowd below. Popping in and out of view, she could catch
glimpses of Sebastian's form on the far end of the line of jostling
horses.

He looked to be having a grand time, laughing with a jockey on an adjacent horse and yelling into the crowd.

In just his white linen shirt and buckskin breeches, he looked particularly relaxed—and strong. The mare, Red Swallow, a tall, sleek black horse, was antsy and proud—Brianna could easily discern that from this distance.

Sebastian had said Red Swallow was built for racing—one of the finest they had produced at Notlund—and if the posturing of the mare was any indication, Sebastian was very right.

"Have you ever watched the races, Lady Luhaunt?"

Looking to her right, Brianna pulled herself back behind the railing, turning to smile at the rotund man stopping next to her. "No, Lord Bayton. This is my first time." Brianna glanced over her shoulder to the line of horses, trying to keep an eye on Sebastian.

"Truly?" Lord Bayton handed her one of the full wine glasses he held in his hands. "For your husband mentioned you were quite the horsewoman."

"He did? I am positive he exaggerated my abilities." Brianna clutched the glass, holding it by her belly. She couldn't even imagine the liquid touching her lips in that second.

"Luhaunt does not pansy about the truth when it comes to the subject of horses—his reputation is the only reason I am even considering allowing a match with my stud and that mare." Lifting his glass of wine, he pointed with his pinky to the horse Sebastian sat atop. "So I imagine he was earnest in the compliment he paid you."

Brianna offered a humble smile. "It was a generous thing for him to say. I do appreciate the stables at Notlund. I have truly never ridden such a lot of fast horses. It took me some time to decide which one I favored most."

"Which one did you choose?"

"Moonlight—she is at the stables by the tavern if you would like to see her. She is as fast as the wind, and her nature fits me quite well. I believe the duke told me she shares a sire two generations back with Red Swallow. Though she does not have the obvious swagger like Red Swallow." Brianna looked out to the line of horses, finding Sebastian. "Moonlight just wants to be ridden for the sake of running fast."

"A horse pure of spirit?"

Brianna laughed. "Something akin to that. Although I imagine my husband would think me fanciful if he heard that."

"Understanding horses is not fanciful, Lady Luhaunt," Lord Bayton said, the tone of his voice heavy with the utmost seriousness.

"You sound as if you know them well, Lord Bayton. Do tell me about your studhorse that Sebastian is so keen to match with two of his mares." Smiling, she shifted the wine glass to her other hand. "However did you come about him? He must be something special if Sebastian cares deeply enough about impressing you that he is riding in the race."

Lord Bayton's mouth cracked with a wide smile, his plump ruddy cheeks rising high on his face. "My dear, it is a grand story. I am sure you will delight in it."

Brianna spent the next half hour listening to Lord Bayton and wondering two things. One, she wondered if the man would ever take a breath. And two, she wondered how long it took a horse race to start.

Just when Brianna was about to break and take a sip of her wine for the thirst that had consumed her, she was saved.

Lord Bayton interrupted himself, pointing out to the course. "They are to begin. It is the final straight-away up the hill at the end I am most interested in."

"Where is that?" Brianna asked.

"There." He pointed to the hill leading up to the finish line, marked with a slew of ribbons fluttering in the wind from a rope strung between two trees.

Lord Bayton turned back to the line of horses, tracing the course with his finger. "They run the straight course, then turn to the right behind those trees and make their way past the adjacent side of this platform. The track is almost V-shaped. And then that—that hill will determine the stamina of any horse. That is what I came to see." The excitement on Lord Bayton's face had him sputtering words.

Brianna nodded just as the crowd cheered. Her eyes whipped to the starting line in time to see the frenzy of the horses bursting into action.

Nine horses hit the straight-away, and Brianna searched until she found Sebastian riding hard in the middle of the pack, angling for a space to break out and set Red Swallow free.

Brianna went to her tiptoes, one hand gripping the railing as she found herself nearly bouncing with the excitement. The set of horses disappeared behind the trees.

"Come, come, Lady Luhaunt." Lord Bayton grabbed her elbow, dragging her to the other wide area of the platform that faced the finish line.

Breath held, Brianna leaned back and forth off the railing on the new side, trying to gain position to where she could clearly see the horses past the jostling heads in front of her.

The first horses rounded the trees, breaking into view, and the crowd erupted. Screaming, chanting, the masses below Brianna went frenzied, cheering for their chosen horses.

Her eyes scanned the field. The string of horses had thinned around the corner, the fastest four breaking forth while the other five fell back. Sebastian was one of the four, jammed between two horses and trailing the leader as they rumbled past the crowd and the high platform.

Her eyes flew to the finish line and back to Sebastian. The horses were just hitting the bottom of the hill. If Sebastian was going to break free, he needed to do it now.

Whipping his horse hard, the jockey to Sebastian's left made a break to push his horse past the frontrunner. It gave Sebastian an opening, and he followed suit, going for the opening to the frontrunner's left.

Halfway up the hill, the jockey in the lead yanked his horse hard to the left, ramming into Red Swallow.

A mass of jumbling horse-flesh, and Sebastian went flying.

He crashed to the ground, tumbling down the hill into the path of the trailing horses—horses thundering down at him.

Brianna's world froze in horror.

The first two horses cleared Sebastian, jumping over his prone, still-rolling body. But the next horse didn't veer, didn't jump, and Brianna watched in terror as one hoof came down on Sebastian's leg, and then a hoof came down at his head.

Her wine glass shattering on the platform, she flew to the ground, shoving her way through the crowd, screaming Sebastian's name before the last horse passed him.

Full speed onto the course, she could see several men had already reached Sebastian, surrounding him, blocking her view.

Her feet lead, she ran. Slow. Too slow. She needed to get to him.

Seconds that felt like an eternity passed and she ripped her way in-between two men blocking her from Sebastian, skidding onto her knees. His head turned away from her, she grabbed his face, hovering over the top of him.

He blinked, looking up at her.

"Se—" Her voice choked, no air to speak.

Her fingers ran over his face, his head—his cheeks, forehead, muddy. But the whites of his eyes were there. His brown eyes. His beautiful, kind, mischievous brown eyes looking up at her.

"Seb." The word came out this time.

He grimaced a smile at her.

"You are not dead?"

He shook his head the slight bit he could with her hands clamped to his face.

She collapsed, her forehead falling onto his chest.

Not dead.

Her heart pounding, it took excruciating seconds for her to lift her head. "Are you hurt?"

Without an instant answer, her hands immediately ran over his body, searching frantically for broken bones, for blood. Brianna didn't stop until Sebastian pushed himself up onto an elbow, grabbing her wrist to still her.

"I am whole, Bree. Roughed up, but I will survive." He looked up at the small crowd surrounding them, shooing with his head. "I am in one piece, everyone. Go congratulate the winner. Gather Red Swallow."

The men surrounding them dispersed slowly.

Her breath still out of control, Brianna waited until the last man ambled away, her hands resting on Sebastian's thigh. Squeezing his leg, she moved so her eyes were in front of his.

"Your face, Seb. You are in pain and you do not want anyone to know."

His eyes narrowed at her. "How do you see that?"

"How could I not? I do see you, Seb, even if you may think I try everything to avoid doing so."

Sebastian sighed, pushing up from his elbow to sit upright, gingerly bending his left knee to rest his elbow on. He flicked a finger out toward the leg still flat on the ground. "My ankle. The horse stepped on it. I do not think it is broken, but it is in wicked pain."

Brianna moved sideways to look at it, then started to stand. "Let me go get one of the men."

"No."

She dropped back to her knees.

"Not in front of Bayton. I need to walk off this course. The man is judging me right now, Bree, and I do not want to forfeit my chance with him because I cannot stand a little pain."

A quick glance back to the platform above the crowd told Brianna that Lord Bayton was indeed, watching them. "What do you need me to do?"

"Be my crutch. Can I wedge you under my arm?"

"Of course."

"Can you handle my weight? I do not want to crush you."

"Do I look crushable?"

That brought a smile to his face. "Proven once more, the excellent choice in a wife I have made."

He nodded to the platform. "Will you stand and block the view to Bayton while I get to my feet? But no helping me—not until I am up and it looks like I am just strolling down the hill with my lovely bride."

Brianna stood, her fingers twitching to help him, but she forced them to stay at her sides.

With a grunt, agony crossed Sebastian's face as he heaved himself to standing.

She waited until he stood solid on his good leg before springing forth, wrapping her arms around his waist, her cheek tight to his chest. She took a moment to listen for his heartbeat.

"A hug?" His hands went around her.

She nodded, her cheek rubbing against his mud-caked linen shirt as she squeezed him without caution to any bruising his ribs may have taken.

Loosening her hold, she looked up at him, slightly embarrassed at her actions. "And easier to slip nonchalantly under your arm."

She released him, sliding one hand across his back for support while spinning so his arm rested atop the back of her shoulders. His weight on her was immediate, and Brianna had to lock her knees.

"Nicely done, my wife." Sebastian motioned with his free hand. "Shall we go speak to Lord Bayton?"

At that moment, a horse and rider crossed their path. Brianna immediately recognized the horse.

She looked up at Sebastian. "Can you hold in place for a moment?"

"Why?"

"I need to speak with that jockey." She started to lift his arm from her shoulders.

Sebastian clamped down on her. "No. You will do no such thing."

"But it is not fair." Brianna tried to wedge up his fingers that tightly gripped her upper arm. "He rammed his horse into you."

"It happens in races, Brianna."

"And it is not fair, and I am going to blast him for it."

His other arm went across the front of her, holding her in place. "That, you are not going to do."

Brianna tried to wiggle from his grasp.

"Why are you so mad about this?"

She gave him a perturbed look, realizing she wasn't going anywhere. "If you must know, I bet on you to win the race and just lost a sizable amount."

"You did?" The devil smirk landed on his face. "You bet? On me? I would not have thought that of you."

"Placing a bet or betting on you?"

"Both."

"Seb, do not be daft, I have full confidence in your abilities on a horse. I have seen you ride, for goodness sake. Aside from the fact that you are my husband—who else would I bet on? And why are you not mad about him unseating you?"

He shrugged. "It was a minor rub. There is nothing to be upset about."

"A minor rub that could have gotten you killed. That hoof missed your head by a hair."

"So you were worried for me?"

"Of course I was." Her head cocked at him, contemplating. "That is what you want to hear, is it not? That I was worried for you?"

His head bowed, his brown eyes slicing into her. "Possibly."

Brianna stared at him for a long moment.

She could lie. She should lie.

Instead, her mouth opened. "My heart stopped, Seb. Everything stopped. I would not have thought it until that moment, but my heart stopped when you fell…and rolled…

and then that horse went over you. I..." She shook her head, her eyes closing as she forced down the lump in her throat. "I cannot describe it...I did not breathe for minutes."

Her eyes still closed, his lips suddenly on hers made her jump. But the instant heat of him, the power of him calmed her, affirmed that he was standing next to her, alive and well.

He pulled away. Soon. Much too soon.

One look at her face and he chuckled. "I would continue, but we are about to become a spectacle."

Brianna took a deep breath, looking around, her anger still not sated. "Well, I still would like to yell at that fool jockey. You may be walking, but I did lose a pretty coin from it."

He laughed, loud and hearty as he pulled her even tighter into him. "Help me hobble over to Lord Bayton and then prop me up so I do not look weak. That showing of Red Swallow—at least until I was tossed—was hopefully enough to convince him of the mare's worth."

They started walking, and Brianna was surprised at how very much weight Sebastian was putting on her. But as long as her spine stayed straight, she could handle it.

"I think you could have every bone in your body broken and you still would not look weak, Seb."

He squeezed her shoulders. "Thank you for saying so. Let us hope Bayton agrees. And if the horse's performance was not enough, I might have to leverage your charms to convince him."

Brianna guffawed. "My charms? I think you know full well how my charms lack."

"On the contrary, I saw you speaking with Lord Bayton for some time before the race. He looked quite interested in what you were saying, and I happen to know Bayton has very little interest in talking to females—unless they are mares. He is of the distinct belief that the fairer sex should be docile, dumb, and mute."

"I gathered that about him. But he was actually quite pleasant to me, and after a few moments we were talking about the horses you and the duke have at Notlund. And then, of course, we spoke of his horses." Her head tilted, thinking. "Possibly, I can help. I did just spend a half hour listening to all of his views on horses and the care of them."

"I can see your mind spinning rampant, my wife."

"Luhaunt." Lord Bayton waved his hand in the air, making his way out of the edge of the crowd, his cane quick through the dirt.

"Luhaunt." Slightly winded, Lord Bayton stopped in front of Brianna and Sebastian. "I dare say, man, your wife is far faster than that horse that trampled you."

Sebastian chuckled, tightening his grip on Brianna's shoulders as he leaned on her. "That she is. She was rather quick to me."

"That she was."

"The privilege of a newlywed," Sebastian said, looking down at Brianna with a twinkle in his eye. His focus went to Lord Bayton. "How did you enjoy the race, Lord Bayton?"

"A fine race—until the end." Both hands clasping his gold-tipped cane, he nodded. "A shame about the end. I would have liked to see your mare finish the hill. But I trust you are unhurt as you are walking about?"

"Nothing for concern. Just a minor tumble." Sebastian motioned to his left. "And there—my man has Red Swallow now. I presume you would like to take a closer look at her? Shall we walk and discuss?"

Lord Bayton looked from Sebastian to Brianna. "Only if your wife will accompany us. I find her perspective on your horses very interesting."

Sebastian smiled. "I dare not let her leave my side."

"Good man, Luhaunt." Bayton slapped his palm on Sebastian's shoulder. "Good man."

CHAPTER 12

"I am concerned about Lord Bayton." Clicking the door closed, Brianna moved back into the room and shoved the table in front of Sebastian to the side, its four legs scraping along the rough floor.

Hands on her hips, she surveyed the private back room of the tavern, then grabbed the wooden chair Lord Bayton had occupied. "He was quite sauced when he stumbled out of here."

"The man can handle his liquor, and his driver will take care of him," Sebastian said, watching Brianna as he leaned against one of the cherubs carved into the high wooden back of the long bench they had both been sitting on. "I am more concerned that he will forget our bargain, come morning. A bargain that would not have been possible without your gentle persuasion, my wife."

She glanced at him, pulling the chair across the floor, and setting it sideways in front of his knees. "Let me try my luck, then, in persuading you to put your leg up. We are alone in here now, the door is closed, and I have been watching your ankle throb—through your boot, mind you—for the past hour."

She bent to grab his right leg, lifting it and setting it on the chair. Sebastian thought for a moment to resist, but then relented. Brianna pampering him was foreign, but he was enjoying it.

"And I can see how tight your shoulders are, my wife." He snatched her wrist, pulling her down to sit next to him on the bench. "You must be in pain after holding me up all day."

His hands went to her shoulders before she could scoot back on the bench. Kneading deep into the muscles, his fingers worked her shoulders, her back, and he could see goosebumps rise along her neck as he brushed aside the tendrils escaping from her upsweep.

"You do realize any success I had with Bayton was due to you, Bree?"

"Me?" She turned her head slightly to look at him. "I merely used what I knew of him to persuade him that you were of like mind."

"Yes. And I am almost afraid of your delicate cunning."

She straightened her head, soft smile on her lips as she leaned into his fingers. "I do not know if that is a compliment."

"It is in this situation—and in most, as far as I have seen. You use your cunning to help your family—it is not used for evil."

She chuckled. "Well, thank you."

"I am just happy I am family—forced or not—and can benefit thusly." The back of her neck so delectable, he leaned forward, kissing the middle divot.

Straightening, Sebastian watched the fire in the deep hearth across from them as Brianna's head fell to the side. He could feel her muscles under his fingers relax, turning to jelly.

"Hmmm. When you are doing this there is no pain—no pain at all." Her words tumbled out, slow, lazy.

Sebastian stared at the bit of her profile he could see from his angle. Her eyes were closed, face relaxed. "You, my wife, are a marvel."

The smile touching her lips slowly faded, and he could see her mind start to work. He kneaded harder into the muscles lining her neck, trying to stave off her thoughts.

"What do you want of me, Seb?" She asked the question without emotion, without moving. Just words sneaking into the room.

His hands stopped.

Her eyes popped open. "Did I say that out loud?"

"Yes. And I have been nothing but honest with you, Brianna." His voice went low.

She straightened her head, turning to look at him on the bench.

"I have been honest about my intentions. Honest about what I want in life. I want you. I want to know you. Fully and completely."

"And that must include my past?"

"Yes."

Her head shook, her hands falling into her lap. "You are not about to let that be an unknown, are you, Seb?"

His head tilted to the side. "For now I am. Until you are ready."

"And if I never am?"

Sebastian shrugged. "I am a patient man, Brianna."

Head dropping, she looked down at her fingernails pressing into her thumbs for long seconds. Her blue eyes came up to him, challenge clear in them. "What about you, Seb—your past? You never speak of your past either." She took a deep breath. "I am fighting myself to want to trust you, Seb, but you left me so quickly at Notlund—you ran. And that is what Wynne said about you. You are the wind. You are always running. Why?"

"Wynne said that?"

"They both did. The duke said this is the longest you have ever stayed in one spot—up until you left a fortnight ago."

Blast it. Wynne, sure, she would share such things—but Rowen as well? Sebastian scratched the back of his neck, his eyes shifting from Brianna to the fire.

"My past is open for exploration, but yours is not, Seb? Truly? You ask me to trust you with things I cannot bear to dredge up, yet you cannot tell me what is in your past. Why do you not stay in one place? Why do you refuse to keep a real home—a place that is yours alone?"

His eyebrow cocked at her. For all he wanted to know of her past, he wasn't sure that he wanted to bare light to his own.

Her left hand slipped from her lap, landing on his thigh. "Tell me."

Still within reach on the table, Sebastian moved forward to grab his glass of brandy, drinking half of it before he leaned back on the carved bench once more.

"My past?"

She nodded.

His eyes went to the fire as he fought down the crushing need to leave. The demanding urgency to get on his horse and move on from this place. But he knew it instantly—it would mean moving on from Brianna. She would never trust him if he left her again. And that, he could not have.

"I had a home once, Brianna. A true home. Father, mother, older brother." He stopped, downing the remainder of the glass, and then looked at her. "You know we were on the continent, in the wars together, Rowe and I?"

"Yes."

"When we came back to England, I stepped off the ship, expecting my family. Someone. Every man around me was greeted by someone. Mothers, sisters, children, fathers, cousins. Someone. Tears. Hugs. Laughter." He shrugged. "But there was not a soul for me. It had been years, yes, since I had been on English soil, but there was no one. So I made my way to our townhouse, expecting to find them there, at least my parents—it was in the middle of the season, and they never missed the season. But the place was empty—only a maid I had never met."

Brianna's right hand silently joined her left on his thigh, giving the slightest caress.

Sebastian's eyes closed, his head shaking. "A complete stranger—a nervous girl with a lisp and a twitchy eye—was the one to tell me my father was dead and that my brother had died in the war."

"Your brother? But he was heir to the earldom, he would not have been allowed near the fighting."

"No. No he was not. He was never supposed to leave England. But that would not have stopped Robert. He came after me and then died on the continent, and I never even knew he was killed—a full year passed, and I never knew."

"What happened to him?"

"Our father was dying—consumption—and my mother sent Robert to find me. My father wanted to see me, and Robert was going to give him that. He was never supposed to be near any battles. Never in harm's way."

His eyes drifted to the fire. "It was stupid—he died in some skirmish over a bridge that meant absolutely nothing to either side. He was only a day behind me." Sebastian drew in a shaking breath. "One day. And I never even knew."

"What happened to Robert is not your fault, Seb."

His look snapped to her. "No? My mother would disagree. She never wanted me to leave in the first place. Begged me not to go. But I was the second son and I had so much to prove." His voice slowed. "Such a need to carve out my own way. She begged, and begged, and begged. But I left. When I found her at our estate in Suffolk, she blamed me for all of it. For leaving, for Robert's death. Even for my father's—his will to live deserted him after Robert died. All of it was my fault. She made me very well aware of that fact, and then demanded I leave and never come back."

"But it has been years since you returned, surely—"

"She still refuses to see me. I have made the attempt several times. The last time I saw her…there was so much hate. She once loved me—adored me—she would have done anything for me. But the last time—there was nothing there—nothing but hate."

Brianna's hands tightened on his leg. "But it is not right—you lost so much and then for her to blame you for all of it—it is unfathomable unfairness."

"Unfair? I was the selfish one. I was the one that left. So I have come to accept it as a cruel twist of fate that I am of the living, after everything I survived in the war, and they are of the dead. I have had to."

He set the empty glass down next to him on the bench before looking to her. "Do you not see, Bree? I had everything. A family that loved me. A home. A mother that adored me. A proud father. A brother that was my partner in everything. And gone. Just like that" —he snapped his fingers— "gone. Everything I was. Everything I knew and loved. Gone."

A tear slipped from the corner of Brianna's eye, sliding down her cheek. Sebastian watched it, wanting to wipe it away but afraid to touch her.

Unable to watch his pain reflected in her face, his eyes moved to the fireplace to stare at the dancing flames. "So I left. I started moving and have not stopped. And I have never wanted a home since then. Never wanted to settle in one place. Never wanted a wife."

He had to force his eyes to leave the glowing embers and look at Brianna.

"Not until you, Bree. Not until you."

Her blue eyes solid on him, she took a deep breath. "And I asked you why you ran from Notlund. I am so sorry, Seb. I did not know."

"I could not stay and chance you hating me, Bree. So I left. It was all I could think to do."

"No. No more." Her hand went to his cheek, her palm rubbing along the stubble. "I understand. I do."

Her hand dropped from his face and she went to her feet. For a moment, Sebastian thought she would leave the room. Leave him. But then she turned to him, pulling up the middle of her skirts as she brought her leg up, straddling him. She settled onto his lap, her shins on the bench as she scooted forward until her chest was touching him.

Both of her hands came up, capturing his face, her clear blue eyes intense on him. "I understand. But do not leave me like that again, Seb. Ever."

He gave her one nod. "I will not."

She leaned forward, her lips meeting his. Her mouth opened to him without any provocation, her tongue slipping out, melding with his. Her lips sweet, he took her, hungry, needing to feel her, be part of her, be more than just himself.

Her hands dropped from his face and Sebastian grabbed her about the waist, thinking she was to escape him. But she made no motion to stop the kiss, instead, stripping off her riding jacket and setting loose the pearl buttons down the front of her silk habit shirt.

Her hands busy, she did not leave his mouth, deepening the kiss, taking his lips between her teeth, teasing with her tongue. His hands moving along her back, Sebastian helped her shirt disappear and shimmied down her short stays and chemise, freeing her chest.

Brianna leaned forward, her fingers wrapping around his head as she offered her right breast to his mouth, her voice heated. "Kiss me, Seb. Here. Everywhere."

He needed no further invitation, taking her nipple into his mouth, harsh, ravaging with every breathless rumble from her chest. One nipple satisfied, he moved to the other, continuing the onslaught. Her fingers deep in his hair, she held him fast, hard to her skin as her hips gyrated on his lap.

The sudden hand around his cock stunned him. He hadn't even noticed Brianna unbuttoning his breeches.

Hard, straining for her, he let her fingers move along him for a few glorious seconds before he pulled away from her chest, realizing they had already gone too far.

He looked up at her face, her lips, red and bruised, her blue eyes smoldering as she looked down at him. Her hair had come undone, the long glossy curls falling around his head, hiding them from the world.

"Not here, Bree."

"Here."

"The door—"

"Did I mention I locked it?"

A smile, straight from the bowels of debauchery crossed his face. "Temptress."

"Yes."

She curled down to him, her mouth capturing his just as she lifted her skirts and her hand guided him through her folds, deep into her.

Sebastian nearly exploded at the tightness surrounding him, but he held. This was far too delicious to end overly soon.

She pulled up, tugging at his shirt, pulling it over his head. It gave him just enough time to gain control of his body. He wasn't about to let Brianna have all the control, to leave her unsatisfied.

Her hands going to his chest, she lifted herself, then slid down slowly on him. Twice more, and her head fell back, deep moans exhaling from her chest.

Sebastian grabbed a nipple in his teeth, rolling his tongue on it as he yanked up on her skirts, finding his way through the cloth to her skin. Fingers splaying along her hip, his thumb went inward, diving to her core, circling the nubbin.

A scream, and her body convulsed at the touch. Sebastian gave a savage chuckle. His thumb sped.

But Brianna was not about to go easily. She looked down at him, challenge in her blue eyes as she increased her own pace, gliding up and down. Harsh, demanding with every stroke. Taking him to the edge of abandon and then thrusting downward.

Gritting, his muscles—his entire being—demanding release, he reached up with his free hand, grabbing the back of her neck. He pulled her down into him, his tongue invading her mouth, making her succumb, his thumb forcing her body to twist, agonized above him.

She could only fight it for another moment, and then she broke, tearing her mouth from his as her restraint vanished. Her muscles contracted as her core tightened around him, drawing him long and solid, even farther into her body.

Control instantly lost, Sebastian growled, coming deep within her, unable to tell his own racking spasms from hers.

Gripping Brianna's back, he pulled her down tight, captive on his chest. Not letting her limp body move from his, he forced her to ride the last unrestrained waves of his contractions, feel every bit of what she had done to him.

What she could do to him.

What she could make him feel.

His lips fell onto the top of her head.

Damn if he wasn't falling completely in love with his wife.

Chest heaving, he didn't move for long minutes. Didn't let her move for long minutes. Not that she tried.

Minutes, hours—enough time for the fire to die down to embers—Sebastian wasn't sure how much time passed as he sat there, sated and in silence. Brianna in his arms and that one thought running through his head. Coming to uneasy terms with that one thought.

Uneasy, because he knew too well the pain of losing happiness. Losing what he loved. He had trusted fate, trusted that Brianna and he were meant to be together. But love. He had not anticipated that.

And if he dared to let himself love her…

The sudden thought of losing her cut deep into his chest. His hold tightened around her back.

She rustled, turning her head, her lips settling onto the skin of his chest.

"I thought you were asleep."

"No." Her voice came up to him, soft, lazy. "Thinking."

"Of?"

It took her a long moment to speak. So long, he almost wondered if she had fallen back asleep. "Where do you put your pain, Seb? All that happened to you. All you lost. What do you do with the pain?"

The question startled him. His hand went to the back of her head, fingers trailing down her hair. "I honestly do not know, Bree. It has never caught up to me. Not until now."

She kissed his skin, then tilted her face up to him. "Do you wish the pain gone—wish it bad enough to leave, banishing it to the wind behind you once more?"

"No. I will take it, Bree. If this is my destiny—if you are my reward. I will take it. Gladly."

~ ~ ~

Brianna hurried up the circular stone stairwell at Notlund to her sister's room on the third floor. According to the first maid Brianna had encountered, Lily was supposedly dressing for dinner.

She slipped into Lily's room, only to be greeted with the usual mayhem that accompanied Lily's change of clothing. Dresses piled high upon the bed, a rainbow of silk and lace. A harried maid running about the room. Lily barking out orders for her hair, accessories, and the next dress she needed to try on before she would be fit to be seen.

And this was just a simple dinner.

Brianna closed the door quietly behind her back, smiling to herself. People thought she was the controlling one—but they had never witnessed this scene. Lily's maids would have a far different story to tell.

In her stays and shift, her sister spun at the sound of the door clicking. "Bree, you are back—thank goodness."

"We just arrived. Is something amiss? Lord Bepton's visit is not going well?"

"Bepton?" Her sister looked momentarily confused, then waved her hand in the air. "No, nothing to do with Lord Bepton—he is well and settled. No, I have been waiting for you. There was a letter."

Lily looked over at her maid digging through a box of ribbons. "Prudence, can you please excuse us? I need to speak with my sister in private."

"Of course, miss." The maid scurried out of the room.

Before the maid closed the door, Lily was across the room, opening the top drawer of a walnut inlaid desk, digging into the far back corners. She pulled out a folded piece of thick paper, the black seal on it broken.

"It was for you, but I took it." Clutching the letter, her sister walked to Brianna. "I am sorry, but I did. I thought it might be a missive about Lord Newdale and I was not about to let you interfere. And then once I read it, I had to hide it."

Brianna's eyes narrowed at her sister. "You stole a letter meant for me? That is not like you, Lils, to sneak about. We may have argued about Lord Newdale, but for you to—"

"Stop. Never mind all of that, Bree." She flung the paper into Brianna's hands. "You have to read the letter. We can discuss at a different time how disappointed you are in me."

Lily's frantic agitation stopped Brianna from her scolding, and she looked down at the letter, quickly scanning the short note.

The blood draining from her face, she reread it three times before Lily interrupted her thoughts.

"Who is Mr. Flemming, Bree? What was he investigating and why is he reporting that a Mr. Welbury is dead? Who is Mr. Welbury?"

Brianna's legs went soft, and she swayed, but she forced herself to stand in place. She couldn't scare Lily.

She looked up to her sister, a wooden smile on her face. "It is nothing to concern you, Lily."

"I do not believe you." Lily's arms folded over chest. "A man is dead, Bree. Tell me this instant who Mr. Welbury is."

Brianna looked down, folding the note carefully along its original lines. It only gained her a few seconds. She met Lily's accusing stare. "It concerns the one thing I will not talk about, Lils. And I will tell you no more. Nor can you speak of this note to anyone."

Lily stepped to her, grabbing her forearm. "What are you doing, Bree? You said the past was the past and we were to not think of it. Not speak of it. Never again."

"I will tell you no more, Lily." Brianna twisted her arm free and stepped backward. "And you can be as angry with me as you need to be. But no more. I am doing this to protect you. That is all you need to know."

Brianna spun, going to the door before Lily could continue her assault.

"But who will protect you, Bree?" Lily's words trailed her into the hallway.

Eyes closed, Brianna clicked the door shut.

She had no answer for the question.

CHAPTER 13

She had known this day would come for long time.

That no matter how long she waited, no matter how she would try to forget, no matter that she prayed him dead, he would show himself again. Gregory.

It was almost a relief. Almost.

The first ray of light appeared along the edge of the draperies, and Brianna slid to the edge of the bed, slipping out from under Sebastian's bare arm over her belly.

She had debated all night about whether she would try to sneak out from Notlund without him knowing, or whether she would tell him of her plans. Neither side winning, she tiptoed across the room, leaving it up to fate to decide.

If he awoke, fine, but she wasn't going to go out of her way to startle him from sleep.

Her breath held, she set her fingers on the doorknob, turning it slowly, pulling, waiting for the squeak that always started when the door swung.

"Is it a ride this morning, or do you have other questionable plans afoot?" Sebastian's sleepy voice cut through the dark room.

Her held breath escaped. Relief, or something very similar, filled her. She closed the door, going back to the bed, her fingertips tapping the edge of the coverlet.

"I do not want you to worry, so I will tell you. I have a meeting with Mr. Flemming near Pepperton again."

Sebastian sat up in the bed. "Why did you not tell me? I am coming with."

"It is not necessary, Seb. It is a simple meeting, just like the one before."

"I am not about to let you go by yourself, Bree. I think you know that."

"I have made this trip a number of times, Seb, I will be fine."

He pushed the coverlet from his waist, swinging his naked legs off the side of the bed. "Think of it as me just accompanying you on a ride, then."

"You will let me speak to Mr. Flemming in private?"

Even in the dim light, Brianna could see the lines on his forehead appear as he looked up at her. "Why would you need to speak to him in private, Brianna?"

"Accompanying me on a ride is just that—a ride, Seb. I would welcome that. But my dealings with Mr. Flemming are private—my business—and I would like it to remain so."

Sebastian rubbed his forehead, his hand moving along his scalp to scratch the back of his head. He sighed. "As it is still well before the roosters are even roused, I do not have the mind to argue with you. But I will accompany you. That is not to be negotiated."

Brianna nodded, silent.

Relief. It was definitely relief she felt.

~ ~ ~

Three hours later, Brianna stepped through the doorway to the abandoned mill, tugging closed the half-attached door, awkwardly lifting it to wedge it into place.

Ignoring Mr. Flemming standing in the middle of the room, she walked straight to a small slit in the far stone wall, peeking through it, searching until she found Sebastian. Leaning on a tree, staring at the stone structure, he didn't look particularly pleased she had held him to his word.

But she could not let him interfere. He had promised to stay with the horses, a good stretch away by the woods, and she was going to make sure he did so.

"Miss Silverton?"

She turned sideways, taking a step backward to make sure she could both see Mr. Flemming and keep an eye on Sebastian.

"Mr. Flemming, your associate, Mr. Welbury, I am so saddened to read of his death."

"Thank you for saying so, Miss Silverton. He is a loss. But Mr. Welbury knew well the risk of our profession."

A quick glance to Mr. Flemming, and then she looked back out the slit. "Do you have any idea what happened?"

"It was foulness that took Welbury out, that be for sure. And he was only working on one case, Miss Silverton—yours."

Brianna's eyes closed, her chin dropping to her chest. She nodded, her eyes first going out to Sebastian, then to Mr. Flemming. "I understand. What had he discovered before he was killed?"

"Beyond what he told me, I do not know. His papers were gone—all out the window into the Thames."

Brianna's arms came up, wrapping her ribcage. This was exactly what she had feared. "That you sent the letter directly to Notlund—it was a risk—a risk you promised you would not take, Mr. Flemming."

"Yes, but I thought you needed to be warned straight away, Miss Silverton. I have been here three days, waiting for you."

"I apologize. I was away from Notlund or I would have been here sooner." Her head dropped and she rubbed her forehead, giving a sideways glance to Mr. Flemming. "What is it that you know from Mr. Welbury?"

"Just that he was close. He said he would have true news for you soon. A location. That the man, Gregory, had been found."

That shook Brianna, shook her to her core, and she stumbled backward. She had guessed it was the case, but to hear the words. To hear that Gregory was alive. Found. Her head spun.

Mr. Flemming grabbed her elbow, his thick hands steadying her.

"Are you solid again?"

It took her long seconds before she nodded and he released her.

"Do you know anything else, Mr. Flemming? Anything at all?"

"No. I am afraid not. Are you safe at Notlund, Miss Silverton? If not, I have places I can hide you. You and your sister."

Brianna's hand waved back and forth. "No, it is all right, Mr. Flemming. We are safe at Notlund." She said the words, only half believing their truth.

"Shall I pick up on what little trail Welbury left?"

"No. Please do not. I do not wish another life to be at risk. Do nothing. Please just concentrate on Lord Newdale. And distance yourself from Mr. Welbury's investigation."

Mr. Flemming gave a nod. "I will."

"And Mr. Welbury—did he have a family? Anyone he supported? I would like to make arrangements for their well-being."

"No. It is kind Miss Silverton, but Mr. Welbury was alone. As are most of us in the trade."

"Please be safe, Mr. Flemming."

"To you as well, Miss Silverton." Mr. Flemming moved next to her, pointing out the slit. "And this man that you rode up here with, can he be trusted, or do I need to determine a new place to meet with you?"

Brianna glanced out the slit. Sebastian still leaned against the tree, arms crossed over his chest. He had kept his promise—she truly hadn't been sure if he would allow her privacy. "He can be trusted, Mr. Flemming. That man is my new husband."

"A husband? That is a surprise. Congratulations on your nuptials."

"Thank you, Mr. Flemming." She pulled on the bottom edges of her gloves, tightening them to her fingertips. "I must leave now, but I trust that you will have definitive news on Lord Newdale for me soon?"

"Yes. Godspeed, and do keep a wary eye out."

With a nod, Brianna walked over to the door, lifting it while kicking it open with the toe of her boot. Once outside in the fresh air, she stopped, her hand on the stone wall for support. She only made it five more steps before she had to bend over, swallowing silent sobs of terror that threatened to overtake her.

But she only allowed herself a few precious seconds.

Pulling her spine straight, her hand dropped from the rough stone. Walking slowly, her feet deliberate with each step, she took a deep breath, smoothing the skirt of her riding habit before she rounded the corner. She had to compose herself before Sebastian saw her. Which meant locking thoughts of Gregory into the back of her mind.

Sebastian would see the worry on her face immediately.

And that, she could not have.

~ ~ ~

"You have not wanted to ride in days, Brianna. Not once since you met with Mr. Flemming." His shirt and buckskin breeches already on, Sebastian sat on the chair by the fire, pulling his dark boots up.

"And?" Brianna rolled from her side where she was watching him onto her back. Her bare arm came up, flopping across her forehead and covering her eyes.

"And it is not like you." He stood, walking over to the bed to hover above her. "While I have enjoyed you not waking me at the break of dawn—and keeping you naked and warm in my bed until a reasonable hour—I am beginning to wonder what is rumbling about in that mind of yours."

Her arm shifted to let one eye find his face. "It is Lily."

"Planning something drastic?"

"No. And I take offense." Her arm moved further up her forehead as she rolled her eyes. "I have come to realize how very soon our lives will be lived apart. She has been the one constant in my life—for as far back as I can remember. So I am trying to get in as much time as possible with her before Lord Newdale comes back to sweep her away."

"So Lord Bepton has made no impression upon her in his time here?" Sebastian asked.

"None. She still talks about Newdale every chance she gets. Bepton is dull—she did not exaggerate that point. As safe a husband as he would be for her, even I would not wish a life with him upon Lily. She is far too vivacious for a man such as him, although I imagine there is a match out there somewhere for him."

She lifted her arm from her forehead, her fingers slipping under the top seam of Sebastian's breeches to pull him closer. "But do not let me keep you from riding. I know how very much you would like to break that new filly in. Maybe today luck will be with you."

"Hopefully." He tapped the tip of her nose. "This one is more stubborn than you."

"Impossible." She sat up, digging her fingers into his side, laughing.

He jumped away, grabbing her hand. "So quick to argue, my wife."

Her fun squelched, she conceded her attack and pulled the coverlet up over her bare chest. "I do not know what Lily has planned for the day with Lord Bepton. If it is conducive, I shall be down to the stables to at least watch your trials with SilverStar."

"To watch me get thrown repeatedly?"

She shuddered. "I have seen you get thrown in the worst possible way, so watching the little game that you and SilverStar have been playing with each other has been amusing. You are very good at falling."

"A graceful faller, am I?"

She reached up, patting his cheek. "The epitome of a fall well done."

He chuckled, leaning in to kiss her. "Later, then, my wife."

"Yes." Smile on her face, she watched him walk out the door. The door had not even closed before her smile failed.

Two hours later, Brianna had escaped Lily and was walking around the stables. After passing by the empty pen by the first pasture, she found little Tommy poking at some hay, pretending to work.

"Tommy, where is the earl?"

Her sudden voice made him jump, and he spun to her, a sheepish look on his face. "'E break the new filly, mi' lady. 'E been out on her, riding 'er good."

"Will he be back soon?"

Tommy shrugged. "Don't know, mi' lady. Maybe a few hours?"

Brianna nodded, her face going hard. It was time. She had been anxiously waiting for just this opportunity—Sebastian far from the stables—since meeting with Mr. Flemming.

"Saddle Firesprite for me, Tommy—quickly."

"Not Moonlight, mi' lady?"

"No. Not today. I need to go up to the castle and will be back within a few minutes, please have her ready."

Before her words ended, Brianna was already racing up to the castle.

CHAPTER 14

Brianna turned her horse to the left, sending it up along the path next to the church in Hoppleton. They moved upward between the buildings, passing the hill holding the graveyard.

The sleepy village was sized perfectly—large enough to welcome newcomers without suspicion, but small enough that the people would protect their neighbors.

She was going to have a hard time finding another village as perfect. Especially one within a few hours travel of Notlund.

Eyes going back over her shoulder, she scanned the main road through town. Normal activity. A few wagons. Several horses. People walking about. Her gaze swept back and forth on the empty hillside on either side of her. Nothing except for gravestones.

Clicking Firesprite forward, her eyes flickered to the middle of the five cottages positioned just above the graveyard. She guided the horse around to the rear of the row of cottages and slid down from her sidesaddle.

Tying her horse to the post near the well, she left enough rein for Firesprite to drink from the nearby trough and to nibble the tall grasses alongside it.

Her look still darting about, Brianna slipped between the middle houses, knocking on the side door to the center cottage. Before there was an answer, she opened the door, entering the house.

Brianna looked around the empty drawing room, ears straining in the quiet house. "Cousin Frannie?"

Footsteps echoed down the center hallway. "Thank goodness, child." Frannie appeared in the doorway, a carving knife in one hand. "You had me scared half to Hades."

Brianna went across the room, pulling Frannie into a quick hug. "Were you cooking, cutting meat? I did not mean to interrupt."

Frannie pulled away, flashing the fat knife. "This? Oh no, child, I was snapping peas." She wiped her hand on her apron, then smoothed her grey hair into her bun. "I grabbed this when I heard the side door open."

Brianna looked down the empty hall. "Where is Harry?"

"Just up the woods a bit. With some other rapscallions from town. They have young Mary with them—she is the Horten boy's older sister, so she should keep them in line. They are supposed to be picking berries. But I doubt Harry will come back with many. He is a snitcher, that one. Cannot hardly keep a tart intact for dessert these days." Frannie's kind eyes narrowed at Brianna. "You do not look right, child. Do I need to round up Harry?"

Brianna shook her head. "Do not fret, Frannie. It is not an emergency, but I do think it is time to move you again. We have a few days while I find something suitable."

"Harry is not going to take kindly to it. He is happy here."

Brianna bit her lip. "I know. I saw last time I was here how very much he likes this place. But I am worried."

Frannie put her thick hand on Brianna's shoulder, squeezing it. "If you are worried, child, then we should move. Harry will be happy anywhere, you have taken care of that."

Sighing, Brianna set her palm on the back of Frannie's hand. "Thank you for that. But I realize that as he gets older—he remembers so much more now—I fear he will become less resilient."

"He will be fine, child. Do not worry on it." Frannie's hand dropped from Brianna's shoulder, and she turned, going down the hallway to the back room.

Brianna trailed her, passing the big pile of peas mounded on a table. "Can you be ready in two days' time? I am afraid I do not have extra time today to help you pack. I only have a moment, truly, for this conversation, but I would like to say hello to Harry before I leave."

Frannie pointed with the tip of the knife out the back window. "He is in those woods, not too far in. He knows to pop in and out so I can see him. He should be showing up again soon."

"Excellent." Brianna wrapped an arm around Frannie's shoulder, leaning over her plump frame to peck her cheek. "Thank you for being so understanding. I will return within a few days when I have everything settled."

"You always do well at it, child. No move has been as traumatic as that first time." Frannie nodded at her. "We will be ready."

Brianna opened the back door of the cottage, walking up the slight hill toward the trees. The woods were sparse, giving perfect dappled shade for growing wild berries. She looked through the trees, trying to spot movement.

"Nama, Nama, Nama."

Brianna heard Harry's squealing voice before she saw him. And then a tumbling tornado burst out of the woods, his short little legs carrying him as fast as possible down the hill. His head flew forward, his torso almost overtaking the pace of his feet.

Berries were smeared on his hands and across the lower part of his face. Brianna watched, cringing as Harry's legs almost tangled under him several times. But he managed to keep upright, stumbling, then jumping at the last possible second into her.

Laughing, Brianna caught him from his flying leap in midair. She bent, her knees on the ground so she could balance him in her lap.

"Nama, Nama." He yanked away, his blackberry hands pushing on her grey riding jacket so he could see her face. "Nama, I missed you." A big purple smack of his lips went onto her cheek.

Brianna couldn't stop laughing at his beard of purple berry juice while trying to avoid his sticky hands. Little hands he was determined to get all over her. Frannie had been quite right about the snitching.

"Brianna."

The voice was so out of place for the moment, for where she was, that Brianna almost didn't note it.

But then it sank in.

Sebastian.

She jumped to her feet, spinning, still holding Harry in her arms.

Sebastian stood ten paces from her, his hands clenched in fists, his chest heaving. Seething.

"Seb—"

"You have a blasted child?"

He turned, running down past the houses and out of view before Brianna could even take a breath, much less utter a word.

Dammit.

In shock, Brianna dropped Harry to his feet.

He grabbed her hand. "What wrong, Nama?"

Brianna looked down to see his cherub cheeks had gone from smiling to serious concern.

She had to shake herself into movement as his face turned panicked.

Scruffing his head, she bent down to his eye level, attempting to keep her voice light. "Nothing is wrong, Harry. I am very happy to see you, but I have to leave right now. I promise to be back in a few days. Can you please run inside to Auntie Frannie?"

He nodded, giving her a quick hug around the neck and running the rest of the way down the hill to his cottage.

Brianna's feet started moving, slowly, then picked up speed until she was in a full run. Onto Firesprite within a minute, she tore through town, aimed in the direction of Notlund, praying that was where Sebastian disappeared.

Pushing the horse, her breakneck speed rewarded her a mile outside of Hoppleton when she caught a glimpse of Sebastian disappearing over the crest of a far-off hill.

She pressed Firesprite even harder, willing the horse to find wings on its hooves.

She had to catch up to Sebastian.

She had to.

An hour later, Brianna lifted her hand from the reins, trying to quickly wipe away stinging sweat from her eyes with the back of her glove. It only smeared the sweat further into her eye, blurring her vision.

"No one will find you, Brianna. No one cares. The only one that did was me, and even that was a lie you fell too easily for. Worthless chit. You do not even know what love looks like."

The sneered words attacked her frazzled mind, and Brianna fought them, shoved them away, wiping her eyes from the stinging sweat again. She had to reach Sebastian. She had to.

Sebastian had been impossible to catch, much less gain any length on. She could see his cloud of dust, his fresh tracks, an occasional glimpse of him, but he didn't slow. Didn't stop.

And why should he? Not after what he saw. What he thought.

She pushed Firesprite down and through the stream again, crossing over to the switchback trail through the woods. It would slow her, but it was slowing Sebastian as well, as she could see the fresh broken branches, and still hear his horse echoing through the trees.

"Seb." She screamed his name, hoping the echo of her voice would reach him. Slow him just enough for her to catch him. "Seb."

Still movement ahead. If anything, the echoes of branches crunching came faster, more brutal.

Brianna clicked Firesprite on, encouraging as much speed as she could as they dodged, whipping back and forth through the scrawny trail.

And then she saw him.

Saw the tail of his black horse. Saw him crouched low, pushing his horse through the last thin line in the woods before the land opened onto fields once more.

She could cut him off. She saw it in an instant. If she cut through the low brush, forging a straight trail, she could cut him off. Firesprite was nimble. She knew the horse could do it.

Brianna yanked on the reins, pulling Firesprite off the trail. The horse, exhausted, at first resisted, then put its head down, picking its way over the shrubbery. Firesprite fought Brianna with every step, but Brianna just held the horse on course. She could see Sebastian was near to the edge of the woods, and she had to get there first.

She dug her heel into Firesprite hard, something she never did with the horses, and Firesprite sprang forward into a full gallop.

Instantly realizing her mistake, Brianna sank forward on the horse, trying to avoid the low branches scratching at her. Firesprite's brown mane flew into Brianna's eyes, blocking her view, but she could see she was close again to the main trail.

"Seb." She screamed again, lifting her head.

She saw him clearly. For just one moment he glanced her way and she saw it all—rage, betrayal ravaging his face, his entire being a mass of fury.

And then a tree limb blasted her straight across her chest.

It ripped her from Firesprite's back, the limb cracking from the tree as she doubled over it. She floated for the tiniest second and then crashed into the ground.

Flailing, her body rolling, pain screeching through her limbs, she skidded to a stop on her side.

Her cheek in the decay of the forest floor, she caught sight of Sebastian's horse thundering away.

Away, and away.

Away until he dropped out of sight.

And she knew. In that very moment—the moment he vanished—she knew.

She loved him.

More than she had ever loved Gregory. More than she had ever loved anything.

But he had disappeared.

Gone.

And she had no one to blame but herself.

Her eyes closed, words from the past flooding her mind. And she could not fight them away.

"You will always be unlovable, Brianna. Utterly worthless to walk this earth."

~ ~ ~

Sebastian stormed out of his room at Notlund, clutching a wide leather satchel. The sleeve of a shirt flopped half out from under the top flap of the bag. One shirt. All he needed. And he wouldn't have even come up to the castle to grab that, had he not needed his papers and notes that were in his room.

The rest of his things he would have Rowe send, as he would never be back to this place.

Moving quickly through the stone corridor, Sebastian almost bowled over the duke when he suddenly appeared from a set of side stairs.

Sebastian attempted to sidestep him without a word.

"Seb, where are you barreling off to?" Not allowing Sebastian to pass, the duke caught his forearm. "Wait. Where is Brianna?"

"I do not know."

"You have lost your wife so easily?"

Sebastian ripped his arm from the duke's hand, stomping away. "Leave me alone, Rowe."

"Why?" At his heels, Rowen wasn't letting him escape. "You have packed to go somewhere?"

"None of your damn business, Rowe." Sebastian didn't break stride, keeping his eyes straight ahead.

"Where is Brianna, Seb? We need her. Her sister needs to talk to her."

Sebastian kept walking.

The duke grabbed his arm, whipping Sebastian around. "Seb, where the hell is your—"

Sebastian's fist went swinging at the duke's cheek, crushing it at contact. It sent Rowen flying backward, hitting the stone wall behind him.

Left hand on his jaw, the duke's right hand clenched, but he held it in check at his side. His glare at Sebastian was deadly.

"Hit me." Sebastian dropped his bag to the floor, bracing himself. "Just hit me, Rowe."

"I repeat, Seb." Rowen pushed off the wall, straightening to his full height, his eyes pinning Sebastian. "Where the hell is your wife?"

"I do not know. In the woods."

The duke's glare went even deadlier. "You left Brianna in the woods?"

"Yes, I damn well left her in the woods. There are things you do not know about her, Rowe. And I am done with her."

"Like hell you are, Seb." Rowen's fist made contact with Sebastian's eye.

Sebastian flew backward. Blast it. He had forgotten Rowen could hit that hard.

"You are not done, Seb. She is your wife. Your wife. You made that happen. You bloody well forced that upon her, and now you think to abandon her?"

Sebastian seethed, pushing off from the wall to part his legs in stance for another blow.

"What blasted idiocy is this?" The duke moved in on him. "You do not get to just abandon her, Seb."

"What I do with my wife is none of your business, Rowe."

"It damn well is. More than you will ever know."

Sebastian's eyebrow cocked. "What the hell does that mean?"

"Nothing." The duke's growl eased slightly and he took a step back. "It means that you are a better man than this, Seb. Of all the things I know of you, you are a better man than this. You would never abandon a friend. And you are not about to abandon your wife."

"She has a child—a bastard child hidden away, Rowe."

"What?"

"A child—a boy—she has been hiding him from me—from all of you."

"No."

"Yes." Sebastian's arms crossed over his chest.

A long moment passed with Rowen shaking his head, his eyes to the heavy oak rafters above them. His look dropped to Sebastian. "It does not matter. You are not about to abandon her, Seb."

"It damn well does matter and I am bloody well leaving." Sebastian shoved Rowen to the side of the corridor, barging around him.

Just as he bent to pick up his bag, the duke's fist caught the side of his jaw, sending him sprawling, hands on the stone wall to catch himself.

"I repeat, Seb, you are not about to abandon Brianna."

Sebastian could taste the blood flooding his mouth. He looked at the duke. "Why the hell do you even care, Rowe?"

"Brianna is my sister."

"What?" Sebastian reeled, spinning so his back was on the stone, propping himself up. "How?"

"Both Brianna and Lily—they are my sisters. My father arranged for their mother to marry Wallace Silverton."

Sebastian's head dropped back onto the stone wall, his eyes high on the ceiling. Several heaving breaths, and his gaze fell to the duke. "Do they know?"

"No." The duke took a step toward Sebastian. "And I prefer it to remain so. They both loved their father, and he loved them. I do not want their memories of him tarnished."

"So that was why you took them in here. Brought them to London."

Rowen nodded. "Yes. And that is why I am not about to let you abandon Brianna."

Sebastian shook his head, the back of his scalp rubbing on the rough stone. "I have forgiven everything Brianna has thrown my way, Rowe. But this…a child…I cannot forgive a secret—a betrayal—such as this."

"You can." The duke moved directly in front of him, his eyes determined. "And you will. Whatever happened to Brianna in the past, you will come to terms with it. And you will bloody well go and find her right now."

Sebastian's jaw clenched, sending fresh waves of pain across his face. "I do not need this, Rowe. I do not need the lies. I do not need her."

The duke stared at him. Stared at him for several seconds. So long that Sebastian thought about just walking away. But Rowen wasn't judging—Sebastian could see that.

Finally, the duke opened his mouth, the slightest smile touching his face. "You do. You need it more than any man I have ever come across."

Sebastian sighed, his head tilting. "What the bloody hell makes you think that?"

Rowen took a step backward, leaning against the wall opposite Sebastian. His arms crossed over his chest.

"Do you know, Seb, that I had always imagined, one day, I would be sitting at my desk, and a missive would appear. I have always, honestly, been waiting for it. A note that told me you had died, somewhere out there." His arm swung wide before resettling across his chest. "Only god knows where. And I would wonder whether you were alone at the end, if you were afraid, if it was a relief for you."

"That is your reasoning? My imaginary impending death?" Sebastian forced a chuckle. "Your persuasion has a lot to be desired, my friend."

"I know it is odd—does not make sense. But you have run from life for as long as I have known you, Seb." He shook his head. "Then one day you got this crazy idea in your brain that Brianna was the one. Though I scoffed at it—I thought maybe, just maybe. And then what I saw next, after you married her…"

"What did you see?" Sebastian could not keep the sarcasm from his voice.

"I saw you still. I saw you stop. I saw you smile and laugh, and not constantly looking over other people's shoulders to decide where you were off to next. I saw you stop running from life, and start living it." The duke shrugged. "As inelegant as it sounds, I cannot say it with enough gravity—I saw you genuinely happy, Seb."

"But her lies—"

"We all lie, Seb. Some are big. Some are little. This is a big one. But are you truly going to trade away your own happiness for something that happened well before you knew her?"

Sebastian stared at him.

"Go back and find her, Seb." The duke stepped forward, patting Sebastian's upper arm. "Find her. Talk to her."

Rowen turned, walking down the corridor, his boots clicking on the stone floor.

Sebastian watched him disappear into the stairwell.

Damn that Rowen's words hit too closely to the truth. Truth Sebastian didn't want to admit to himself.

With a deep breath, Sebastian pushed off the wall. Dropping his bag back in his room, he went down to the stables.

Just as he was approaching the far right stable, a brown mare ambled into the field across from him, going over to munch on a swath of tall grasses.

Nobody by the horse, Sebastian squinted, trying to see it clearly. It had on a saddle. A sidesaddle.

His eyes not leaving the horse, Sebastian yelled into the stable closest to him. "Tommy. Tommy."

The boy came running, skidding to a stop in front of Sebastian. "Yes, mi' lord?"

"That horse." Sebastian pointed across the field. "Why does that horse have a sidesaddle on it?"

"Oh, that be Firesprite—Lady Luhaunt took 'er this morn. First I seen of 'er since then. I gettin' right on it, mi' lord." Tommy looked up to Sebastian. "Lady Luhaunt is with ye, mi' lord, right? She's right good 'bout carin' for the horses and findin' me when she returns. So that be odd."

Sebastian looked across the field, trying to control the panicked beating of his heart as his eyes searched the grasses.

Empty.

Shit.

CHAPTER 15

Sebastian found the trail Brianna's horse had forged through the edge of the woods.

He had heard her in there, screaming his name, her voice echoing through the woods. He had heard her and had kept going.

Pulling up on the reins, Sebastian stopped his horse, looking in all directions. His heart had not stopped pounding since the stables.

What the hell had happened to her?

He had searched every nook along the trail to this spot but had not found Brianna. This was the last area where he knew for sure she was.

Setting his horse forward, Sebastian followed the trampled underbrush into the woods.

An hour passed, searching the woods with no luck, when Sebastian set his horse to the stream to drink.

Then, noise. Thankfully, noise.

He heard the sobs before he saw her, and he followed them, reaching the high bank of the creek. Desperate, he searched the rocky streamside below.

Half-hidden behind a wild shrub, the back of her white shirt popped into view. Her riding jacket gone, she sat curled over, shaking with the sobs, her head tucked down and her hair wild, fallen from the pins.

And then he saw the blood.

"Good God, Bree. You are injured." Sebastian jumped from his horse, racing down the bankside to her. He skidded, rocks flying as his hands landed on the back of her shoulders.

She didn't look up at him, her body rocking back and forth, words mumbling from her mouth. It took him hearing the repeated words again and again to hear them correctly.

"Not like this. I do not want to be like this. Not this." Her mouth rambled, whispering repeatedly.

Her skirt pulled high and her boot gone, her focus stayed down on the pointed bloody rock she dragged back and forth across the back of her left calf. Digging into her own skin.

"Not like this. Not like this."

Sebastian's stomach churned when he realized what she was doing. Maiming her own leg. Blood covering every spot of her skin.

He snatched her wrist, ripping the sharp rock from her hand and whipping it into the stream.

"What the hell are you doing, Bree?" He grabbed her ankle, dropping to his knees as he pulled her leg away from her body so he could look at it. Fingers running along the back of her calf, he tried to discern open wounds from seeping blood.

Her blue eyes, wet with tears but vacant, moved up, finding his face. Finding his face but not truly seeing him. "Not like this. I do not want to be like this."

Her right hand was already searching for another rock. Finding one, her body jerking in sobs, she bent forward, going after her calf once more.

He smacked the rock out of her hand, hard, sending it flying. "Dammit, Bree. Like what? What the blasted hell have you done to yourself?"

Before she could move again, Sebastian stood, picking her up and setting her none too gently at the edge of the water. He grasped her leg, thrusting it into the water to wash away the blood.

Anger so thick ran through him that he didn't trust himself to not injure her further. He looked up at her face. "Why in the hell would you do this to yourself, Bree?"

"I just want it all to be gone, Seb." Her voice came out small, a wooden whisper. "Gone. I do not want to be like this anymore."

"Like what?" Sebastian's attention stayed on her leg in the water, his hands running up and down it, clearing all the blood. Dammit. Five major gashes and numerous smaller ones. But thank the heavens the blood had made it look worse than it was.

His initial panic quelled, he looked up to Brianna's face, fury that she would do this to herself peaking. She sat, hands in her lap, palms up, her shoulders slumped in defeat. Broken. Completely broken. The sobs had ceased, leaving only an ashen shell of his wife.

It tempered his rage. He forced his voice even. "Like what? You do not want to be like what, Bree?"

"Not able to tell you. Not able to trust you. To have to control everything. When I cannot...I cannot even control myself." Her eyes dropped down to her leg. "The scars. I want them gone. Gone. I do not want them anymore, Seb. I do not want what they do to me."

"Tell me what I can do, Bree. You need to trust me to help you."

Silent, her eyes stayed on her leg.

Sebastian wanted to move to her, to hold her face, to demand answers, to shake her until her eyes lit up and she spit fire at him. But he did not trust her enough in that moment to not pick up another rock. To not mar her own body even further.

He stayed where he was, the water soaking through his boots, her leg cradled in his hands.

"Brianna."

"I see...I know what a fine man you are, Seb. How you take care of me." Eyes downcast, she took a quivering breath. "But you do not know what it takes...what I have to overcome to be with you...to trust you."

"Tell me, Bree. Just speak the words. There is nothing left to do but that."

Her blue eyes flew up to him, sudden panic crossing her face. "He is not my child. The boy. Harry. You need to know he is not my child."

Sebastian froze. "But I heard him say 'mama.'"

"No. Nama. You heard him say Nama. It is what he has always called me—his mother died a month after he was born, so I was like his mother in his early years and I allowed it—he could not say Brianna, so that is what he called me. I know I am not his mother, but he needed one so badly."

"Who is he?"

"He is the viscount's son."

"Viscount Friellway? Why did you not just tell me? Why did you sneak off?"

"Why...why..." Her eyes went to the sky. "You cannot imagine what I have had to forget in order just to be near you, Seb. The position I have had to force myself into."

"Dammit, Bree, I will fight a hundred—a thousand demons for you, but I do not know what they are—what to fight. You need to tell me."

She took a deep breath, her gaze dropping to him, and Sebastian could see sanity return to her eyes. See her pull away from the very dark place her mind was suffering when he found her.

"It is time, Bree. You need to tell me. Trust me."

"You left me."

"I came back. I am sorry. I was furious. Done." He dared to set her leg down, letting the water run over it. He moved toward her, settling on his knees as his hand went to the side of her face.

"But I was not back to the castle for ten minutes before I realized I was an idiot." His forefinger rubbed against her temple. "Whatever you have in here, whatever it is—you need to trust me with it, Bree. I will not leave you again. Will not repeat idiocy. I swear it. But you have to tell me, Bree—what the hell is going on?"

Her head shook against his words. "Why did you find me, Seb? Why could you not just leave me?"

"I love you, Brianna."

Her eyes went wide with a slight gasp, disbelief clear. She studied him for a long moment, and Sebastian accepted it in silence.

Whatever it took for her to believe his sincerity. He did love her. What had begun as lust—as fate calling him—had without a doubt, turned into love.

He watched as her face ran through emotions—shock, wonder, landing on softness, and for a moment—one tiny moment—he thought he saw love.

But then she blinked, her face turning hard.

She pulled away from him, tugging his hand from her face. "This is not your problem, Seb. I did not want to involve you. I did not want to put you in danger. And now   " She hiccupped a breath, her words cut. She had to swallow hard to continue. "Now you say that to me. I could not involve you before, and now it is even more so that I cannot tell you."

"Dammit, Bree, do not—"

"Not knowing what was happening was the only reason I was left alive." Her voice arced into a yell as she cut him off. "I will not put you in that danger, Seb. I watched my father die because of this. I almost died because of this. Lily does not even know, and neither can you…I cannot…I cannot lose you."

Sebastian's head fell. He tried to draw up reasoning, draw up anything that would make Brianna see the reality around her.

She was not alone. Not anymore. And she damn well needed to tell him what was going on.

His head lifted, and he studied her blue eyes. "Brianna, that fortune teller, what she said to you—I always thought it was your head that was stopping you—keeping you from me. But I see it now. It is your heart. You heart is what stops you."

He ventured to bring both of his hands up, capturing her face. "This is the time, Bree. You need to let your heart lead. You need to trust me enough to tell me what is happening. Trust me enough to take care of you—take care of myself. I cannot protect you if I do not know what I am protecting you from. What I am protecting myself from."

It took the longest moment, her eyes not leaving his, for her mouth to open. "I did not tell you about Harry…" Words faltering, she took a deep breath.

Silent, Sebastian dragged his thumb across her cheeks, wiping away fresh tears.

"I did not tell you because the last time I trusted someone—loved someone—he almost killed me." Her voice crept out, tiny.

"Gregory?"

She nodded. "And then he killed my father. I loved him—I was going to marry him—and he…he tortured me…cut me."

"Hell, Bree. The scars?"

"He was after Harry. Sent to kill him." Her eyes dropped to his chest, her voice a whisper. "It was through me. All of it. It was how Gregory got into our lives, into the viscount's house. It was through me. He convinced me he loved me. He was in our home all the time. He ate at our table. Drank port with my father and the viscount. Again and again. And I never suspected. Never. I was so stupid."

Her eyes came up to Sebastian's. "Gregory was the one that killed the viscount. Papa saw him come from the viscount's room, bloody knife in hand. Gregory was going into Harry's room, but Papa scared him off. Papa woke me up with Harry in his arms. He knew I could ride. Ride fast. He told me to take Harry and go to the village, wait in the back of the church, let no one see us. We waited, Harry and I. We waited all night until Papa came to us. Then he sent me back to the estate and moved on with Harry. He only said that Harry was in danger. And Harry was so little then—so little. He had just started to walk, talk. I knew that Papa had hidden him away, far from the estate, but I did not know where. When he came back, he told me, told Lily to never speak Harry's name again. But he did not tell me who had killed the viscount, who was after Harry, only that it was a man. If only—if only he would have told me."

"Why did he not tell you?"

"Why did he not tell me?" Her eyes flew to the sky, head shaking. "To spare my feelings? To protect me? I do not know. If only he had told me immediately that the man was Gregory. I never would have walked into that deserted abbey."

Her head slowly fell, her look glazing over. "I was so sad that day. It was after the viscount's funeral, and I missed Harry, and I was so sad. I had not seen Gregory in days—I missed him so much and was wondering where he was. The abbey was where we would meet, Gregory and I. So that was where I went. I would not have gone…Gregory was hiding in there and he thought I knew where Harry was. He tied me down, and he had the knife and…he…he…"

Her left leg jerked.

"You do not need to say the words, Bree."

She swallowed back a sob, and Sebastian could see the horror of the memory filling her head. Her eyes shut tight, tears still escaping as her head trembled between his hands.

"I did not understand what was happening. Hours. Hours of pain. Hours of his words, his viciousness, tearing at me. Hours before I understood what was happening. He would cut me and ask. Make me scream and ask. Even then, I did not believe it. That he had never loved me. That the sight of me sickened him. I could not believe it. And I could tell him nothing—I knew nothing of where Harry was, but it did not stop him. To the very end, I could not believe what was happening—I loved him. He loved me. But it was a lie. A lie. All of it. Every moment we had shared was replaced with hours of his knife…of pain. What he said. And then Papa found me. He tried to save me, he came in—"

A sob escaped, cutting her words.

His heart breaking for the terror his wife had suffered, Sebastian's hands went down around her shaking body and he pulled her close, holding her head to his chest.

"Papa shot him—the bullet hit his eye and Gregory dropped. But it did not kill him. Papa had turned to free me, and Gregory attacked him from behind. I was still tied down. He slit Papa's throat in front of me. And then he disappeared—stumbled out of the abbey."

"He did not try to kill you as well?"

She took a deep breath, steadying herself. Her voice became the tiniest bit stronger. "No. For the longest time, I did not understand why he did not kill me. I thought it was his wound that made him leave, but then I realized after he killed Papa, I was his only connection to where Harry might be. I was the one that took Harry away from the estate, even though I did not know at the time where Papa brought him."

She wedged her head upward to look at him. "That, Seb, that was the only reason I survived—I did not know where Harry was. Through the torture, it was the only thing that saved me. Had I known, I would have broken—I would have told him, and he would have killed me. And then he would have found and killed Harry. That is why Lily knows nothing of this—and can never know—it may be the only thing that saves her. No one can know. It is why I did not want you to know."

Sebastian's hand clamped onto the back of her head. "Dammit, Bree. You have hidden all of this from everyone? Lily, the duke, Wynne, me? This is madness, Bree. Sheer madness."

She pushed back from his chest, her eyes on fire. "Is it, Seb? Is it? Gregory is still out there. Still in the woods, in the towns, in the fields. Still everywhere. How else am I to protect Harry? Lily? And I have not—for one second—not been afraid he would appear. Appear and tie me down…the only difference is that I know this time—I know where Harry is, and I do not think I could suffer his knife again…the pain…not without breaking.

And if I break, then I am helping him to murder an innocent little boy."

"But to not ask for help—"

"You may think my decisions stupid, Seb, but has someone you loved—more than life—ever died in front of you? Taken their last breaths before you?"

"No."

"I was bound to that chair, Seb. Watching my father look up at me. Blood seeping from his neck. His eyes—his beautiful blue eyes—to the very end, telling me all would be well—that I would survive. And I could not go to him. Could do nothing. Could only watch the last breath leave his body. Watch his eyes flicker out, still fixed upon me, even in death." She swallowed hard and had to force her next words out. "You do not know the horror of it—what you would give to never have to feel that pain again. But I do. So do not judge what you think are misguided decisions, Seb. I have only done what I needed to. I am never going to feel that pain again."

"Bree, you should not do this alone."

"Who then, Seb? Who? Who should I set in harm's way for my own gain? Lily? The duke and duchess who have taken us in and very generously given Lily the life she wanted?"

"Me?"

A sharp intake of breath, and her head shook instantly, horrified. "No. Not you, Seb. I could never forgive myself if…"

He grabbed her head in a growl. "Stop, Bree. Stop your damn mind. Stop trying to see into the future and fight it—protect everyone from it. Nothing is going to happen to me and you damn well need to start trusting me as your husband. Trusting me to protect you."

Her hands came up, gripping his wrists. "But this is not your problem, Seb."

His palms moved down, cupping her face. "Are you my wife, Bree?"

She nodded.

"Then it damn well is my problem."

A shuddered breath, and her eyes closed to him. She was still resisting him. Still unable to let him protect her.

Sebastian let his hands fall from her face. "There must be others that can take care of the boy, Bree. Others that can keep him safe."

"There is not. And I am not about to sacrifice an innocent child, Seb. I love that boy. We were a family—we are family—why would I not protect him?"

"There is not an uncle, a cousin?"

Her eyes narrowed at him. "Who do you think sent Gregory?"

"No. You do not mean."

"I do. Harry has only one living relative, an uncle. An uncle that very swiftly had Harry declared dead and taken over the title and the estate. I could not stop that. But I could keep Harry safe. Papa knew it was the uncle—it was why he sent me away that night with Harry. He knew the uncle would be notified right away about the viscount's death, and papa could not chance Harry being given to his uncle's care. Papa told him Harry had disappeared, most likely taken by the man that killed the viscount. But I do not know if the uncle truly believes Harry to be dead or not. So what do you think would happen if Harry resurfaced?"

Sebastian exhaled a long sigh. "Nothing good."

"Exactly. Gregory or not, the threat has not gone away."

"So who is Harry with now?"

"It took months of digging through Papa's papers and searching, but I found he had hidden Harry with his fourth cousin, Frannie. She was the only person he trusted. But when I found them, I did not know if Gregory was still alive, still after Harry. Or if his uncle would send someone else. The threat on Harry still exists. So I have kept them hidden and every six months or so I have moved them to a new town—I cannot chance them being in one place for long. Chance his uncle or

Gregory following a trail to them. This is the only way I can think of to keep Harry safe."

Sebastian stared at Brianna's face. She was still holding back. "But what happened, Bree? Why did you go to them today?"

For a moment, she resisted, but than a small acquiescing sigh escaped. "I need to move them. There was a death. I had hired an associate of Mr. Flemming's, Mr. Welbury, to track down Gregory, to discover if he was dead or alive. It was why I had to meet Mr. Flemming several days ago. Mr. Welbury was not only trying to find Gregory, but he was also looking for evidence that Gregory was working for Harry's uncle."

She stopped herself, her head dropping.

"Did he discover anything?"

Brianna did not look up at him. "Yes. Gregory is alive. And then Mr. Welbury was killed."

"Dammit, Bree."

Her hands came up, hiding her face. "His death is upon me, I know that Seb."

"Brianna, you do realize it is not a secret that you and your sister are living at Notlund with the duke and duchess? That Gregory can easily find you?"

"Of course I know that, Seb." Her hands dropped from her face, her blue eyes snapping to him. "But I thought he was dead…I hoped it…but then…"

Her voice started to tremble. "All of it—it is too much—this has spiraled so far out of control, Seb. I do not know for certain if Harry's uncle truly believes him to be dead. And I thought we would visit the duke and duchess and that would be the end of it—I did not think we would end up in London, and that Lily would become a sensation, and that I would have to marry, and that Mr. Welbury would be killed, and that Gregory…I…I had planned that if he was alive, he would be caught and hung by now. And I have been holding on, Seb. I have been holding so tight, but now—"

Her voice caught, swallowing a panicked sob. "I am tired, Seb. So very tired and I do not want any of this. I do not want what happened. What I have become. I cannot be all of this—trying to keep Lily and Harry safe—and then you, your face when you found me with Harry."

Sebastian grabbed her, yanking her into him, his hand deep in her hair, stilling her words. Stilling her mind.

"Hell, Bree. I do not know whether to keep you wrapped in my arms for finally telling me this or to condemn you for keeping this from me."

He could feel her swallow hard against his chest. "I have just been trying to keep everyone safe, Seb. You included. If anything happened to you, I…"

He gripped her tighter onto his chest, his lips going to the top of her head. "I say it again, Bree, nothing is going to happen to me. And this is no longer your battle to fight."

She angled her face upward. "I will not give up Harry to anyone, Seb."

"I know. I will keep him safe. I swear it." His fingers went through her hair, landing on the nape of her neck. "I will keep you safe, Bree. You must believe that."

"I do." She nodded, her blue eyes, for the very first time, clearly trusting. "But I did not want you in danger. I did not want this to become your trouble."

"I married you, Bree. All of you. I do not take the good parts, and leave you with the bad." He tucked her head under his chin, his gaze going upstream. The rushing water instantly reminded him of her calf, and he glanced at her leg, still in the stream.

Her scars. The bastard lying to her. Cutting her.

Watching his wife try to cut away the past with a rock.

The rage that had been pulsating in his belly reignited. He gripped Brianna tighter.

"Hell, Bree, how did you ever let me touch you?"

"I resisted, if you recall."

"As you should have." His fingers clamped around the back of her neck. "I understand, and I am astounded that you ever managed to let me do so."

"As am I, Seb." He could feel her smile against his chest, even if her words were weary. "But you and fate had something very different in mind, and I was no match."

CHAPTER 16

Watching the early morning rays through the open window in Sebastian's bedroom, Brianna loosened the laces of her left riding boot wide. Bending, she gingerly pulled the boot up over her left calf. It was wrapped from ankle to knee, a constant pain that nagged at her, but she could feel the scabs healing well.

Once they had arrived back at Notlund in the darkness, Sebastian had gently wrapped her bloody leg in linen without a word, and after, had not mentioned what she had done to herself, other than to ask her how her leg was faring.

For that, she was grateful.

In the moment by the stream, she had been so desperate, so despondent, that she did not know what she was doing. But now she was mortified at her lack of control—what she had done to herself.

"I can see you cringing." Sebastian's hands clasped onto her shoulders from behind. "Are you sure you can ride with your leg as it is? It has only had one day to heal, and Plarington is a distance. The ride will be long."

Brianna looked up over shoulder at him, her fingers still clutching the laces. "I will suffer it. I need to move them as soon as possible."

"I can go by myself and find a suitable home to rent, Bree. You do not need to come."

"I do. For my own assurances. It is not that I do not trust you…"

"But you do not trust me?"

"I am trying, Seb. I truly am. And I do trust you. But it is not a card I can so easily flip over in my mind—the control. After everything that has happened, what I have done to keep Harry safe, I cannot just absolve myself from the responsibility."

"Responsibility that never should have been yours."

"Responsibility that I chose to take on." She gently tightened the laces on her boot, tying them. "I could not just walk away from an innocent child I love, Seb. I know it riles you that I am in this mess, but there was no other choice I could make. No one else to trust."

"But you have me now."

"I do." She looked up at him. "And I cannot tell you how much of a relief it is to not have to bear this secret alone. Just know that the control I cannot let go of is a reflection upon a flaw in my nature, not yours, Seb."

"You, my wife, are not flawed."

She scoffed, rolling her eyes at him. "Do not try to charm me into staying here, as we both know that statement is wildly untrue."

He gave her his devil smirk. "I know no such thing."

She sighed, a smile playing on her lips as she stood from the leather chair, slipping her arms around his waist and looking up at him. "As long as I can make it to Plarington with bearable pain, I would like to do so. Besides, I did ask you for advice on the town and location, did I not?"

"Yes, but only after a lengthy argument—I still think Harry will be safe here at Notlund."

"There are too many servants, too many visitors coming through, Seb, and you know I refuse to put danger anywhere near Lily. The most inconspicuous life is the easiest to hide. And you yourself said Plarington would be the perfect place for them, and from what you told me of it, I agree. That must show some sign of my surrender."

"Surrender?" He wrapped his arms around her. "Now that, I like the sound of from your lips. It is a shame you are fully dressed."

Her eyebrows cocked, her own devil smirk appearing. "My skirts do lift, my husband."

Twelve hours later, Brianna was damning her own insistence on accompanying Sebastian to Plarington.

It had been a long ride, and they had had to visit five cottages in Plarington to find a suitable one to rent for Harry and Frannie. The whole of it had taken much longer than Brianna had anticipated.

She adjusted her left leg on the leather of the sidesaddle once more, trying to push the waves of pain from her mind. Looking about, she tried to concentrate on something—anything else. Anything that didn't include the overwhelming thoughts of Harry, or Lily, or Sebastian—as each one of those thoughts only meandered back to the pain in her leg.

Anything else. Trees. A squirrel teetering on a branch above. The drips of rain falling from the front of her hood. The long black tail of Sebastian's horse swooshing in front of her.

The rain had begun midday and slowed them on their return, the trails turning mucky. But now they were within an hour of Notlund, and Brianna couldn't get there fast enough. Food. A warm fire. Her leg stretched out free, unbound on the bed.

The pain. She was back to the pain.

"Hold here." Sebastian pulled up on his horse in front of her.

Brianna looked around. Grey sky above them, they were to the area of the trail that ran between the stream and the forest. An enormous willow to their left, Brianna set back her hood to find that the rain had eased into a drizzle.

"What is it?" Brianna asked as Sebastian jumped off his horse, coming back to her.

His hands came up, gripping her about the waist. "You are exhausted." He lifted her down from the saddle, not giving her a chance to argue. "And you are in pain. My stomach rolls every time I look back and see the grit in your teeth."

"I grit?" Her feet hit the ground, the impact sending a wave of pain up her leg.

"Yes. Exactly what is on your face at the moment. Gritting. So we are stopping for a moment so you can stretch your leg. Maybe loosen your boot."

He tucked her under his arm, steering her from the horses. "Here. It should be drier in here." Sebastian moved forward, parting the wall of willow branches in front of them, and then ushered her through.

The wide canopy of the willow tree created a somewhat dry, secluded spot. Sebastian disappeared out through the branches to secure the horses, and Brianna took off her gloves and opened the silver clasp at the top of her black cloak, shaking droplets free as she took it off.

Laying the cloak open near the base of the tree, Brianna sat heavily upon it, pulling her wet skirt upward to expose her left leg. Fingers working down the leather laces, she loosened her boot and immediate relief flowed through her calf.

She stretched her leg out in front of her as Sebastian came back through the wall of leaves, shaking his arms out of his dark coat. Holding the coat by the collar, he snapped it a few times, sending water splattering, and then set it on the ground next to hers.

He stood, gazing down at her, a peculiar look on his face. Brianna couldn't help being immediately suspicious.

His arms went wide, taking a deep breath. "This. This is what I wanted with you, Bree."

"What?"

"Listen. Look around."

She shook her head. "What? I hear nothing."

"Stillness. This is what I wanted." He dropped to his knees in front of her, his brown eyes bright. "A moment of stillness in all that is swirling about us. Stillness. Just us."

Brianna leaned back on the trunk of the tree, her gaze going about. She had to admit the leaves of the willow made an effective barrier to everything looming in her mind. "Yes, but for how long?"

"For as long as we dare to make this moment last." He smirked, his eyes scolding her. "Let me look at your leg to make sure it is not too dire."

Sebastian moved to the side of her leg, gently slipping off her tall riding boot and rolling down her stocking. His fingers, gentle, grabbed the end of the linen and unwrapped her calf. She could see spots of fresh blood dotting the white cloth.

"Dammit, Bree, I knew I should have demanded you stay at Notlund."

"I was not about to let that happen, Seb, and you know it." She tried to bend her leg up, pulling it from his inspection.

He snatched her ankle, keeping her from escaping him. His fingers prodded about the cuts on her calf. "Then we should have at least spent the night at Plarington." He glanced at her face. "You hide too much from me, Bree."

"Apparently, not enough." Her chin tilted up, the top of her head hitting the bark of the tree. Air reaching her wounds was welcomed, but they still panged, even though Sebastian's hands were beyond soft on her skin.

"You are riding in front of me on my horse the rest of the way home. I will not allow that boot to go back on your leg. And do not even attempt to argue with me, Bree."

Her eyes dropped to him. Concentration furrowing his brow, he tended to the bloody spots as though it were a newborn babe he dabbed at. Considering the anger in his voice, Brianna shook her head, awed that he could still be so gentle with her.

Her throat swelled.

"I want this, Seb."

"The stillness?" His focus stayed on her leg.

"Yes." She watched him, his brown eyes intent on her calf, his hands large against her skin, his heat flowing into her. So much strength, he had, but for her, so much gentle kindness. "And us, Seb. I want us, but I am so afraid."

His gaze came up to her. "Afraid of what?"

"When you told me about your family, Seb—about your life before the war. How happy you were. How content. And then how it all just disappeared—how you lost all of it."

"Yes."

"It was the very same for me. I was happy. I knew how to laugh. I knew how to have fun. We all did, my family. We were content." On her lap, her fingernails started to dig into her thumbs, one by one, as her eyes went to her skirts. "But then the viscount was killed. Then my father. And in a moment, it was gone—all of the joy. All of the happiness. It was so incredibly hard to move on from that. And I have not, for one day, felt right since the moment Gregory killed my father."

Her head rose as she found his brown eyes. "Not until you. I get glimpses of what happiness is. When I allow myself to see the moments, they are moments of happiness. Moments of right."

Sebastian tenderly set her leg down, moving up alongside her. "Brianna, that is a good thing."

"That is a terrifying thing." Her head shook slowly. "I do not know if I want happiness."

"Madness, Bree." His brow furrowed. "Why not?"

"I cannot have happiness again, only to lose it."

For a moment, his mouth opened, but words did not escape. With a quiet nod, his mouth closed.

"You are the same as me, are you not?"

"Yes." He grabbed her hands, stilling her fingers. "But I am trying extremely hard not to be. To allow myself this—you—us—without letting the ghosts of the past steal the present."

"How do you manage to do it?"

"Unfounded arrogance." Sebastian shrugged. "I do not believe fate will do it to me again—rip my life apart. Not now."

"I need some of that arrogance." She shook her head, her eyes going up to the long swaying branches. "It is little things from those days. Little things that haunt me. Little things I did not do at the end, take the time to care about."

A soft smile came to her lips. "Papa—the day before he died he wanted to walk with me in the gardens—just a simple stroll like we always used to do when I was a child. Just walk along, the two of us, him plucking blooms and tucking them all throughout my hair. I loved those walks."

Her smile evaporated. "But that day before he died—I wanted to do something else—something that had so little importance that I do not even remember what it was. So I did not go. A walk. One walk. Simple. And it is the one thing I would move heaven and earth to do over. Say yes."

"Brandy."

Her look fell to him. "Brandy?"

"Brandy. One more." Sebastian's cheek lifted in a grim half smile. "The night before I left for the war, my brother wanted to have one more brandy with me. It was already well into the dark morning. The tavern empty. One more, he said. Just one. But I resisted. I did not want to be tired when I left in the morning. So I retired. It was the last time I saw him."

Sebastian's gaze dropped, his hands tightening on hers. "Ten more minutes with him. What would it have hurt? Ten minutes."

Brianna tilted her head back, trying to drown gathering tears. "Plucking flowers—what would it have hurt?"

Silence fell upon them, thick, torments of the past heavy until Brianna could take the memories no longer. Her gaze went down to her lap as her hands flipped over under his, her palms sliding onto his wrists. "I wish…"

"You wish what?"

"I just wish all of this was gone. I wish Harry was safe. I wish Lily was married to a man that adored her. I wish you had mended ways with your mother."

"And what about you, Bree? What do you wish for yourself?"

She closed her eyes, swallowing hard. What did she wish for herself?

She knew it. Knew it, but could barely speak the words. Her eyes came up to his. "I wish I could tell you I love you, Seb, without part of me resisting—refusing it because I am so scared to live a life that could be ripped from me at any moment."

"You love me—except for that one part?" His voice was rough.

"I do. Save for that part that cannot bear it, I do." Her fingers came up, resting on the dark stubble along his cheek. She could not control the tears that swelled in her eyes. "But do you not see how wrong this is, that I cannot tell you this with freedom—with a happy heart?"

His hands captured her face, thumbs wiping the edges of her eyes. "I will make another deal with you, Bree. You hold onto the part that loves me without hesitation. And that troublesome part of you—the part that holds so fast to the fear—that part you need to leave to me. It is for me to whittle away at—whittle down until there is no fear left."

Brianna's chest tightened at his words, her heart aching.

If he could do that, truly do that for her... impossible. She swallowed hard. But she wanted to believe. Believe for him.

She nodded.

~ ~ ~

Not wanting Sebastian to see the motion, Brianna adjusted her leg on the sidesaddle as minutely as she could. Now was not the time for him to demand they take a break.

She looked over at Sebastian in the twilight. They were finally close to Plarington, only a few minutes away, and it had been an exhausting day—getting to Harry and Frannie in Hoppleton, packing up the few belongings they could take with them, and then traveling to the new town.

Their horses side-by-side, Frannie rode behind them alongside the horse carrying the belongings. Aside from it being the fastest way to get them to Plarington, Sebastian had not wanted to chance a carriage that could be identified delivering Frannie and Henry to the new home.

Brianna's heart tightened as she looked at her husband's profile. Harry was tucked in front of him, squirrelled up on his side, his cheek on Sebastian's chest. The boy was fast asleep, and had been for the last hour of the ride. As comfortable and peaceful as Harry looked, she realized the awkward position Sebastian had to hold himself in just to keep Harry settled.

Harry murmured something, snuggling his head further into the crook between Sebastian's chest and arm. If there was one thing Brianna had learned about her husband today, it was that he had a well of incredible patience—both with Harry and the entire situation. The last time she had moved Frannie and Harry, it had not gone nearly this well.

Sebastian glanced at her, a soft smile on his face.

Brianna's heart tightened even further. That he did all of this, all of this just to help her, to ease her burden—she could not thank enough the fate that he was always talking about.

Minutes later, Sebastian was sliding Harry down from his lap to Frannie's waiting arms. They had stopped all of the horses behind the new cottage so as to not draw attention to their arrival.

On the edge of Plarington, in the middle of a row of seven matching cottages, the home they had rented for Harry and Frannie was clean and bright, and there were other children in neighboring cottages for Harry to play with. Brianna knew she never would have found such a perfect place for them on her own.

Frannie carried Harry, still sleeping, in through the back door of the cottage as Brianna started to tie the horses to the post. Sebastian went right to the mound of belongings on the back of the fourth horse, removing them and piling them by the back door.

Brianna went to help him, but he caught her arm, stopping her from grabbing a heavy bag. "No. Let me. You can help unpack inside, but I do not want any more strain upon your leg." He stopped, looking at her as he held a large satchel in front of his chest. "How is your leg? It was a long ride and you were fidgeting at the end of it."

So much for hiding anything from him. Brianna shrugged. "It is not the most comfortable thing. But neither is it the worst."

Sebastian's eyes narrowed at her, and then with an acquiescing nod, he continued to move the belongings. Brianna stood by the door, watching him go back and forth from the horse.

"Harry quite adores you, Seb. It only took him a short time to warm to you, and then he could not leave you alone." She fingered the twine wrapped around a burlap bag on the increasing mound next to her. She caught his eye as he set down his next load. "And you are very natural around him, Seb."

"People are unnatural around children?"

"You would be surprised."

He stacked three iron pots next to the pile. "Were these truly necessary?"

Brianna shrugged. "Frannie thinks they are. They have made every move, so I doubted you would be able to convince her otherwise. I never have."

He turned back to the horse, head shaking. "Harry is a fine lad. And entertaining with his stories."

She chuckled. "And he had a thousand to tell you."

"That he did." Sebastian continued his unloading.

"It makes me wish they could come with us to Notlund as you suggested, but we cannot risk it." She watched Sebastian untie the last bundle from the horse. "Not now. Maybe someday."

"You would like that, Brianna? Harry to live with us?"

She bit her tongue, afraid to utter the words. It was an unattainable dream, Harry living with them, safe, with no threat. No threat to Harry meant no threat to her. No threat to Lily. A dream.

Sebastian came to her, stopping in front of her. He set the last bundle next to his feet, and stood, looking down at her as he smacked his hands clean. "We will fix this, Bree—I will fix this. This—for you, for Harry, for Frannie—this is not what life should be."

His voice hard, his hand went along her neck, fingers running up her spine in the exact spot that always sent shivers along her scalp. "I swear I will fix this, Bree. And I would like very much for Harry to live with us, if it will make you happy."

She nodded, eyes closed. How very much she wanted to believe that. Believe this could be over. "Seb, seeing you today with Harry…"

"Yes?"

"It has made me think beyond this summer. Beyond today. I imagine Lily will be married soon, if she has anything to say on the matter. So our need to stay at Notlund will have ended, save for your business there with the horses, of course."

"And you are wondering where our home will be?"

"Yes. We cannot live at Notlund forever."

Sebastian's hand dropped from her and he rubbed the scruff along his jawline. "I had not considered it. For the first time I have honestly been happy being in one place, and I had not thought past today. But you are right. I do believe it is time to consider the future."

"What about your lands in Suffolk, your ancestral home?"

Sebastian instantly shook his head. "Mother is at Callish Hall, so I leave that domain to her. She has made it understood that I should not step foot on the Callish estate."

Brianna stepped closer to him, grabbing the lapels of his dark jacket. "Is there no way to mend the break between you two?"

His jaw stiffened. "No."

"Are you positive?"

"I have not been able to convince her of it, Bree. I destroyed everything she held dear, and there is no recovery from it."

"But it is still unfair. It is your home. Maybe if—"

"Do not push this, Brianna."

Her mouth snapped shut, stung.

His arms went around her before she could take a step backward. "I am sorry." He sighed. "We could settle in Goldton, my secondary estate near Newmarket. I have not been by there in years, and I imagine it will need repairs. But it is within a hard, two-day ride from Notlund, which is convenient."

He angled his head downward so she had to look into his eyes. "Why has Harry made you think of all this?"

She shook her head. "It is just dreams—thoughts—I know I cannot afford to have. Not now."

"Thoughts of a simple life in the country?"

Her hand went up to his face, fingertips curling along the hair behind his temple. "Honestly, thoughts of you as a father. How could I see Harry with you and not imagine you as a father? You will be amazing—I can already see that."

Silent, he looked at her stiffly, his eyebrows collapsing together as if she had just spoken in a foreign language to him.

Hand dropping from his temple, Brianna filled her lungs deep, her chest rising as a frown settled on her face and words rushed out. "My mind has wandered into waters it should not have. I know you are just becoming accustomed to staying in one place, to a wife—to not travelling—and I should not speak of a future that may never be, not with the threat on Harry, and not with—"

His fingers went over her mouth, stilling her words. "You speak of babes, Bree, and I do not know what to say."

Her mouth moved beneath his fingertips. "You do not?"

"I do not know what to say," his voice went low, heated, "because it makes me want to kick Frannie and Harry out of the cottage this very instant so I can throw you down on a bed and guarantee our first babe is well on his way. We will have that future, Bree. Harry with us. More babes than you can imagine. Half of them tumbling rapscallion boys, half of them the image of you. We will have all of that. Safe. Secure. Happy. You did not come into my life, Bree, not to make it so."

He wiped the lone tear that had escaped from the corner of her eye.

"But I cannot build that life by myself—not without you, Bree. So I need you to believe in me. Believe that I can make that happen for you."

Her breath stolen, Brianna could only stare at him, the light from within the cottage reflecting the acute vehemence in his brown eyes.

Slowly, the slight movement holding the weight of all she had ever wanted and had been forced to deny, she nodded.

Words found their way through her clenched throat. "I do. I believe in you, Seb."

She did. Beyond any reason. Beyond the dread still hanging in her mind. Beyond her once shattered heart, now whole again.

She did believe.

CHAPTER 17

Sebastian set the silver serving spoon for the eggs on a saucer, glancing at Lily piling her plate high with marmalade-smeared rolls and bacon.

"You are positive, Lily? I do not want to put you in an awkward position, but I do not have a handy excuse to get her to stay here at Notlund."

Lily waved her hand, turning from the breakfast-laden sideboard to move to a seat at the table. "Do not worry on it. Of course I will help. Whatever surprise you have for Bree, I cannot wait to see it. Besides, she has more than neglected her duties with me as of late. And our guests. Not that I have minded. I only hope my future husband will be as thoughtful as you are to Bree."

"How are things progressing with Lord Bepton?" Sebastian set his plate on the table and sat down next to her.

Lily glanced quickly about the room, and seeing only a footman, leaned toward Sebastian, her voice low. "Dull. Dull as the day is long."

"Did you not realize that in London? How did he gain an invite here to Notlund?"

She shrugged. "Honestly, I was foxed during most of our encounters, and Bree somehow convinced me he would make a steadfast, attentive husband. Since she had better memory of him than I, I agreed."

"So he is not all that you hoped for?"

"He is sweet, and will make a wonderful husband for someone."

"Someone other than you?"

She smiled, popping a bite of bacon into her mouth.

The click of the side door to the dining hall sent both of their heads swinging to the doorway.

Brianna stepped into the room, her eyes flickering between Sebastian and Lily. "You two look…suspicious."

Sebastian stood, moving over to the sideboard to collect a plate for his wife. "We do not usually get the company of Lily this early in the morning. It is a novelty."

Brianna joined him at the sideboard, setting eggs and ham onto her plate. Sebastian set her across the table from Lily and went to his seat.

"My new brother-in-law was teasing me," Lily said. "It makes me thankful I only had you, Bree, and not an older brother to contend with growing up."

"I did not torture you enough when we were children?" Brianna asked, smile on her face.

"You did remarkably well, in that regard, sister," Lily said.

"I was just explaining to Lily where we are going for the next week, to deliver Red Swallow to Lord Bayton's estate for breeding, since he will not let his prize stud leave his sight," Sebastian said. "But I was also regaling her with news of your exploits with Lord Bayton."

"It seems your husband wants you to go along because you have Lord Bayton smitten," Lily said. "But I do not see the necessity of it, Bree. The deal has already been made, so why do you have to go as well? You would not leave my side when Lord Newdale was here at Notlund, and now that Lord Bepton is here, I have barely seen you."

"You are not interested in Lord Bepton, Lily. It is as simple as that," Brianna said. "I have no fear that you will find yourself in a compromising situation with him—most directly because you yourself would not allow it."

"And you feared I would compromise myself with Lord Newdale?"

Brianna shot her a wry look.

"What little you must think of me." Lily's face set to a pout.

"We will only be away for a week, Lily," Brianna said. "By then, Lord Bepton will have departed, and you will be preparing for Lord Rallager and his cousins."

"Which is exactly why I want you to stay, Bree. How will it appear if you are not present for both Bepton's departure and Rallager's arrival? It will appear dismissive, and you are the one that wanted me to give each of them a true chance."

Brianna sighed, setting her fork, full of fluffy eggs, down and looking to Sebastian. "I fear Lily is right. Is it necessary for me to accompany you?"

"No. I will miss your company, by large." Sebastian gave her a reassuring smile. "But I will be able to handle Lord Bayton. Though he will miss you as well, I imagine. I will just have to promise him another visit in the near future."

"And that will give you an opportunity to bring a new mare with for breeding." Brianna's eyes lit up. "It is the perfect excuse to sneak in another match with his studhorse."

Sebastian nodded with a smile. "Perfect. I do enjoy how your mind works, my wife."

~ ~ ~

Brianna scanned the sideways titles of the books on the shelf in front of her. She looked over the leather-bound volumes slowly, enjoying the moment of silence in the empty library. She had, admittedly, been so consumed by her own commotion during the past month that she had momentarily forgotten about all of the drama that spun around her sister.

In the week since Sebastian had been gone, Brianna was reminded quite quickly of the whirlwind Lily twirled in the center of.

At least Sebastian would be back in another two days. Only two more nights in his cold bed without him. With the frenzy surrounding Lord Rallager and his family's arrival, Sebastian would give her a harbor in the middle of the storm. A harbor she missed desperately. The past week had surprised her in how very much she had grown to depend on his presence—on how he stilled her mind.

"Brianna, here you are." Wynne walked into the library. "Are you collecting the classics for Lord Rallager's aunt? She just sent me after the very same thing. Cannot do without her Plato and Homer, she insists."

Brianna chuckled. "Is it too early to persuade Lily away from Lord Rallager, merely because I do not want to wait upon his aunt hand and foot?" Brianna normally would not have uttered such a disparaging comment out loud, but Wynne was one person Brianna felt completely unfiltered around. Maybe because Wynne was an American, or maybe because no matter what Brianna told her, Wynne had never judged her. Not once.

"I think one more day like this, and that is well within proper bounds." Wynne pointed at a tall shelf further into the library and slipped her hand into the crook of Brianna's elbow, walking them toward it. "Forgive me, I feel as though I have neglected you and not spoken to you in weeks—other than to discuss menus. I am not accustomed to entertaining such as this, and it is taking a dreadful amount of time. Especially since Rowe had to travel to London. So many expectations to be managed, and beyond his aunt, several of Lord Rallager's cousins have extremely exacting tastes in how they like to pass their time."

Brianna nodded, pulling tomes from the shelf where Wynne stopped. "Yes. And I fear his aunt is here only to spoil any hopes Lily has of Rallager—if she even has any hopes with him."

Wynne glanced up from the book she was flipping through. "Lily is still tethered to Lord Newdale?"

"I fear so, though she has been tight-lipped about Newdale as of late. Has she said anything to you?"

"No."

"More importantly, have you been able to paint?"

Wynne offered a half-smile with a shrug. "Very little. But the end is in sight."

"I am so sorry we have upended your life as much as we have done, Wynne."

"Nonsense. I was able to enjoy the season—and both Rowe and I adore you and Lily. We both just want to see you two happy. Plus, I will be attending to other things when the next season comes about."

Brianna looked from the spine of the book her hand was on to Wynne. "Already planning for next year? Why so far ahead?"

"What I am planning for has a very set timeline to it." Wynne set two books down on the heavy oak table in the middle of the room and turned back to Brianna. "I am with child."

Brianna spun to her, a shocked smile on her face as she grabbed Wynne in a tight hug. "I am so happy for you. When is the babe due?"

"It is still early—another five months, or so."

"This is wonderful news, Wynne. Both you and the duke must be delighted." Brianna's smile faltered. "But you should not be run so ragged by these guests—I am suddenly overwhelmed with guilt."

"We are—delighted. And there is no need for guilt. I am managing well. I have not been ill—something I am thankful for." Wynne motioned to the bookcase, and they both turned to pull several more volumes. "Speaking of happiness, things are going well with you and Sebastian?"

"They are. It is unexpected, but they are." Brianna added three more books to Wynne's pile.

Wynne smiled. "I never, in the farthest reaches of my mind, expected that I would end up in such a place as Notlund." Her finger twirled about the room. "Never. Who would? But it has been the unexpected in life that has brought me the most incredible happiness. Brought me Rowe. I hope for the same for both you and Lily."

"Seb would say fate brought Lily and me here, and on that accord, I have to agree with him. You and the duke have become our family, and I am eternally grateful to fate for making that so."

"Seb is making you believe in fate, is he?"

"Possibly."

"Then your marriage must be going well." Wynne smiled, picking up the stack of books. "Let me bring these up, and you can take a moment of respite."

"You are the one that should be taking a moment of rest, Wynne."

"I am not an invalid yet." Wynne smirked. "Plus, have you seen me all morning?"

"No."

"Exactly. I already have taken my escape for the day." She winked at Brianna. "Your turn."

Wynne walked to the door, but then stopped abruptly and turned back to Brianna, shuffling the books into one arm to free a hand. "I almost forgot. This arrived for you earlier today, but this is the first I have seen of you." Her hand went into a pocket buried in her skirt, fishing out a sealed letter.

Brianna went to take the letter from her, waiting until Wynne walked down the hall to close the doors to the library. She had refused to look down at the letter in her hand until she was closed off from the world.

Dread building, she glanced down to her already shaking hands.

Thick paper. Black seal.

Her legs heavy under her, Brianna went to the table in the middle of the library, breaking the black wax of the seal over the wood.

A simple note, the words were scratched out quickly with not much care. She recognized Mr. Flemming's handwriting immediately.

Miss Silverton,
Gregory has travelled to Yorkshire. I have found and followed him, against your advisement. Justice for Welbury. I shadowed him until I lost his trail in a town called Hoppleton.

Brianna's breath stopped. Her eyes blurred for a moment, and she sank to a wooden chair next to the table. It wasn't until air reached her lungs and her eyes cleared that she could look down to finish the note.

As the proximity is close to your current residence, I thought it a necessity to warn you in the quickest manner. I lost him on the 16th. Even as I write, I am still searching for him. If you can, please meet me on the 18th at the usual location. I will review with you all I know.
Regards,
Flemming

Hands trembling so violently she had a hard time folding the note, Brianna had to use the table to push herself to standing. She took a back winding staircase to avoid everyone milling about the castle and made her way to her room.

Sinking to the side of her bed, her hand crushed the paper, the wax crumbling onto the peach coverlet.

Time passed, and Brianna wasn't sure how long. An hour. Maybe three. She sat there in shock, only one thought reverberating through her brain.

She needed Sebastian. Needed him like she never had before.

"Bree? Bree?"

Brianna's head snapped up. Lily.

She slid her hand along the bed, shoving the crumpled note under the closest pillow just as the door opened.

Lily's head poked into the room.

Hell. Lily. Her sister's smiling face busted through the shock that had enveloped Brianna, holding her hostage.

Her mind started churning.

She needed Sebastian, but he wasn't here. And she had to keep Lily safe. She had to keep Harry safe.

There was nothing more important. She had been silly to think telling Sebastian would absolve her of that responsibility. And time was not her ally. The eighteenth was tomorrow.

If Gregory was in Yorkshire, he was close—far too close. As much as she wanted—needed—to wait for Sebastian to get back, she had to at least meet with Mr. Flemming. Had to know what he knew. Had to have something to tell Sebastian, some detail, however small, to give him a trail.

And she had to get to Harry and Frannie as quickly as she possibly could. Her face swung to the window. Dark. She couldn't leave now. She would have to go to them after Mr. Flemming. There was no one else. Sebastian was gone. The duke was in London. Just her.

Brianna jumped to her feet.

"What are you doing in here, Bree? You have not been in here since you married." Her sister came into the room. "I have been looking everywhere for you. You were supposed to meet us at the stables an hour past."

"I was?"

"Yes." Lily's eyebrows cocked at Brianna. "Bree, what is amiss?"

Brianna shook her head, pasting a wide smile on her face. "I am sorry. I was diverted."

"By what?"

Brianna shrugged. "Thoughts."

"Thoughts of what?"

"You, most recently."

Lily moved to stand in front of Brianna. "Just what thoughts have you been having about me?"

Brianna motioned to the chairs in front of the fireplace. "Sit with me a moment?"

Lily's head tilted, suspicious, but she went to sit in front of the fireplace.

Brianna moved to sit across from Lily, her fingernails on her right hand digging into her thumb. Where to start? What to tell her sister? Brianna cleared her throat. "Did you know I visited a fortune teller?"

"You did?" Lily's eyes went wide. "You? When? I cannot believe it."

Brianna nodded. "I did. When I was at that horse race with Sebastian. I thought it would be fun, so she read my palm."

"Was it? I have always wanted my cards read by someone other than an old hen in a card room."

"It was, to an extent." Brianna leaned forward, grabbing Lily's hands. "The fortune teller told me to make a good decision when it came to choosing between following my heart or my head."

She squeezed Lily's hands. "I want you to do the same, Lils. This decision—who the right man is for you—I want you to follow your heart."

"Bree—"

Brianna cut her off, shaking her head. "No, let me say this. I have been trying to get you to make this decision with your mind, with logic, with safety—but I have been wrong. It is your heart. Your heart is so pure, Lils, so very sure of itself—it has never failed you."

"Yours has failed you, Bree?"

"It did, once, long ago, and I have been suffocated by that very thing for so long. Do you remember when Papa was still alive? How simple everything was? How happy we were?"

"I do. I remember it well." Lily took a deep breath, her blue eyes somber. "I miss it, Bree."

"As do I. But I see it now. I see it so clearly. Our hearts were what we lived for back then. Impulsive and laughing and happy. And now, making this decision about a husband, you need your heart to guide you. It will not fail you."

Lily nodded, but suspicion crept into her eyes. "Why now, Bree? Why tell me this now?"

"Is there a better time than right now?"

Lily held Brianna's look for a long moment. Brianna could see the questions in her eyes, feel her wariness, but then she shrugged. "I suppose not."

"Good." Brianna squeezed Lily's hands one last time and stood, ushering her to the door. "I love you, Lils."

Lily paused with her hand on the half-open door, looking back to Brianna, her head cocked in unspoken curiosity. But then she smiled. "I love you too, Bree."

Brianna wiped a tear away from the corner of her eye, closing the door after her sister.

She had to get down to the stables and talk to little Tommy.

She would need Moonlight to be fresh in the morning.

~ ~ ~

The terror running through her mind morphed as the lips on her neck twisted away the nightmare of a knife in her flesh and replaced it with the tingle of Sebastian caressing her skin.

She could feel him in her dream. Feel his breath hot on her neck, feel his hands running down her body.

Her heart still beating wildly from the horror of her dream, her body came alive in a wild rush as the dream fully transformed from hell, into Sebastian naked above her.

Rolling her from her belly onto her back. Murmuring her name. His fingers slipping her night rail down her body. His mouth capturing her nipple.

She curled in her sleep to him, the cool air sending goosebumps along the back of her arms. His hand went down, making her night rail disappear, then trailed back up her leg, sliding to the curve of her inner thigh. Deep into her folds, he plied, sending her core into a demanding, throbbing need.

It wasn't until he entered her, filling her, slow and methodical, again and again, that Brianna began to meander through the remnants of her dream into reality.

She fought consciousness, not wanting to leave the dream that had come so close, but had not yet finished satisfying her.

A groan, low and rumbling sank into her ears.

This was no dream.

Her eyes fluttered open, only to see Sebastian hovering above her, watching her face.

He smiled. "You are awake."

She nodded, dreams still muddling her mind. Lifting her arm, still heavy with sleep, her palm went to his cheek. He was real.

"You are home. Seb—"

He slid into her, stealing her words.

"I am." His hand slipped under her knee, drawing her leg up. "And I am ready to explode, Bree, so brace yourself."

He withdrew, and Brianna arched, not willing to let him leave her. Her hand went above her head, palm wedged on the headboard. "Yes, Seb, yes. Please."

He slammed into her full force.

"Hell, Bree. Come. Now."

He gave no quarter to the delicate balance she held between sleep and consciousness, demanding she join him, fully cognizant to what he was doing to her body.

He filled her repeatedly, harder, his breath strained, until Brianna screamed, fingernails ripping into his back as her body contracted underneath him, drawing him into the same tortured release.

Brianna went limp, both her mind and body still jumbled between Sebastian's hard chest above her and the weightless state of her dreams.

He collapsed next to her, pulling her onto his bare chest and tugging the coverlet over her backside.

Nuzzling her cool cheek onto the warmth of his skin, she inhaled, breathing him in as his muscles twitched under her. "You are home early," she murmured, starting to drift back to sleep.

"I did not want to waste another night without you."

"Hmmm, I am lucky." The words slid out slowly, her head nodding, her eyes already sliding shut.

Sebastian's fingers played in the thick of her hair as his voice rumbled low from his chest. "Do not fall asleep on me yet, Bree. I have to talk to you."

It took a long time for the reply in her mind to make its way to her lips. "No? Why?"

"You need to know what I did."

A deep breath and she snuggled closer to him, her arm tightening around his waist.

"Bree. Brianna."

Eyes closed, she had to force her heavy head to nod on his chest. "Yes?"

"I moved Harry to a new location. I am not going to tell you where."

His voice barely made it through the fog filling her head. "What?"

"I moved Harry and Frannie."

The words sank into her mind. But it still took a full ten seconds to realize what Sebastian said.

She jolted upright.

"You what?"

"I moved Harry and Frannie to a new location. And I am not telling you where they went. They are safe. That is all you need to know."

Her hand on his chest, she shoved away from him, eyes wide in the low light of the candle he had lit next to the bed. "What are you talking about, Seb? We just moved them to Plarington." She gripped his arm as he sat up in the bed. "Are they in danger? I have to get to them. We have to leave right now, Seb."

She shoved down the covers, starting to move out of the bed. Sebastian grabbed her upper arm, stopping her. "Bree, stop, listen. I moved them. I was not convinced of their safety in Plarington. That was where I was—what I was doing this past week."

"You were not with Lord Bayton?"

"No."

Full understanding dawned on Brianna. "You moved them without telling me? Without asking me?"

"Yes."

She ripped her arm from his grip, scampering off the bed. "Why in the hell would you do that, Seb?" She leaned back over the bed, fishing under the covers to find her night rail and then yanking it over her head. "Tell me this instant what you did, where they are, Seb."

"No."

"No?" Her eyes went impossibly wide. "You moved them and you are not going to tell me to where?"

"Correct."

Brianna looked down, her chin hitting her chest as she tried to control the panic seizing her lungs. A dream. This was still a dream. It had to be. The perfect dream that had veered back into a nightmare.

She shut her eyes tight, shaking her head. No. He couldn't have done this to her.

Opening her eyelids, she looked up.

Sebastian still sat in bed, watching her like a hawk. "Whether you admit to it or not, Bree, you are terrified of knowing where they are, of having to protect them. I have removed that responsibility from your shoulders until Gregory is found and I can decide what to do about Harry's uncle."

"Take…take my responsibility? No." She didn't bother to curb her voice. "You would not do this to me. You have no right to do this. Frannie would not have let you—not without my permission."

"She did. She trusts me. And you need to do the same, Bree."

"No. No. No." Brianna's hand went to her forehead as she tried to fight the wave of panicked fury overtaking her. "Tell me where the hell they are, Seb—this instant. Tell me."

"I will do no such thing. You said yourself not knowing where Harry was, was the only thing that saved him—saved you. This is me saving you, Brianna."

"But you cannot—you cannot just barge into my life and take over everything, Seb. You are not saving me. This does nothing of the kind—I have to know where they are." Her fist slammed down on the side of the bed. "You need to tell me, Seb. You cannot just sneak behind my back and move them. Tell me where the hell you took them."

Sebastian moved to the edge of the bed to stand up, his look crushing down upon her. "You gave me no margin not to go behind your back, Bree. And I am not telling you—I am damn well protecting you, whether you like it or not."

She stared up at him, her breath seething. "No. You cannot do this to me. You are not a brute like this."

"In this I am." His arms folded over his chest, setting a wall between them.

It took a long second for the finality of his words, of his voice to hit her, and it stole her breath—sent her gasping, curling over as she stumbled backward.

"Brianna." He lunged, trying to grasp her shoulders, but she twisted viciously from him, bolting for the door.

"Leave me the hell alone, Seb."

Clutching her stomach, bile threatening to rise, she staggered down the dark hallway, hand running along the cold stone, searching for the path away from Sebastian.

Blackness surrounded her, smothering her.

How had it happened again?

Everything she had guarded against. Everything.

Her heart, her mind, given to a man.

A man who betrayed her.

CHAPTER 18

Three brandies chasing down his throat and two hours spent stewing, and his wife still hadn't made it back to his chambers.

Though Sebastian wasn't about to tell her where he moved Harry, he also wasn't about to allow her to escape him—allow her to blow this out of proportion.

He had been away from her for more than a week, and he damn well wanted her back in his bed. He was protecting her, and he was going to force her to see that.

Sebastian set his candlestick down on the bureau in Brianna's room, looking at the huddled mound on the bed. Though her room was mostly empty—she had moved most of her belongings to his chambers in the castle weeks ago—the bed had remained ready for her, should she need it.

It twisted his stomach that she had retreated to the room. He loathed that she had felt the need to run from him. He was protecting her, and she was being far too stubborn in her reaction.

The coverlet only covering her legs, Sebastian walked to the side of the bed, watching the mound quiver. Sleeping on her side, her body was curled into a ball away from him, her face buried deep in a pillow, hidden from view.

Just as he stretched a hand out to touch the edge of her bare shoulder, a shuddered breath shook her body.

Sebastian froze.

She had clearly been crying for some time, and sleep had not tamed her breathing.

His hand drew back to his side. She wasn't ready yet. Not ready to listen to him. To listen to logic. He had been trying to take all worry from her mind, she had to understand that—and she would understand that. But not in that moment.

In the light of day, with a clear mind and hours of sleep tempering her reactions, she would understand. See the wisdom of his actions.

Sebastian turned from the bed, his toe crunching on a piece of paper. He cringed, hoping the sudden sound wouldn't wake Brianna. Another shuddered breath, but she made no other movement.

He bent to pick up the crumpled paper, curiosity striking when he saw the broken seal crumbling from it. Grabbing his candlestick, he eased into the hallway as quietly as he could, then opened the paper, flattening it the best he could with one hand.

He scanned the note.

His heart suddenly racing, he looked up, blinking, then read the note once more with slow care.

Gregory was in Yorkshire?

Shit. How had his own man not discovered this piece of information?

And why in the damned hell hadn't Brianna said anything about it? Flemming would be waiting for her in the morning.

With a quick glance into the room at her still form, Sebastian shook his head, muttering incoherent blasphemies as he spun on his heel and disappeared down the hall.

~ ~ ~

Brianna pulled Moonlight into a slower gait, even though the mare wanted to fly. She had never held back the horse before, but Brianna was in no mood for speed. No mood to get to Mr. Flemming as quickly as she could.

At least she didn't need to rush to Harry and Frannie in Plarington. It would serve no purpose since Sebastian had moved them. A small favor that there hadn't been enough daylight to start off to them the previous evening.

Brianna looked up at the leaves rustling in the wind under the grey sky. She had not come through these woods, along this stream alone for some time—not without Sebastian—and where once she had reveled in the solitude, she was now struck by how very lonely the ride was.

Alone. She was absolutely alone.

And now, not just alone—hollow as well. She had so very little left. No emotion. No thoughts. No energy. Just the dull ache of hollowness.

She had slept the night in her old room and Sebastian had let her, did not come for her—and that had cut through her heart even more than his betrayal. And even though it had galled her to do so, she went to Sebastian's room at daybreak, willing to trade her pride for his help, to ask him to accompany her on the ride to meet Flemming. To not have to go alone.

But Sebastian was gone. She had searched the castle. The stables. He was gone. No note. Nothing.

He had left her again.

"You thought I loved you? Imbecile little twit."

Gregory's voice filled her head.

She swallowed hard, holding back a well of panic at his words. His voice had not haunted her for so long. But he was back. Back full force, filling her mind. His mocking laughter. His sneer. His wicked enjoyment of her agony.

A sob tore from her throat, her pain echoing through the woods. Her head dropped, defeated, the leather of the reins digging into her skin as her fists tightened.

Gregory. Sebastian.

She had to stop.

She had to put all of it—both of them—out of her mind.

She could not wallow in her crushed heart. She still had to meet Mr. Flemming. Still had to come up with a plan. A plan to keep Lily far from danger and Harry safe—and a way to have Gregory found and hung for his crimes. As for Harry's uncle, she knew he was untouchable, she could think of no way to prove he had hired Gregory to kill the viscount, but she also hoped he still fully believed Harry to be dead.

Maybe the duke could help. If he returned from London soon…she shook her head. Now that Wynne was with child, entangling him in the danger did not sit well with Brianna. She could not be the cause of Wynne becoming a widowed new mother.

Brianna's mind wandered to the blade buried along her skirts. She had grabbed a dagger from the display of weaponry in the library—a small modicum of safety should she need to use it for protection.

Though she tested the blade for sharpness against her thumb, she ignored the fact that it was a bold lie she told herself—she had no experience with a dagger and would truly not know what to do with it. She hadn't even had a proper way to attach the sheath to her body, so she had secured it to a pouch tied around her waist.

With a sigh, she scolded herself. *Do not move ahead in time.* She was getting far, far ahead of herself. It was not as if Gregory was going to just jump from behind a bush and attack her. It was not going to happen. He was far too cunning for that.

She was just going to meet Mr. Flemming. A simple meeting. Something she had done before without incident. And depending on what he told her, if she was desperate, she could always still go to the duke for help if it was warranted. Sebastian had deserted her, so the duke was her last option for help. Maybe he could find out where Sebastian had moved Harry.

Moonlight tugged at the reins.

With a sigh, Brianna relented, letting her quicken the pace. Best to get this meeting with Mr. Flemming done quickly.

~ ~ ~

Brianna tied Moonlight to the tree behind the abandoned mill, looking around. Mr. Flemming's horse was not where he usually tied it. She was late, she knew that, but he had always waited for her in the past.

Maybe he had gotten his day wrong, although she had never known him to miss a detail. The man was as thorough as could be—that was why she had hired him to begin with.

She walked around the mill and lifted the tilted old door to wedge it free of the stone frame. Hinges creaking, she pulled it open, poking her head inside the main room. It was quiet, only dust moving through the air as she stepped in.

Wood scraping against stone caught her ear, and Brianna followed the sound, moving around the giant millstones in the middle of the room.

Sebastian.

Her breath stopped. Fear, like nothing she had ever experienced, shook through her body, freezing her in place.

Sebastian tied to a chair. His arms yanked behind him. Feet tied to the legs of the chair. His head hanging limp. Blood covering his body. His white linen shirt, shredded and red.

Brianna tried to rush forward, but it took seconds for her feet to respond to her brain. And when they did, they were out of control, skidding, falling to the bumpy stone floor in front of Sebastian. She crashed into him, landing on her knees as her forehead banged into his chest.

His body jerked with a slight cough.

He was alive.

Brianna gulped air. Alive. He was alive.

"Seb." Her hands went to his face, gripping him, shaking his head back and forth—harshly, too harshly, but she couldn't control herself. "Seb."

His right eye cracked open, his left one too swollen and bloody to see through.

Another cough. "Bree?"

"Seb—"

"Get out of here, Bree." Even with the ragged whisper, he managed to cut her off. "Out. Run."

She dropped his face, her hands scrambling down to the pouch hanging from her waist, digging out the dagger she had brought.

Stumbling, crawling on her hands and knees to get behind him, she set to sawing at the rope around his wrists, not caring that she sliced his skin as she went. She just needed him freed. Needed him out of there.

Blade through only half of the rope threads, the door creaked and, hell, footsteps. It only gave her seconds, but it was enough time to slip the dagger behind Sebastian's arm, hiding it as she clasped the rounded end of the hilt into his palm.

Don't drop it, Seb, she willed him. Please, just don't drop it.

A thick hand yanked her away from Sebastian, her body viciously snapping. Cold steel landed long on her throat. Brianna scratched at the arm, a vise across her chest, trying to look back at Sebastian, trying to make sure he was still there. Still alive.

The arm spun her out, turning her, but the blade only left her neck for an instant. Her lower back cracked into the millstone, jolting her to a stop just as the knife landed on her neck again.

She looked up.

Gregory.

No. God, no.

Brianna swayed. The blade pressed into her neck, and she nearly dropped, unable to control her spinning head.

Gregory. Still handsome. Still brutally strong. Still the same dark blond hair.

And still the same sneer on his face. The sneer she'd never recognized as evil—not until he had almost killed her.

The only thing that marred his appearance now was the scar that arched across his temple to his right eye. A right eye that was now glass. An eerie blue eye that stared at her, not moving, cautioning her to look away. To flee.

If only she could.

"My love."

The two words, low in his gravelly voice, slammed into her, doing more damage than the blade pinning her neck. Words that cut off all breath, cut off all hope.

Two words that told her he was about to wreak devastation.

Gregory glanced over at Sebastian. "Good. I can kill him now that I have you."

Brianna forced her eyes to Sebastian. His head had fallen down, his body drooping.

"No," Brianna screamed, grabbing Gregory's wrist with both hands, trying to wedge the knife from her neck. It only made the blade pinch tighter to her skin.

"He is of no use, my love. The bastard was not forthcoming with information, and I have a job to finish." Gregory's one good eye stayed on Sebastian as his glass eye stared into nothingness.

"No. He does not need to die, Gregory. He is not a part of this. He does not know where Harry is." She swallowed hard. "But I do. That is what you want—Harry? Only I know, so you can let him go."

Gregory's good eye swung back to her. "Interesting. Since that is the same sentiment he has expressed—he claims he knows where little Harry is, and that you have no knowledge. So I should leave you be." Gregory chuckled. "Have I stumbled upon a love affair, my dearest Brianna?"

She met his good eye, her fingers dropping from his wrist as her voice turned to calm threat. "I know where Harry is, Gregory. But if you kill him, you will never find Harry. I will not tell you on principle alone." Her eyes narrowed at him. "Do not think I cannot withstand you again, Gregory. I can."

His one good blue eye flickered.

He remembered.

She could see it instantly in his eye. The pleasure. The gleam of vileness.

Her gut churned at the sight.

But there it was. She needed time, precious moments, and in her sea of desperation, a singular beacon. One thing—the only thing she could think of.

She stole a glance at Sebastian. Still limp. Still not moving. Time. He needed time.

Brianna closed her eyes, taking the slightest second to steel herself. She had to do this. It didn't matter that Sebastian had left her. It didn't matter if he had betrayed her. If he didn't love her. She loved him, and she wasn't about to see him die. That was the last thing she would let happen.

She needed time. Time for Sebastian to wake up. Time for him to cut his ropes.

She opened her mouth, talking before she had even formulated a plan. Keeping her eyes on Gregory, she ignored the perversity of her own words. "I remember, Gregory. I remember how it lit up your eyes. How my screams pleased you."

Ever so slowly, her hand went forward, palm lightly onto his chest, her fingertips caressing the smooth linen of his shirt. To her surprise, he allowed the movement.

He was interested now. His good eye fully on her. No more flickering looks to Sebastian.

This was good. This would work.

It would work as long as she could stomach it.

Brianna swallowed down the rock in her throat, forcing her voice even, sultry. She had to make him believe it.

"I saw, Gregory. I saw how you liked it. Even through my pain. The agony. How it tore me. Even through that. I saw it." Her other hand went up to his chest. "I never wanted to admit it. But it…it awoke something in me. Something I cannot name. Something I have tried to deny. I liked it."

"Do not think you can lie to me, my love. You will not save him." Gregory's jaw set hard, even though the gleam of interest didn't leave his eye.

"Your control. How you made me bend to you. Scream." Her palms flattened on his chest. She could feel his heart thumping, his muscles twitching at her words. "What you drew out of me. The blood. The begging."

Not breaking eye contact, she moved her right hand down to her skirt, pulling, bunching the fabric up as she exposed her right leg. Boot. Knee. Thigh.

Fist wrapped around the fabric, her bare thigh fully exposed, she bent her leg, lifting it as she wedged her heel onto the stone behind her.

"We can do it again, Gregory. Again and again. I can hold out, just as before. You can punish me."

He swallowed, and Brianna could see him nearly salivate at the mere suggestion.

She had him now. But there was still a flicker of doubt. She needed to prove it.

Movement numb with disbelief at her own actions, but hardened against stopping—against weakness she couldn't afford—Brianna's left hand slid across his chest.

Slowly, her fingers trailed to his shoulder and along his outstretched arm toward the blade at her neck. She snaked her hand along the back of his forearm gently, causing no alarm, until she gripped the dagger through his hold, fingers entwined with his.

Bringing his hand down, she set the blade on her thigh. He didn't halt her motion.

Brianna didn't stop to take a breath. Didn't slow. She couldn't or she wouldn't be able to do this.

She pressed the blade into her thigh.

Hand tightening over his, digging the sharp edge into her skin, she dragged the dagger across her thigh, cutting deep.

A gasp she couldn't control choked out. Instant fire in her leg, her head dropped and she grimaced, trying to overcome the pain.

Her eyes cracked. She could see the blood dripping down her leg, puddling on the floor. The bulge in Gregory's pants pulsating, huge.

"You cut too deep, my love." His gravelly voice sank to her ears. "We will have to ensure we enjoy this fully before you faint."

Bile rushed to her throat.

She swallowed the vileness. She couldn't break. Not now.

Teeth gritted, she sucked air. She could do this. She had to.

When she could breathe again, she looked up, her eyes meeting his. His glass eye had slipped, looking off to the side, but his good eye stayed fixed on her, his face throbbing with hunger. Sick desire.

"I want it again," Brianna choked out, her voice surprisingly even. "Make me scream, Gregory. Like you did before."

"No. Shit, Bree. Stop. Stop." Sebastian's ragged shout cut through the room. "Good God, Bree, stop it. God no."

Gregory's head swung to Sebastian.

Sebastian went frantic trying to free himself from the ropes holding him to the chair.

"He does not matter, Gregory." Brianna's voice cut sharp over the noise, her hand tightening over his fingers on the blade.

Gregory looked back to her.

"This is not enough for me, Gregory. You know how to do it. Make me scream. Make him hear it."

She dropped his right hand with the blade and grabbed his left hand, setting his fingers over the open wound. She leaned forward, making sure Gregory could look nowhere but at her. "Make. Me. Scream."

Gregory's mouth curled as his fingers slid through the blood on her thigh to the cut. With a grunt and a sinister sneer, he slid three of his fingers deep into the wound, tearing at her flesh.

Her scream pierced the mill.

Waves of pain ripped through her body. Her agony echoed off the stone walls.

She doubled over, falling, but Gregory quickly pinned her shoulder to the stone before she slipped from his fingers deep in her flesh.

"Well done, my love."

He twisted his fingers, scratching his nails into her thigh muscle.

Fresh shrieks. Gasping for air.

But in the middle of it, calm.

She had been terrorized by this for years. This very thing. But this time it was freeing. This time it was to save Sebastian. This time for love. Love she knew, without fail, was true.

This time, she could endure.

"Do tell me, my love. Where is the boy?"

Brianna's head swung side to side, and then she managed to lift her chin, finding his good eye. "No."

He twisted his hand.

"No," she screamed, collapsing again, her convulsing eyes shut tight against the wretchedness.

He shoved his body into hers, his fingers dragging through the length of the wound.

And then his mass was on her, crushing her against the curved millstone behind her, dragging her downward. A blade passed in front of her eyes.

She crumpled under his body, fighting for breath beneath his weight. Shoving, kicking, she tried to free herself from suffocating, her head banging into the stone floor.

He rolled off her, his body thunking to the ground.

It took Brianna a gasping breath to realize Gregory was limp beside her. Blood seeped from the side of his neck. Slowly at first, then fast.

She looked up.

Sebastian stood over her, heaving, bloody, straddling her body, her knife gripped solid in his hand.

Neither of them moved for seconds. Sebastian's eyes stayed trained on Gregory. Brianna's eyes stayed trained on Sebastian.

Slowly, Sebastian's eyes swung to Brianna.

"Bloody hell, Bree."

He stepped off from above her, going to the door.

Brianna's head rolled to the side, her temple hitting stone.

Sebastian kicked open the door and disappeared.

Leaving her.

Again.

CHAPTER 19

"Seb?"

Sebastian's head popped up. He scrambled to get his face above Brianna's. "Bree. I am here. Right here."

Her blue eyes, searching, vacant, found him for a moment before falling closed.

Sebastian smoothed the wet strands of hair back from her forehead. Waiting. Watching. Searching her face for movement.

Surprised that her skin was hotter than he remembered it before he fell asleep, he reached to the wet cloth in a bowl by the bed, dragging it across her forehead, her cheeks.

He waited. Hoping. Watching for the slightest quiver. Something to tell him Brianna was still in there. Still fighting.

In the very second that he thought she had drifted away again, her mouth cracked, but her eyelids did not even attempt to flutter open.

"I love you." Nothing but her mouth moved, her words sparse whispers. "Every last part of me, Seb. No hesitation. You are here. I am happy… I do not care if it is this minute alone, or a lifetime. As long as I have it, I do not care. I can go. Happy."

The last of her raspy words slipped into nothingness, barely perceivable.

Sebastian's head bowed, tears slipping from his eyes to land on her shift, already soaked with fever. He had to swallow the lump in his throat several times before he could trust himself to speak.

He bent, setting his mouth to her ear, making sure she could hear his words. "You will not die here, Brianna. Do you understand? You are the love of my life, Bree. And you will not go anywhere. You will not die. Do not think you are leaving me. Ever."

No movement.

Her breath shallow once more.

She was gone again.

~ ~ ~

"Seb. You need to sleep."

Sebastian's head swung slowly to the door. He hadn't heard anyone come in. Eyes bleary, he could just make out Wynne coming in through the dark and lighting a wall sconce by the door.

Carrying a candle-stick, she brought it to the side of the bed, setting it on the bedside table next to the bowl of cool water.

"You need to sleep, Seb. You can barely keep your head aloft."

Sebastian did not move from the simple wooden chair he sat in, his eyes going back to Brianna's face. "I sleep fine beside her."

"Yes, but you have not even done that." Wynne moved to stand in front of him. "And you have not moved your arm from atop her belly in days."

"She needs to know I have not left her." He did not bother to look up at Wynne.

Sebastian could hear Wynne swallow hard before her hand went gently to his shoulder. "Seb, Rowe talked to the physician." Her head fell as she took a deep breath, her hand tightening on his shoulder. "She is slipping, Seb. The physician says there is little hope. You need to...to ready yourself."

His eyes turned to daggers slowly moving up to Wynne. "Leave, Wynne. Leave this damn room."

She shook her head, refusing to budge. "Seb, you have not left this room since you came back with her, it has been days—a week. I will sit with Brianna. You need to go outside. Breathe fresh air. It is a clear night. Cool. Just for five minutes, Seb. I will sit with her."

His gaze dropped back to Brianna. "I told her I would not leave her."

"You are not leaving her, Seb. You are taking five minutes to stand. To breathe. Your own wounds—they are not healing as they should."

Sebastian's eyes flickered down to his left arm draped over her belly. The strips of linen wrapping the cuts in his arm were tinged with spots of blood. "They are fine."

"Seb, we are all worried about you. Rowe, Lily, me."

"Worried for what?"

Wynne's hand slipped from his shoulder, her fingers clasping in front of her belly. "Worried that you are searching for death with her."

"If death comes for her, I am not going to let her be alone." His voice caught as his fingers dug in around Brianna's waist, his forearm pressing down on her belly. "I am not going to let her breathe her last breath without me, Wynne. Not without me holding her. I will not allow it."

"Seb...she does not know you are even here. It has been days since she has spoken, since there has been any sign."

He glanced at Wynne, his eyes almost instantly drawn back to Brianna's face as his voice turned ragged. "I know. I know I am here. And she will not leave this earth without knowing I am here."

Wynne's hand went gently to his shoulder, squeezing.

Silently, she stepped to the side and left the room.

Sebastian waited minutes, an hour, staring at Brianna's face, the grey tint to her skin making the shadows on her cheeks appear even darker than the day before. Wynne's words hung in the air, haunting him. Whispered talk of death that weighed upon his chest, suffocating his lungs.

He drew a shuddered breath, moving forward to sit on the side of the bed and dip a fresh cloth in the basin of water in front of him.

Achingly slow, he set the wet cloth to Brianna's lips, letting the water slip into her mouth. His head fell, his shoulders following as his forehead landed on her shoulder. He sat there, his head on her chest, willing her to fight, to breathe.

But there was nothing. He could feel the cold stillness of her body.

He lifted his head, his face next to hers as his arm rose from her belly, and he smoothed the hair along her brow. "I can feel it in your body, Bree. Did you hear what Wynne said? You are failing. And I see. I see you have so little left—nothing."

His eyes closed as he fought the words he abhorred having to speak. "But you are holding on, Bree. You are holding on for something." His head shook, his voice cracking. "God, how I do not want to say this. But if you are doing it for me, Bree—holding on—you can stop. You do not need to stay here for me. You can go. I want you to stay—god, how I need you to stay. I want you to fight, and I will never let you go. But I cannot have you suffering for me. Suffering because you are afraid for what I will become. I know the pain you are in, and it is not fair, me keeping you here."

He stopped, looking away from his wife as he took long minutes to force his chest into submission, his voice into strength. Strength he knew Brianna needed from him.

His gaze fell back upon her. "You have to let me go, Bree. Let your body go. Let the pain go. We will be together again, for you are the love of my life in this world, and in any other. Fate will make it so. We are destined to be together again. And I will be whole again when that time comes. Trust in that, my wife. Trust in that."

He broke, all words, all thoughts failing him. Crumbling, he could only move enough to stretch himself out beside her, holding her limp body tight to him.

If these were to be her last minutes, he would hold her. Hold her until the end.

His head dropped, his face touching hers. His breath mingled with what little she had left.

And he let the pain consume him.

CHAPTER 20

"Seb."

The sound floated into the room, so soft, Sebastian mistook it for the breeze from the window Lily had opened hours ago in the middle of the night.

"Seb."

Sebastian opened his eyes. It took him a full breath to realize he had fallen asleep, Brianna still tight to his body, his head tucked in next to hers on the pillow.

He pushed himself up, his arm dragging across Brianna's belly. Blinking the sleep from his eyes, he looked to the open window to see morning sun streaming in.

"Seb."

Sebastian suddenly realized the sound came from the bed. Brianna. He looked down to see her eyes open, the light blue in them clear, watching him, puzzled.

"Bree." He moved fully upright on the bed, his hands going to her face, holding her, proving to himself that she was awake and looking at him.

Her mouth opened, but no sound came out. She tried again, but again, no sound, only what looked like the word "water."

Sebastian spun, grabbing the pitcher from the table at the side of the bed, and poured water into a glass. He turned to her, slipping his hand behind her neck and lifting her from the bed.

She was light. Too light.

Gently, he set the glass to her lips, tipping it until water drained into her mouth.

She nodded, and Sebastian gently set her back onto the pillows. He placed the glass back on the side table, almost afraid to turn to her. Afraid this was a dream. Not real.

"Lily? Harry?" A whisper floated from her.

Sebastian turned around. "Both are safe, Bree."

"Seb..."

"Bree, do not talk." He slid his hand along her neck. "You are too weak."

The confusion in her eyes thickened. "I have been sick?"

"Yes. A fever. It has been days. Many days."

She gave one nod of her head, her blue eyes not leaving him. "I remember. I wanted to go." Her left hand rose, weak, shaking, and landed on his cheek. "You kept me here. Your arm...it held me down. You would not let me leave."

Sebastian exhaled, his head dropping as tears started slipping down his cheeks.

She was back. Back with him. Alive.

A minute passed before he could raise his head to look at her. "No. I was not about to leave you, Bree. Never."

Her mouth curved into a slight smile, the tiniest touch of pink filling her lips, contrasting against the grey set to her skin. "Thank you. I am happy you made me stay."

The words, the miniscule movement drained her, and her eyes closed as she drew a shaky breath. Her face went still.

For a moment, Sebastian froze, afraid she was about to slip from him again.

But then her eyes opened. "I hurt."

He grabbed the glass, lifting her head again to pour more water into her mouth. "The fever—it ravaged your body." He laid her back.

"Why did I have a fever?"

Sebastian searched her face, not wanting to tell her anything it would be far better for her not to recall. "Do you remember the mill?"

Her eyes closed, and Sebastian could see her straining to remember.

A long moment passed.

"Yes. Gregory. My leg." Her eyes flew open, sparked. "The knife—it went right in front of my eyes—you could have killed me, Seb."

Sebastian could not hold back a relieved chuckle. She truly was back. "I am better with a blade than you, my wife. And I owe you my life for bringing that dagger."

Brianna's eyes searched his body. "You were bloody. I could not tell where it all came from. You are injured? Your arm?"

"It is nothing." He glanced down at the wrapping around his arm. "I have healed fine."

"Gregory… "

"Is dead. Yes. And Harry's uncle is currently residing in Newgate, awaiting trial. Gregory made no secret as to who had hired him when he tried to persuade me to give up Harry."

"Persuade?" Fear flooded Brianna's face. "What did he do to you, Seb?"

"Nothing I could not survive. I was more worried about what he was doing to you." Sebastian had to force his still simmering rage to stay even and not explode in front of Brianna. "The knife was far too good for him, as I would have gladly ripped him limb from limb."

Her hand lifted, weak, and she grabbed his left wrist just below the bandages wrapping his arm. "Seb—what I said—I did not mean it. I was only trying to gain time. Give you a chance to cut free. I—"

"Stop. I knew exactly what you were doing, Bree. And I have been in awe of your courage ever since. You knew what was coming, the pain, and you did it anyway."

Eyes closing, her head shook as her face twisted. Her fingers dropped from his wrist. "But at the mill. You left me. I saw you leave. I thought…"

"Brianna, look at me." His palm went to her cheek and she opened her eyes. "I only went to get a horse. I did not know how far I could carry you."

"You were not leaving me?"

"No. Never." He leaned in, his face just above hers, his hand cupping her jaw. "You are my love, my happiness, Bree. For today and tomorrow. You are my fate. Never doubt that."

Tears welled in her eyes, a single drop slipping out and trailing down to his fingers. But her smile went wide. "Today and tomorrow. I will not forget. Not now that my head and heart are finally working in accord."

"They are?"

"Yes. All of me leading to you."

Words had never meant as much as those few from Brianna. Her head and her heart—all he had ever wanted from her.

A knock at the door interrupted his thoughts, the door opening before he could reply. Lily came rushing into the room.

"I heard voices." Lily's frantic eyes found Brianna. "Bree? Bree? Are you awake?"

Lily rushed to the side of the bed.

"How did you hear voices?" Sebastian asked, startled, as he pulled back so Lily could see her sister.

"I was sleeping in the hallway." Lily landed on the bed, her hands gripping Brianna's face. "Bree? You are back to us?"

"Gentle." Sebastian put his hand on Lily's shoulder, cautioning her.

She merely shrugged his hand away. "Bree?"

A smile came to Brianna's lips. "I am, Lils."

Lily's head dropped onto Brianna's chest, a sob racking her body. Brianna's shaking hand went to the back of Lily's head, caressing it.

Lily looked up to Brianna, her voice vehement. "Do not ever do this to me again, Bree. The first time was hard enough, but then this." Her head swung back and forth. "This was beyond... you were a step away from death. From leaving us. From leaving me."

"I am sorry, Lils."

Sebastian stood up from the bed, his hand going to Lily's shoulder once more. "Do not harangue your sister any longer. She just awoke and is weak."

Lily glanced up over her shoulder at him, her annoyed glare telling Sebastian she would scold her sister any time she chose to, and he had nothing to say about it.

Sebastian almost had to laugh—he was holding his own scolding at his wife in check until she was recovered enough to hear it properly. Lily just did not have the same restraint as he.

He squeezed Lily's shoulder. "Watch your sister? I am going to gather some broth and the physician, and find Wynne and Rowe to tell them Bree is awake."

"They are across the hallway—Wynne and the duke," Lily said, still looking up at Sebastian. "All of us moved to this hall after the first days. You did not notice?"

"No."

"Seb, you have not left the room?" Brianna asked, concern in her voice evident. "How many days?"

Sebastian shrugged against the two women staring at him. He honestly didn't know how long Brianna had been prisoner to the darkness. He had lost track days ago.

Lily turned back to Brianna. "No, your husband has not left this room. And it has been nine days."

Sebastian stepped in front of Lily, moving to kiss Brianna's forehead. "I will be back in moments. Do not let your sister tire you."

Sebastian gave Lily a pointed look, then stood. He wondered if he looked as haggard as Lily did. Probably more so. He left the room, leaving Brianna in Lily's care.

~ ~ ~

Brianna's head went to the side, watching Sebastian leave the room. The door clicked closed, and her eyes landed on Lily. "You were sleeping in the hall?"

"Yes." Lily scooted further onto the bed, tucking one of her legs underneath her. "The duke set a bedroll out there for me days ago after he tripped over me."

"You look like it." Even though Lily's blue eyes seemed bright, Brianna had never seen her sister with such dark circles under her eyes.

"And you do not look exactly radiant, either, my sister."

A breathless chuckle escaped Brianna. "I do not imagine. Nine days?"

Lily nodded, her face suddenly solemn.

"And the duke tripped over you?"

"It was dark and I was sleeping." A smirk reached Lily's lips. "He crashed down right on top of me. It was awkward for all involved."

"I can imagine," Brianna said. "Sebastian made you sleep in the hall?"

"He did no such thing, Bree." Lily leaned over Brianna's lap, pulling the coverlet down to expose Brianna's thigh. She fiddled with the thick linen covering the wound that stretched across Brianna's thigh, her bottom lip jutting out in a frown. "Your husband is many things, Bree but an ogre he is not. I could not sleep in here—it was too much...too much to bear, watching Sebastian."

"Why?" Brianna tried to bend her leg to see the wound when Lily lifted the linen, but Lily pushed her thigh down, holding it to the bed with a scolding glance. Brianna had no strength to fight her.

Not answering her question, Lily reset the linen in place, pulling the coverlet back over Brianna's leg. Setting the cover just right, it took her long moments before she took a breath and looked up at Brianna.

"He was destroyed, Bree. There is no other word for it." Lily's eyes glazed over. "Utterly destroyed. He barely ate. Did not sleep. But it was his face. I could not bear to look at his face—I cannot even describe it. It was as though he landed in hell and could not quite accept the fact that he was there. Fighting it, but still having to watch the horror of it."

Lily shook her head, snapping her gaze to the present. Her voice took on a forced lightness. "Do not look so heartbroken over it, Bree. It is past. You are alive and here. And he is alive and here. You two are together again."

"But that is not all you are thinking of, Lils, is it?"

Lily shrugged, her hand slipping along Brianna's arm to grip her hand. "It is nothing. Just that…it made me realize things."

"What things?"

Lily sighed. "I want that. Watching Sebastian watch you. I want that. A man that loves me to such an extreme that he would battle death just to hear my voice again. Not leave my side. It made me realize that what I was doing—with the season, with Newdale, Bepton, and Rallager—it is all a sham—a shimmering pretense I am attempting to create upon my life."

"You do not think any of them care for you like that?"

"No. Newdale, maybe. But not yet. Maybe someday, but not now. But I do not know. Maybe you only get one chance at that in life. And I had my chance. So maybe what I want, and what I settle for are to be two different things."

"Do not say that, Lils. Maybe Newdale does feel exactly that for you."

"Maybe." Lily sighed, waving her hand. "It is of no bother. Not now. Not when we need to concentrate on you while you recover. We will deal with the rest of my life at a later date."

"Lord Rallager, is he still here at Notlund?"

"No. I sent him and his relations off a day after you and Sebastian returned. He understood. His aunt of course, bemoaned her inconvenience at their quick departure. It was just another sign that he was not the one—that he did not want to be near me—us—in a time of crisis. He is a good man, but his character is not worth my time."

A half smile came to Brianna's lips. "You do know your mind, little sister."

The door opened and Sebastian walked in, holding a bowl with steam rising from the top.

His look immediately finding Brianna, relief flashed through his brown eyes. He walked across the room, setting the bowl on the bedside table. He turned to Lily. "I want to get some broth into her belly before the physician makes it up here. Can you find a maid to fill the bath?"

Lily stood from the bed. "For you or for Bree?"

Sebastian looked down at himself, giving the question consideration. His nose wrinkled. "Both of us, I suppose."

Lily nodded. "Excellent choice." She stepped around Sebastian with a smirk on her face, going to the door.

Shaking his head, Sebastian grabbed the chair by the bed and settled it close to the head of the bed. "Do you think you can sit up?"

"Yes."

Sebastian slid an arm underneath her shoulders and lifted her, settling a stack of pillows behind her before leaning her back on them.

His face next to hers, Brianna's hand went to the dark gruff of a beard along his jaw. "This is new. Lily says you have not been sleeping."

He sighed, sitting down onto the chair and grabbing the bowl of broth. "Having a shave was the very last thing I have been worried about, Bree."

She smiled. "I like it. It is rugged."

"Then I will keep it around for a while, just for you."

He fingered the spoon in the bowl, stirring it. Steam still wafted up from the liquid.

"Seb, I see that Lily is safe. But Harry—"

"Harry is safe, Bree. Do you not trust me?"

Brianna could hear the note of warning in his voice. "I do. Of course I do. But that does not stop my worry, Seb."

"No. You are already tired, Bree. I can see that. You need to sleep."

"Yes, but—"

"Bree, all I want at the moment is to get this broth into you. See that the physician looks at you and your leg. Give you a bath. Take a bath myself. And then collapse next to you on this bed knowing full well that you are going to wake up and smile at me."

He stuck a pinky into the broth, testing the temperature.

"We will discuss at length any and everything you can imagine up when our heads have been re-attached properly." He nudged a spoonful of broth into her mouth. "Give me that, Bree? Just that?"

The warm broth slid down her throat, warming her chest. A deep breath, and she nodded. "I am under your control, Seb."

CHAPTER 21

"This is a surprise."

Brianna looked up to see Sebastian coming in the door, a smile wide on his face.

It had taken two days of sleeping, eating more and more, and copious amounts of tea before Brianna had managed to move her body in a half normal way.

She couldn't help her own inordinately proud smile as she watched him come across the room. "I know. All by myself I made it over here." She patted the sidearm of the fat chair by the fireplace. "But I have been winded for the last ten minutes for my effort."

"At this pace, you should be back on Moonlight in a month."

"It had better be sooner than that."

Sebastian eased himself onto the sidearm of the chair facing her, his long legs casual in front of him. His left arm landed on his lap.

Brianna hid a cringe. She could see Sebastian's arm still panged him with pain during random movements, even though he hid it well.

"That will suit Moonlight just fine. She has been antsy for you. Wynne took her out yesterday, but she said Moonlight just slumped through the ride, pouting."

"Is it wrong that that makes me slightly happy?"

Sebastian chuckled. "Yes. Wrong. But understandable. And the same goes for Moonlight. That horse is as loyal as they come—you always say that about her, and it is true. Maybe tomorrow I can carry you down to the gardens and have her brought up from the stables. It might put a spring in her step."

"Maybe." Brianna pointed to his left arm, still wrapped tight with strips of white linen from his wrist upward. The bandaging disappeared under the rolled-up sleeve of his shirt, and Brianna wondered just how far up the dressing went. "But you are not carrying me anywhere on that arm."

He glanced down. "It is doing well."

"Well enough for me to look at it?"

"There is no need for you to see it, Bree. The physician has attended to it."

Her left eyebrow arched. "You have been poking and prodding at my leg for days, Seb, and yet you will not let me look at your arm?"

He shrugged. "No."

"I will see it eventually. If not the scabs, the scars."

"Maybe."

Her head tilted, her eyes twinkling. "Do you have plans to never be naked with me again?"

He smirked, chuckling. "Far from it, my wife. And well played. But I do not want any extra worry upon your mind. You need to concentrate on your own healing, not on mine."

"And I will concentrate much better once I do not have to worry on your healing."

Silent to the argument, he moved to bend down in front of her, balancing on his heels as he slid her robe and shift up her leg, exposing her thigh. "Aside from the winding, did your leg suffer the stroll over here well enough?"

Brianna sighed. It was hard to argue with him when he was being this attentive to her. "It did. It swelled a bit with the movement, but at the same time, it also felt good to have a bit of weight on my leg."

She leaned forward, her palm running along his smooth cheek. "And you had the scruff shaved off."

Satisfied with his inspection of her thigh, Sebastian pulled down her robe and looked up to her, rubbing his jaw. "I had to before you thought me a derelict."

"Does this mean your head has been re-attached properly? That you are going to stop avoiding my questions?"

Sebastian groaned, pushing up from the floor and moving backward to sit on the chair opposite Brianna. "Now?"

She nodded.

He looked to the low fire, grumbling something nonsensical under his breath. When his gaze swung back to Brianna, somberness had set into his brown eyes, darkening them. "Go ahead—no, wait."

Sebastian got up, moving to a side table holding a decanter of brandy and several glasses. He poured himself a full glass and then came back to Brianna, sinking heavy into the chair. His free hand flipped into the air as he took a healthy swallow. "There. I am ready. What is it you need to know, Bree?"

"Harry. Where is he?"

Sebastian didn't flinch from the question. "He is with my mother."

"Your mother?" Shock sent Brianna's eyes wide.

"Yes. Both he and Frannie are with her at Callish Hall. They are my mother's 'destitute cousins from Cornwall' that she has generously taken into her home. That is the story they have all committed to living."

"Is it believable?"

"My mother has distant cousins all over England. It makes sense, and no one has questioned the story. That is how we will know them—distant cousins—at least until we are assured all threats to Harry have been removed. Which depends upon, of course, how his uncle's trial goes. Or until Harry comes of age and can accept the title and whatever danger comes with it. Until then they are very well protected at Callish Hall, Bree."

"It is…" Her arms crossed over her belly as she slumped back in the chair, shaking her head.

"What?"

"It is perfect." Her words were in awe. "Perfect and it will work for a length of time. Why would you not tell me, Seb? I would not have fought you on it—not once I knew where they were. I was furious at you for moving them without telling me, but I would not have fought you. I am not so stubborn that I would not have recognized the good sense of it."

He looked taken aback for a moment. "Thank you, for that, I think."

Her eyebrows arched at him. "But you were never going to tell me, were you?"

"No. I was not about to tell you where I moved them until Gregory was found." His voice went hard as he leaned forward in the chair, his forearms balancing on his thighs as he clasped the glass between his palms, rolling it back and forth. "As much as you were going to hate me for it, Bree, I was not about to have you burdened with the knowledge of their whereabouts. Nor was I going to allow you to continue to place yourself in danger."

He sat straight, staring at her as he took a sip of brandy. "I make no apology for it, Bree."

Her eyes closed and her chin dropped to her chest. Loose brown locks slipped in front of her forehead, tickling her eyebrows. After all their time. After everything. Her words slipped out, soft in defeat. "You do not trust me."

"It has nothing to do with trust, Bree. It has to do with you being my wife. It has to do with the fact that I swore I would keep you safe."

He rose from the chair, standing in front of her. Her eyes still downcast, she could see his fingers straining around the rim of the brandy glass.

"It has to do with my heart, my life that I did not want destroyed. My life with you. My life that I almost lost regardless, Bree. But I am still here. Not running. Still fighting to keep this life mine. To keep you mine. I will do anything to keep you safe, Bree. Even have you hate me, if that is what it takes."

"I do not hate you, Seb." Her eyes rose to him, tears slipping to her cheeks. "I could never. I love you. All of me."

"All of you?"

"All of me. You have banished that part that hesitated. You said you would, and you did, Seb. You have done everything you swore to me you would. And I...I..." She drew a shuddered breath, her words failing her.

Sebastian dropped to his knees in front of her, setting the glass down so his hands could capture her face. "You what, Bree?"

"I give you everything, Seb. Everything I am. Even my need for control. It is yours."

His hands tightened along her jaw, his voice rough. "I never wanted control, Bree. Only you. You were all I ever wanted. Your heart and your mind."

He pulled her forward, his lips meeting hers hard, promising her their life together, promising lust they had no right to entertain at the moment. But it still curled her toes and she had to stop herself from wanton thoughts.

All in due time. Patience.

He pulled away, the heat clear in his brown eyes. "And lest I be remiss in saying so, your body is pretty important to me as well."

She laughed. "You kiss me like that, and I do not think you remiss at all. Seb, all of those things—all of them—I happily give to you." Her head tilted, smirk on her face. "But it still gives me margin to...supervise things?"

Sebastian chuckled. "Supervise? That is your new word for it?"

"Kinder, gentler—do you not think?"

"I do, my wife. I do."

EPILOGUE

Brianna smoothed the skirt of the pretty peach gown she had borrowed from Lily. She had wanted to look bright, her best, and had realized earlier in the day that her wardrobe sadly consisted of blacks, browns and greys. Lily had been more than happy to hold Brianna captive in her room, making her try on eight dresses to find what Lily finally determined was the perfect one.

Her silk slippers crunched on the smooth gravel of the circular drive outside the main gate to Notlund, grinding the rocks in place. The air was crisp, fall almost in the wind, and Brianna's eyes swept over the wide rolling hill surrounding the castle, eventually settling on the main drive up from the forest.

"You are anxious, my wife?" Sebastian's arm went along her back to curl around her waist, pulling her tight to him. "Harry will be beyond ecstatic to see you."

"It is not Harry I am anxious about."

"My mother?"

"Yes. I do want to make the best impression I can upon her."

Sebastian's lips went to the top of her head. "She will adore you."

"But the break between you two—you said it was still tenuous, the bridge you have erected to her."

"My mother can very well tell the difference between how I disappointed her, and the woman that is pushing her son to mend the break."

Brianna looked up at him, his warm brown eyes settling her nerves. "You never told me. How was it that you convinced your mother to take in Harry and Frannie and keep them safe?"

"I did not?"

"No, you did not. You distract me too easily, my husband."

He gave her a wicked smile, the devil dancing in it. "And you love how I distract you." His hand slid down, cupping her backside.

"I do." She laughed, grabbing his hand and pulling it up to set it firmly about her waist. "But it is not in good form to get me riled while we are waiting for, of all people, your mother. And you are distracting me again. So tell me, after the direness of your relationship with your mother, I am curious as to what magic you worked with her."

"Magic?"

"I need to know how you managed it, mending the break, lest you use the same magic on me someday."

He wrapped his arms fully about her, spinning her to him as he kissed her forehead. "This particular magic will never work on you, Bree."

"No?"

"I offered her something I could never physically give you."

Confusion crossed Brianna's brow. "What could that possibly be?"

"I merely promised her grandchildren if she did this favor for us."

"You promised her grandchildren?" Brianna slapped her hands on his chest. "Grandchildren that have yet to be created?"

"Yes. So she can love and spoil them. She has been waiting for that very thing for years. She loves babes." He tightened his hold, lifting Brianna from the gravel, as his lips went to her neck. "And as we were, and are, working quite enthusiastically on the mission, I did not think the promise too far off."

Brianna leaned away from him, her mouth pulling to the side. "You realize that puts even more pressure on me in meeting her?"

"Pressure is one thing I have never known you not to handle, my wife." He set her down, swatting her backside through her skirts just as the carriage appeared from the trees.

Brianna resettled herself, hoping the flush in her cheeks would abate in the next seconds. Her heart instantly swelled when she saw Harry, laughing, poke his head out of the side of the closed carriage. Someone was holding him—it looked like Frannie's hands—and he waved with glee, his whole arm flopping up and down and bringing his torso to teetering out of the carriage.

Pure happiness washed over Brianna, and she grabbed Sebastian's arm, leaning into him. "Thank you for this. For everything. For banishing every worry from my life."

"Just to see that smile on your face, my wife, is reward enough for me." Sebastian looked up from her, nodding in the direction of the carriage. "And that little boy—if he only knew all you have done for him."

"And all you have done for him," Brianna said. "Did your mother tell him we are accompanying them back to Callish Hall after the wedding?"

"I do not know. But I do know she has become anxious for us to settle in there."

"I honestly cannot wait. I love Notlund, but the wedding preparations have been enough to drive anyone to bedlam." Brianna waved back at Harry, still flailing his arm about outside the carriage.

"Is Lily ready for tomorrow?"

"I believe so. Your mother, Harry and Frannie are the last guests to arrive."

"And are you still worried about her?"

"I have tried to not be. Even though Mr. Flemming never discovered definitively what Newdale's business was in those brothels, I am attempting to give Newdale healthy leeway. I have only been questioning the decision not to hire another runner to investigate—Mr. Flemming is still moving slowly after his injury."

"The man appreciates your loyalty to him, Bree. Especially for how guilty he felt, not guarding against Gregory following him to you."

"He could not have known what was to happen." Brianna shrugged. "And he paid for it dearly as well. That scar across his forehead is atrocious."

She took a deep breath, giving a shake to her shoulders. "But I do not want to dwell. Lily made the decision to marry Newdale, and I am trying my hardest to respect that." She looked up at her husband out of the corner of her eye. "That said, I may need you to take my mind into a different direction."

His eyebrow cocked. "Distraction?"

"That should work. Distraction as only you can do."

Sebastian chuckled, his hand going to the small of her back, fingers slipping downward.

The carriage stopped before them, and Brianna set her face to innocence.

One last swipe to smooth the front of her skirt, and she stepped forth.

~ ~ ~

"Lily will be ripe to put me on a spit and roast me when I get back up to the castle, Seb." The lantern in his hand glowed, swinging with their gait, and Brianna's mouth pursed. "You promised her it would only be five minutes, but now we are down at the stables. She will think I chose to sneak off with you for fun instead of walking her through every step tonight."

"Your sister can well handle her own steps, Bree. She is just nervous, as anyone would be the eve before they are to be married."

Brianna glanced up at his dimly lit profile as they crunched out of the trail from the woods. "Were you nervous?"

"No." Sebastian smirked, winking at her.

She rolled her eyes, shaking her head.

"Believe me, Bree, this is important. I would not drag you down here and take you away from the festivities if it did not warrant it. It is more important than your sister's need for someone to hold her hand."

Brianna scanned the stables and the fields beyond. Still. Everything seemed still and peaceful in the low light of the cloud-covered moon. "Seb, is something wrong with Moonlight and you have not told me?"

"No, nothing of the kind. Here." Sebastian lifted the lantern, pointing to Wynne's painting studio. "In the studio."

"The studio?" Her eyes whipped to his face. "What is going on, Seb?"

"You will see. I would not have brought you down here, Bree, if it was not necessary."

Brianna quickened her steps. They rounded the side of the studio, soft light spilling from under the door. Her palms suddenly itchy, Brianna stepped to the side as Sebastian opened the door.

"Mr. Flemming?" Shock crossed her face for a moment, but then she composed herself, stepping into the studio. Sebastian closed the door behind them.

"Mr. Flemming, it is so good to see you." Brianna rushed into the room, grabbing his hands as he stood to greet her. "But this is quite unexpected. Whatever are you doing here? But first—" Her hand pulled from his, her fingertips going to the scar that arched over his wrinkled forehead from his eyebrow to his scalp. "First, your head. How is it faring?"

"Better every day, mi' lady." Mr. Flemming's look went over Brianna's shoulder, and he gave Sebastian a short nod.

"Excellent. I am relieved to hear it." She glanced back to Sebastian and then looked to Mr. Flemming. "But why are you here?"

"I know it is a late hour, and late to the activities in the castle, and I apologize. It is about Lord Newdale, mi'lady. I spoke to your husband about it, and he believes you should have the information directly from me."

Sebastian moved to stand next to her, his hand on the small of her back. Always a comfort, her husband. Her hands clasped in front of her. "Do tell me, Mr. Flemming."

"I discovered what Lord Newdale's business was in the many brothels, mi' lady." His eyes flickered to Sebastian. Sebastian offered a nod. "He was purchasing virgins, mi' lady."

"Virgins? Purchasing virgins?" Her eyebrows collapsed, her look going to Sebastian. She glanced back to Mr. Flemming. "Whatever does that mean?"

He coughed. "Virgins. They are sometimes sold for a high price at brothels. Not one's typical business in them."

"He buys virgins?" Brianna's head shook, still trying to wrap her mind around what Mr. Flemming was telling her. "But that… that…that is horrific, Mr. Flemming. Utterly horrible. Vicious."

"It is, mi'lady. All of those things. The sales, they are more common than they should be, but are usually discreet affairs. It is why it took me so long to discover what Lord Newdale's business was in those particular brothels. I apologize again for the late news on the matter, but I did think it imperative that you had all the information before tomorrow."

Brianna's hand clamped over her mouth. "Tomorrow…"

She looked to Sebastian, and at seeing her face, he grabbed the nearest wooden chair, slipping it behind her. He made it just in time for Brianna to sink.

"But tomorrow…Seb, tomorrow…Mr. Flemming, you are sure of this information? Absolutely positive?"

"I am afraid so, Lady Luhaunt."

She nodded, slumping back on the chair, her muscles turning to jelly.

Sebastian stepped in front of her. "Wait here a moment, Bree? Sit, Breathe. I will walk Mr. Flemming to the stable."

Brianna nodded, unable to conjure words.

Sebastian squeezed her shoulder, his fingers sliding along her neck before he left her, ushering Mr. Flemming to the door.

He left the lantern on the table, and Brianna stared at it, stared at the curve of the black iron framing the flickering light. Eyes glassing over, she tried to keep her head from floating away. The wedding was tomorrow. Eleven in the morning. Tomorrow. And Lily was happy. Excited.

Brianna was going to have to do it. She was going to have break Lily's heart again.

The door opened and closed.

It took moments for her heavy head to rise.

But it wasn't Sebastian that walked in through the door.

A man. A man pulling a dark hood back from his head.

His face. A face from the past. A face she almost didn't recognize.

Garek. Garek Harrison.

Lily's Garek.

He smiled at her.

"So what will it be, Brianna? The devil you know, or the devil you don't?"

~ ABOUT THE AUTHOR ~

K.J. Jackson is the author of *The Hold Your Breath Series,*
The Lords of Fate Series, and *The Flame Moon Series.*

She specializes in historical and paranormal romance,
loves to travel (road trips are the best!), and is a sucker for a good
story in any genre. She lives in Minnesota with her husband,
two children, and a dog who has taken the sport of
bed-hogging to new heights.

Visit her at www.kjjackson.com

~ AUTHOR'S NOTE ~

Thank you so much for taking a trip back in time with me.
The next book in the *Lords of Fate* series will debut in
Winter 2015/16.

If you missed the *Hold Your Breath* series or
the first in the *Lords of Fate* series, be sure to check out these
historical romances: **Stone Devil Duke,
Unmasking the Marquess, My Captain, My Earl,
and Worth of a Duke**.

Be sure to sign up for news of my next releases at
www.KJJackson.com (email addresses are precious, so out of
respect, you'll only hear from me when I actually have real news).

Interested in Paranormal Romance?
In the meantime, if you want to switch genres and check out
my Flame Moon paranormal romance series, **Flame Moon #1**,
the first book in the series, is currently free (ebook) at all stores.
Flame Moon is a stand-alone story, so no worries on getting
sucked into a cliffhanger. But number two in the series, **Triple
Infinity**, ends with a fun cliff, so be forewarned. Number three in
the series, **Flux Flame**, ties up that portion of the series.

As always, I love to connect with my readers, you can reach me at:

www.KJJackson.com

https://www.facebook.com/kjjacksonauthor

Twitter: @K_J_Jackson

Thank you for allowing my stories into your life
and time—it is an honor!
~ K.J. Jackson